SCONES AND SPELLS

MIXING UP MAGIC, BOOK 2

ROSIE PEASE

Scones and Spells
Second Edtion

Editor: Word Whisperer Literary Editing
Proofreader: Jasmine Bryner
Cover Designer: Melony Paradise, Paradise Cover Design

PAISLEY PRESS BOOKS
WEST WARWICK, RHODE ISLAND

For Rob.
Thank you for being my biggest supporter as I follow my
dreams.
I love you.

About This Book

Some secrets don't go to the grave... they come to my bakery.

I thought ghosts meddling with the last couple I got together was a one-time situation. But the spirits are interfering again, and my current mystery is more complicated and even a little dangerous.

Nothing is quite what it seems in my small town, and everyone has something to hide. Even me. When the case leads me to a forest where six townspeople disappeared, or worse, I learn I must uncover the truth of what happened there to heal Heartwood Hollow and help my latest match find love. It won't be easy.

To do it, I need to accept there's truth to the rumors about me. I'm a witch. But can I turn to magic I didn't know I had to get my answers?

There's more to Heartwood Hollow and its residents than meets the eye.

AUTHOR'S NOTE

Dear Reader,

Thank you so much for picking *Scones and Spells* as your next read. I hope you fall even further in love with the characters and Heartwood Hollow. It's no secret that the town is full of secrets, and I can't wait for you to uncover them all. They really start to come out of the woodwork in this one.

For example, the story contained within this book is what actually gave the town its name. So in a way, I'm still discovering some of the town's secrets too. Each new book reveals something new, and I'm so glad you are along for the ride.

I love hearing from readers. If you'd like to reach out to me, you can do so across social media @WriteRosiePease.

Happy reading!

Cheers,

Rosie

CHAPTER 1

As Lily stormed into the kitchen, Gina's mouth dropped open as she looked at the clock. "Oh my gosh, you're late!"

"Had to happen eventually," Lily grumbled. Her demeanor seemed in stark contrast to the cheery pinkish hue of her blond ponytail. I assumed she colored it every morning with some sort of chalk. The shade varied nearly that often. She stomped over to her baking station after dumping her bag in the closet.

Bryan divided the lemon-blueberry scone doughball he had formed in half and plopped a portion onto Lily's work surface. "You wake up on the wrong side of the bed this morning?"

Lily immediately pounded it out with her fists. Something was eating at her, and if I didn't put a stop to it, that batch of scones would be no better to eat than the doorstop I used to keep the shop door open, letting the warm spring air in and allowing the bakery smells to waft out to the sidewalk.

I needed Bryan to move so I could hop in and see what

was wrong with my usually punctual and breezy baker. "Bryan, can you pour the batter into these muffin cups, please?" I ticked my head to the side for emphasis.

"Sure thing, Joanie." He stepped away as I approached, then walked around me to the industrial mixer where the muffin batter had seconds left to mix.

Lily pulled out a rolling pin, but before she could do anything, I placed my hand over it to prevent her from flattening the scone dough. Whispering so only she could hear, I asked, "Is everything okay?"

"Yeah, fine," she mumbled.

The kitchen light above her told a different story, dimming slightly while all the others remained the same.

I worked the doughball Bryan had left at his station, forming it into a flat circle. "You sure? Gina's right. Late isn't like you."

"Yeah, I'm fine." She took a deep breath in and slowly let it out before shaking out her shoulders and bending her neck to one side and then the other.

"Okay. Well, I'm here if you need someone to talk to." I pulled the rolling pin out of this station's drawer and flattened the dough disk until it was roughly a half-inch thick and the size of a round dinner plate.

"Thanks, Joanie." She stayed silent as she rolled out her dough with less force than she would have moments before. It was as if the fight had left her.

Not wanting to press her further, I cut my dough into eight wedges and transferred the raw scones to the baking tray between us. I grabbed another hunk of waiting dough, this time cinnamon chip, and formed it into a large ball.

Lily worked her jaw, readying herself to speak. "It's just, why are men so difficult?" She slid her scones onto the baking sheet.

Ah, dating troubles. Although I was a matchmaker, I didn't have a wealth of advice in the dating arena. Until a few weeks ago, I hadn't been on a date since college. Sure, I'd had the opportunity, but my ability to see ghosts complicated my love life. Until I fell—almost literally—for Ken Dawson, a recent transplant to Heartwood Hollow, I'd sworn off dating.

"I wish I could tell you. It's infuriating sometimes, isn't it?"

Lily scrunched up her face as she contemplated this. "I'd thought you'd have some insight. Isn't matchmaking, like, your superpower or something?"

I laughed. "I wouldn't exactly call it a superpower, and it can only tell me when people are meant to be together, not what someone's thinking or why they do what they do."

She sighed, and I took a stab at what was bothering her. "Problems with your boyfriend?"

Aaron had come into the bakery a couple of times over the six months he and Lily had been together, usually when she was particularly proud of whatever she had baked. He was a good guy, but the two weren't right for one another.

"Not anymore," she quipped. "We broke up."

Gina rushed over to Lily. "Oh my gosh, I'm so sorry!" She placed her arm around Lily's back, her hand resting on Lily's far shoulder.

Sam, who had been quiet up to this point, walked by the two rear baking stations with a rolling rack of cookie trays ready for the oven. "He didn't deserve you. You'll find someone so much better."

Lily straightened and considered his statement for a moment. "You know what? You're right, because I'm awesome." She breathed on her knuckles and pretended to shine them on her green apron. The light above her returned to the same brightness as the rest in the room.

"That's the spirit," I said, knowing Lily would recover from this heartbreak and eventually find someone right for her. For the two years she'd been working for me, I'd never known Lily to be upset for long, almost as if she could cast her cares away on the breeze to let them be carried away.

The oven beeped, and as Bryan turned it off, he announced, "Muffins are coming out of the oven, Joanie."

"Great. If you wouldn't mind setting them to cool, then you can get back to these scones while I pack up the morning deliveries.

Bryan nodded. "Sure thing."

Sarah popped into the kitchen shortly before the shop was to open to put away her purse. I was cleaning up my baking station as the rest of my team continued their tasks for the late-morning deliveries and second round of baked goods. What wasn't going to Riverview Inn, we'd pull from throughout the course of the day as the front cases emptied.

"Someone's in the front to see you," Sarah said. "I figured it was close enough to opening that you wouldn't mind me letting him in."

About to reprimand her for leaving the shop unattended —after working for me since I'd opened four years ago, she knew better—I caught her smile. Realizing whom she was talking about, I hurried to the bathroom and quickly washed my hands before checking myself out in the mirror. After wiping a spot of flour off the side of my nose, I deemed myself okay, then pulled my medium-brown hair tighter into its ponytail.

My smile brightened as I walked through the kitchen and

into the shop, the glow of the lights above me intensifying just enough for me to notice.

"What a pleasant surprise this is, Ken," I said, heading toward him. "What are you doing here?"

He straightened and turned toward me, his back now facing the case he had been peering into. "Good morning, Joanie." He wrapped me in a hug and leaned down to kiss me.

I met him halfway, rising onto my toes. "Good morning to you too."

"Hope you don't mind Sarah letting me in." He grinned sheepishly, as if wondering whether his being in here before opening concerned me.

Dismissing the statement with a wave, I said, "Of course not. It's always good to see you. Can I get you anything?" I looked at the clock on the wall opposite the cases. "I know you have to get going to work."

"Originally, I was thinking a cinnamon scone, but then these caught my eye." He shuffled toward the pastry case and pointed to a puff-pastry treat curled into a heart shape.

"One elephant ear coming right up." I'd also heard them called palmiers during my time at culinary school, but I preferred the term I'd grown up with.

I walked behind the counter, then opened the case to pull out an elephant ear. The treat was about twice the size of my hand. I reached behind me and grabbed a white wax paper bag and dropped the pastry inside.

"On the house."

He shook his head as I handed him the bag. "You really need to stop giving me free things. It can't be good for your bottom line."

"You pay me for Ivy's cookies. With how often you get things for her, that's plenty." Ken's seven-year-old daughter had developed a fondness for my cookies after trying them in the basket Ken had received when he closed on his house last month. The partnership with the real estate office had yielded me many loyal customers during my time in Heartwood Hollow.

"I'm pretty sure you give me a discount for those," he replied, chuckling.

I made a motion of zipping my lips and raised my eyebrows. "I will neither confirm nor deny that statement."

"A free breakfast wasn't the reason I came here this morning, but thank you."

"So what else brings you in?" I walked toward the window and raised the blind. The bakery would officially be open in another two minutes.

"Well, Ivy got invited to a sleepover—"

"Oh, how wonderful. Good for her. I'm glad she's making friends." I scooted back around the counter and over to the other window to raise that blind.

"She's really excited for it. Anyway, I was hoping you were free Friday night since I will be free."

"A date night? One without the potential of the babysitter having to leave to find her grandma's dog?"

He nodded enthusiastically.

A smile grew across my face. "Count me in. You pick the spot, though. I've chosen the last two places."

"Fair enough." Ken leaned in and quickly kissed me on my lips. "I hate to run, but I have to go. I'll call you." Then he spun around me and headed for the door.

I followed him and turned the sign on the pink-painted door from *closed* to *open*. "I'll talk to you later."

"Looking forward to it already," he said over his shoulder, waving behind him with the hand holding the pastry bag.

The kitchen door swung open, and Sarah stepped into the

shop, but not before revealing Gina, Lily, and Sam trying to look innocent as they hurried back to their stations.

I laughed at the sight. When had my social life become so interesting? Right—when I met Ken while covered in salad dressing. "Busted. I see all of you snoops. Now get back to work."

Gina and Sam continued to walk away, but Lily drew closer and popped her head into the bakery. "That. I want that."

Noted. I hoped someone would come into her life soon. She deserved a good guy.

After Ken's visit, the first half of the morning continued like any other Wednesday would. By ten thirty, I had sent my bakers home, aside from Sam, who'd left to go to school when we opened. Despite having a free period first thing that allowed him to skip homeroom, he'd likely still be late as a result of his snooping. Since he was graduating in a month, I was sure he wasn't too worried. He was my best worker, and I looked forward to him being available all summer, but sadly I'd be losing him in the fall to culinary school.

The door to the shop swung open, and I glanced up at the clock to see how much time I had before my next round of deliveries. A few minutes. Hopefully this would be quick, but at least Sarah was already in the kitchen packing the orders.

I smiled at the flanneled stranger. "Good morning. Welcome to Suncraft Bakery. How may I delight your sweet tooth today?" I'd never seen him before, which was strange for Heartwood Hollow prior to tourist season. It didn't officially start for another two weeks, and Wednesdays were an odd day for vacationers to pop in no matter the time of year.

He nodded and gave me a nervous "Hullo" as he surveyed the cases.

"We have a wide variety of treats, as you can see." I swept my arm in front of me in a displaying motion.

The man paced the shop, sometimes looking at me, other times looking at the cases or at the clock. He tapped the front pocket of his jeans repeatedly.

"We make everything fresh daily in our kitchen except for what you see on the corner rack over there." I pointed to the little blue shelf that had a small assortment of day-old cupcakes and bags of cookies. There was never much left at the end of the day, but I wanted to provide goodies at a bargain for those who needed it by discounting anything that remained from the day before.

He glanced at the shelf but continued his back and forth of the floor.

As I ran through my list of suggestions, I studied the twenty-something-year-old man in the red flannel button-down and white T-shirt. His carpenter jeans fit well, and his tan boots were the type construction people wore. They weren't dirty or worn, though, and I wondered if this was more a fashion choice than a necessity. "Is there anything that strikes your fancy?"

He shook his head and glanced back toward the kitchen. His caginess was setting me on edge, but then the strangest thing happened. Not because it hadn't happened countless times before but because he was alone when it occurred. My toes tingled, and the sensation spread up my legs and settled in my stomach. It was the feeling I got whenever I came in contact with a couple that was a perfect match for one another. It was a skill I'd had since childhood, one I'd inherited from my mom. In this town alone, I'd matched a dozen couples in about four and a half years.

I had never been wrong.

But this was a first. He was alone, and the skill didn't work on me, so we weren't a match.

Could the match be so strong as to sense Sarah in the kitchen?

I tried again to engage the man. "How about a scone?"

He gave another shake of his head before he spun on his heels and hurried out of the bakery, his hand still pressed against his pants pocket.

CHAPTER 2

What in the world had just happened? I couldn't remember the last time someone had come into the shop and left without getting anything. Had it ever?

As I continued to watch, the mysterious man turned left on Main Street and then disappeared from view as he headed past Dawg Pound, the family-friendly hot dog restaurant on the corner.

I turned away from the window and startled, nearly bumping into the back counter. Where the man had been pacing moments before, a ghost had appeared. The spirit doing the same thing, only his pacing extended through the door and into the kitchen. From my years of experience in seeing ghosts, I knew they rarely walked through things, instead behaving as they once did. Meaning they walked around objects or opened them as needed. This ghost was either smart or experienced in being around the living. He was aware he could freak people out by having the door swing open and shut multiple times seemingly on its own.

Whereas the living man who had left appeared agitated, the ghost looked worried. His head turned slowly this way and that as his gaze scanned the entire room. I had no doubt he was doing the same in the kitchen. He wore nearly an identical outfit to the living man, the only difference being the color of the T-shirt. They had to be related, and judging by the more-salt-than-pepper hair, this ghost easily could have been the living man's grandfather. Did I have a grandfatherly ghost involved in his grandson's life for the second time in a month?

I thought back to Daniel Johnson, the ghost who had been following his grandson, Rich, and was directly interfering with Rich's match to Ashley O'Donnell. I was happy that solving Daniel's problem went hand in hand with securing Rich and Ashley's relationship. All it had taken was figuring out how and why a haunted hairbrush had ended up in Ashley's possession and then setting that spirit—Kate—free so she and Daniel could be together.

Joanie Sunevall, matchmaker for the living and the dead.

I chuckled.

The ghost passed through the kitchen door and into the shop once more. He looked at me quizzically as I laughed, cocking his head to one side as he passed in front of the cases.

"Sorry, you probably wouldn't find it funny."

My statement stopped the ghost in his tracks, and his gaze homed in on me.

"Yes, I can see you . . . and most ghosts. Name's Joanie. You seem to be looking for something. Can I help you?"

He opened his mouth to speak, but no words came out. I wasn't surprised. It took an immense amount of energy to communicate verbally. That had been a problem I'd had when Kate first appeared to me too.

"It's okay. We'll figure out some other way."

He nodded.

"See? We're getting somewhere already."

The door from the kitchen swung open, and Sarah bounded into the bakery. She looked around. "Who are you talking to?"

I glanced to where the ghost had been, but he was gone.

"Customer just left." I slipped my apron off, grabbed my purse from under the counter, and I scooted past her. "I'm taking my lunch after I'm done with deliveries. Donna's, but I should be back shortly after my normal time."

Sarah walked behind the counter. "Okay, sounds good. Everything's packed up and already in your trailer."

"Wow, really?" She'd never packed the trailer without me before.

"I had help," she replied. "Now go before you're late for Libby. You know how she is."

"See you later." I darted into the kitchen, nearly smacking into Lily. She bumped into one of the racks, which was fortunately empty. "Oh, sh . . . ugar! Sorry. Are you okay?"

She straightened. "Yeah, no worries. That's what I get for being too close to the door."

"Guess you were the help Sarah mentioned. Why didn't you go home?"

She shrugged. "Didn't feel like it. Aaron still has some of his stuff there. Not much, but I'm not ready to deal with it."

"Stay as long as you need."

She offered me a small smile. "Thanks, Joanie."

My toes were still tingling from earlier, and as I walked outside to my awaiting bike and trailer, I realized Sarah wasn't the strange young man's match.

Lily was.

CHAPTER 3

Grateful to be dining solo during the lunchtime rush, I stepped into Olde Templeton Diner and snagged the last remaining open seat at the counter. I nodded in greeting at my counter mates. Seats where Walter and Paul sat every morning as I made my muffin delivery were now occupied by Pam and Anthony. Their daughter, Chelsea, was one half of an earlier match I had made.

Pam leaned toward me as I sat down on the stool. "Chelsea gushed about the drawings you did for her cake design. She's so excited."

"Oh, that's so good to hear. I love the theme. It's so unique."

She chuckled but said nothing more, busying herself by counting out change to pay the bill in front of her.

"Joanie!" Donna Templeton exclaimed as she walked out of the kitchen. She waved to Pam and Anthony as they left before returning her attention to me. "Twice in one day. To what do I owe the pleasure?"

I smiled at the diner's owner, one of the town's lead gossipers. Donna knew everything about everyone or at least tried to. She'd lived here her whole life, and I was pretty sure her parents had too. They'd run the diner before her.

"Lunch, for one," I started as she poured me a cup of coffee in a heavy white mug. "But I also came to pick that brain of yours for your vast knowledge of who's who in town."

"Oh, now you have me intrigued. Tell me all the details while you think about what you're gettin'." She grabbed the money Pam had left at her spot, pocketing it in her apron.

"The strangest thing happened in my shop this morning."

Donna wiped down the now-empty spaces at the counter. "That's saying something coming from you."

It didn't surprise me she bought into the rumors about my being a witch. They'd been circulating for almost as long as I'd lived in town. I'd recently come to the understanding that I had witches in my family, namely my mom and my gram, but I wasn't one. At least I didn't think so. Wasn't seeing ghosts and being a matchmaker enough?

"A man came into the bakery, and he was nervous, on edge as if he were waiting for something to happen. I tried talking to him, but he barely answered. Just kept looking around. Then he left without buying anything."

Donna gasped. "Now *that* is strange. No one walks into your shop without getting something. Who was the man?"

Before telling her, I placed my order for a burger and fries. Templeton Diner boasted the best burgers in the county, as well as the biggest. They were an inch thick and deliciously juicy. The hand-cut fries made for the perfect side.

"That's just the thing, Donna. I don't think I've ever seen him before," I said with a slight lift of my shoulders. "He's certainly never been in the bakery before. I make it a point to know everyone who walks through those doors."

"Well, what did he look like?"

"Mid to late twenties, brown hair that's short on the sides but a little curly at the top, a bridge of freckles over his nose. Didn't get a good look at his eyes as he paced the floor. Brown maybe." I lifted my hand a half foot over my head. "Taller than I am too."

"You just described a good quarter of the male population in Heartwood Hollow. What about his clothes?"

I thought back to his flannel shirt, light-blue jeans, and work boots. "Would it make sense to say he looked a bit like a lumberjack?"

"Now we're gettin' somewhere." A bell in the kitchen dinged, and Donna spun around to grab two plates sitting in the window. She delivered them to the corner table and returned, only to grab the pot of coffee and refill the cup of one of the men sitting at the table behind me along the wall.

She walked back and topped off my cup. "My best guess would be that you're talking about John Singer."

My eyes widened. "So he's from here?" How had I not seen him before?

"Sure is. Whole family's been here about as long as mine. Alfred Dunmore sold them the mill before he died."

I scrunched my lips to the side. The mill hadn't been in operation for at least half a generation from what I'd been told. "What does he do?"

"He's a fabulous furniture maker. Ya've seen the beautiful furniture in the library, haven't you?"

"Sure. Those chairs are super comfortable. I even wanted to buy one for my house, but it was too expensive to justify at the time." I'd have to look into it again now that I had some money saved up. "He's the Singer of Singer Furniture?"

Donna nodded. "One and the same."

The bell in the kitchen rang once more, and Donna reached behind her for a plate with a large burger and a heaping of fries on it. She placed it in front of me with a *thunk.*

"The behavior seems a bit off, though," she explained. "The anxiousness seems more like his dad and granddad. They never were the same after the mill closed. John's turned the family name back around, that's for sure. Well, at least in the job department. Can't say much in the relationship department, although I guess *no* relationship *is* an improvement."

I didn't like the sound of that. "What do you mean?"

"You've been here how long now?" a female voice from behind me asked. I thought I recognized it, and my guess was confirmed when Holly from Leafs and Grounds sat on the stool next to me.

"Almost four years and a half years," I answered, then took a bite of my burger. Perfect.

"And you've not heard about that family's cursed relationships? I would have figured you'd know all about it," Donna said.

Holly nodded in agreement as Donna poured her a cup of coffee.

Cursed relationships? As a rule, I tried not to gossip—although it seemed like I'd been doing a lot of it since working to cement Ashley and Rich's match—but I had to find out more. I shook my head as I took another bite of my burger, hoping one of them would continue.

Holly quickly ordered, then pivoted on her stool to face me. "That whole family is plagued by failed relationships, and that might be putting it lightly."

I popped a fry into my mouth. "Come on, the whole family? They can't all have been bad. There wouldn't be any of them left if that was the case."

Holly made a face, raising both eyebrows, her mouth

drawn into a thin line. "John's the only one in his generation. No siblings. No cousins." Holly took a small sip of her coffee before adding in cream and sugar. She tried it again and let out a contented sigh.

Donna set Holly's plate of food in front of her. "Some relationships even ended bloody. I'm telling you. They're cursed."

"Bloody?" I held up my hand to keep either of them from going into detail.

The thought of setting John Singer up with Lily began to gnaw at my gut. I'd never ignored the matchmaking feeling before, but perhaps it wasn't the best idea to get these two together even if they were perfect for one another. What would happen if I did nothing to get this couple together?

I pushed my plate away, no longer hungry for the remaining half of my burger. I had to get back to the bakery anyway.

"Well, ladies, thank you for enlightening me about John and his family." I stood, placing fifteen dollars next to my plate. Even though I always looked at the menu, I'd gotten this same thing so many times, I knew how much it cost along with a tip. I always gave a little extra to cover the free coffee Donna gave me when I delivered muffins in the morning too.

"It's a shame, really," Holly said between bites. "He's a nice guy, good looking too, but I can't blame him for staying single."

Donna nodded. "Although, maybe you could work your magic on him, Joanie." She quickly wiggled her fingers at me.

"We'll see what happens." I waved at both of them. "Have a good day."

Gray clouds dotted the sky, partially obscuring the sun as I exited the diner and walked around the old stone building to where I'd hidden my bike. Many people around town had told me hiding it wasn't necessary, but even four years into living here, doing so made me feel better, especially as we got closer to tourist season. I climbed onto the bike and took off toward the bakery, going the long way around to clear my head. It wouldn't be fair to deny John a chance at true love just because no one in his family had ever had a successful relationship. That wasn't his fault. But my first impression of him on top of what I knew now about his family made me question the match all the same.

Several minutes later, I pedaled into the parking lot behind the bakery. As I stowed my bike and trailer, the ghost from earlier reappeared before me, making me jump . . . again.

"Hello, there. You're back." I hoped he'd be able to talk this time.

He nodded, smiling, and opened his mouth to speak. No sound came out, but I could read the words on his lips. "I am." His brow furrowed and he tried again. Nothing. After a couple more tries, he clenched his hand into a fist.

I held up my hands in front of my chest and slowly lowered them in a calm-down motion. "It's okay, we'll get there. It takes a lot of energy to talk. How about you act it out?"

He pointed to the door leading into the kitchen.

"There's something in my kitchen?"

He shook his head, still pointing at the door but pushing his arm forward.

"The bakery?"

He nodded.

"What about it?"

He jabbed his arm forward repeatedly, his hand clenched as if holding something. But what? And what did that have to do with my bakery?

"I, um, I'm not sure what you're doing."

He opened his hand and pointed at his palm with the other. He closed his hand and resumed thrusting it toward the bakery.

"I'm sorry. This isn't working either. All I know is that you're holding something. But I don't think I have anything you'd make that motion with in the shop."

He shook his head.

"So it's not in the bakery?"

He shook his head again.

First it was in the bakery, and then it wasn't. I was at a loss. What could he have been talking about? "I really want to help you, but we need to find another way. Rest up. Gather some more energy. We'll try again soon, okay?"

He nodded and blinked out of sight.

It wouldn't be the last I'd see of him.

CHAPTER 4

Lily had already left by the time I entered the bakery kitchen. I wondered if she had gone home. She'd have to eventually to decide what to do with her ex's things. Although I hadn't ever been in her position, I felt for her. Maybe I could make her favorite baked good to cheer her up. I'd have to look through my files to find her application. It was a question I asked everyone who applied.

I grabbed my green apron from the kitchen closet, then pushed through the cream-colored door leading into the shop. "Hey, Sarah. How'd things go in here?"

We swapped places behind the counter, and she filled me in on the near hour I'd been gone. Eating at Olde Templeton Diner had extended my time out of the shop, but talking to Donna and Holly had been worth it.

"When did Lily leave?" I asked, stowing my purse under the front counter.

Sarah slipped off her apron. "Shortly after you left."

"How'd she seem?"

"Okay." She shrugged. "She'll bounce back from this soon enough. She's not one to stay single for long."

"Oh?" I'd never gotten that vibe from Lily, and she'd been with Aaron for a while. But before that? No idea. Then again, I mostly saw her in the kitchen. No significant other needed there.

"Yeah. I think she prefers having someone else around."

I nodded. Not everyone liked to be alone. If my calico cat, Saffy, hadn't come into my life when she did, I would have had to get a pet to keep me company by now. I liked having my own space, but I could never do without some sort of companionship for long. The four-footed kind had proven to be the best over the years. Saffy never minded my early hours or the fact I could see ghosts. Part of me thought she could see them too. Especially with her involvement in helping Kate and Daniel. My mom's cat, Paige, hadn't minded my abilities either, but she'd never shown an interest in my otherworldly visitors.

My thoughts momentarily drifted toward companions of the human variety, and I smiled. Though he'd been skeptical at first, once he saw my abilities in action, Ken fortunately wasn't bothered by them. Amazed was more like it. I was glad I didn't need to hide that part of my life from him. Ashley and Rich had also proven to be open to what I could do. Maybe I needed to let more people in, but part of me worried about trusting the wrong person.

"Am I good to go to lunch?" Sarah asked, half-concerned as if it weren't the first time she'd done so, bringing me out of my thoughts.

Waving her off and giving a small smile, I said, "Enjoy. I'll see you when you get back."

She studied me another moment before heading into the kitchen. A minute later, the back door closed with a loud thud. Part of me expected for the lumberjack ghost to reappear now that I was alone, but he didn't. Perhaps he had taken my suggestion to heart.

As I condensed a few trays of cookies and pastries, my mind wandered back to when I'd last helped a ghost. Kate had only been able to talk to me after an influx of energy from a recipe I'd learned from my gram. She'd call it *a divination spell*, but spells were for witches like her and my mom. I wasn't a witch, so I referred to it as a *recipe*, a more comfortable term for me. Before, I'd used the recipe in a time of need, eager to free Kate from the object that anchored her to this human plane so she could be with her true love, Daniel.

Could a recipe like that help this ghost even though it didn't seem like he was anchored to anything? But if I were a betting woman, then the ghost was somehow connected to what I'd been told was odd behavior for John. Especially if it was his grandfather. Like with the ghost, I knew I'd be seeing John again soon. Both had come to the shop for a reason.

Although I needed more information on this new spirit, research wasn't my forte. I'd proven that searching through newspapers on microfilm with Rich and Ashley a few weeks before. I thought about calling Rich since he enjoyed sorting through historical records, but school was still in session, and teachers were exceptionally busy toward the end of the school year. We were still in the first half of May, but June was right around the corner. The high school's honors banquet was already this weekend.

That left me with one other option off the top of my head. I picked up the shop's phone and dialed it.

"Hey, Steph, it's Joanie. Got a sec?" Steph had lived across the hall from me when I first moved to Heartwood Hollow. We'd become friends and hung out a lot over the year I'd lived in that apartment before getting my house. Although our girls' nights had become far fewer as we moved across town, I tried to catch up with her regularly somehow, even if with a phonecall.

"Sure, what's up?"

"I'm hoping you'd be able to get your hands on some 'dirt' as they say in your business. They do say that, right?" I wasn't sure of the exact terminology, but if anyone could dig up the information, it would be one of the town's newspaper reporters.

Her lilting laughter filled my ear. "Who could *you* possibly need dirt on?

I explained the weird occurrence with John this morning and how Donna and Holly had mentioned it could be related to his family.

"Oh, interesting." Her tone had turned serious. "That dirt I can do. I'll call you later with what I turn up."

"Thanks so much. If I don't answer, it's because I'm on a date."

Her tone shifted once more and sounded almost teasing as she asked, "Another date with the hot doc?"

She couldn't see me roll my eyes, but that didn't prevent it from happening. "Not you too."

Steph laughed again. "I'm a reporter. I make it my busi-ness to know everything."

"Then you know he's not a doctor."

"Of course I do, but it has a ring to it. And he *is* hot." She had a point about that.

"He is. Okay, I don't want to keep you while you're at work."

"Eh, don't worry about it. But, hey, let's get together soon. Have a girls' night. It's been a while. You can tell me all about your new man. Plus, I miss your cat."

"That sounds fabulous. I'll talk to you later."

"Bye, Joanie. Have fun on your date."

CHAPTER 5

"I can't wear the black one again," I told Saffy, who stared at me from my bed as I held up two outfit choices for my date. I'd worn my black dress twice already in the few weeks I'd been dating Ken—Saffy had picked it out the first time—and I wasn't willing to consider it again so soon.

Saffy swished her tail back and forth, then let out a short chirp. I had no idea what she'd said. Not that she could talk, but I was usually able to figure out what all of her noises meant. This one, however, had me stumped.

"Pink or yellow?"

She squinted at me and stopped flicking her tail. It was wrapped around her, the black tip pointing at the buttercup-yellow dress in my left hand.

"You think?" I brought the dress up and studied the delicate floral pattern. I had the perfect blue cardigan to wear with it.

Decision final, Saffy ambled in a circle and lay down, her back to me.

"All right. Thanks, Saffy. Let me finish getting ready, and I'll feed you before I go."

No sooner had I stepped into the half bath connected to my bedroom than my landline rang. Thinking it might be Ken, I shuffled across the floor, hoping I could grab the cordless phone from its cradle before it stopped ringing.

I glanced at the caller ID, then put the phone to my ear. "Hey, Steph."

"I didn't catch you at a bad time, did I? You sound a bit out of breath."

"Just getting ready for my date. I was in the other room and rushed over. Did you find anything?"

"Maybe. As I'm sure you know, John's family used to own the old lumber mill in town," she began matter-of-factly.

"Yeah, Donna and Holly mentioned that today."

"But do you know *why* it closed?"

Forgetting for a moment that she couldn't see me, I shook my head before replying, "No clue."

I sat on the bed, disturbing Saffy's nap. She jumped off the bed and darted out the room, likely thinking I was done getting ready. Silly cat.

"Well," Steph began. "Do I have a story for you. John's father, Joe, was the last to run the mill. Before him, it was his father, Dale. It goes back a few generations prior to that, to when the Singers got it from the Dunmores. Singer Lumber was a family venture. Everyone worked there, wives included. Business boomed for years until a couple decades ago."

"What happened?" I asked, glancing at the clock to see how much time I had left to get ready for my date. Another forty-five minutes, including the time I needed to put makeup on. Poor Saffy had quite the wait still. One look at me and she'd have realized I wasn't close to done. Now instead of a comfy spot, she'd stay sitting in front of her bowl, tapping it harder and harder the longer I took.

"Things were going so well, the family purchased land to

a new grove west of the land they had. It was untouched forest. Plenty of old wood. They expected to make a killing, and with the first harvest, they started to. But then they didn't. We're talking multiple freak accidents with equipment, theft, a couple of bad business deals—lightning even struck one of the storage barns. After the accidents and business deals gone wrong, insurance costs rose and I guess no banks would lend Dale or Joe Singer more money to keep the business afloat. They shuttered when John was a teen."

That was an impressive string of bad luck, but there was one thing she hadn't touched upon. "Nothing about any of their romantic relationships?"

"Well, the normal run-of-the-mill relationship stuff wouldn't make the papers." She chuckled. "Mill pun totally intended, by the way. One of the accidents involved Dale's wife during a supposed argument. I won't go into details about that, although police deemed it to be just a freak thing, no mal-intent. She survived. Another Singer wife ran off with a foreman . . ." The hesitation in her voice was clear. "John's mom."

"That might explain some things, then. Thank you so much for all your help, Steph. I owe you."

"Mmm . . . I accept payment in the form of baked goods or wine."

I laughed. "How about both for girls' night?"

"Deal. Okay, I'll let you finish getting ready for your date. Later."

Never one to waste words, she hung up before I had the chance to say goodbye.

I checked the clock again. Talking to Steph had eaten into much of my prep time. Nothing she'd said had struck me as a ghost's motive to get involved with John even if they were related. I doubted a ghost would interfere with a relationship that had yet to even begin. But after my last matchmaking case, I knew the reason would reveal itself eventually. Oh well, I couldn't dwell on it or else I'd never get ready. I still needed to get dressed, run a brush through my hair, and put on some lip gloss. Time to apply more makeup than that had run out.

Almost ready several minutes later, I rushed downstairs to my kitchen escorted by the sounds of clinking metal. As expected, Saffy sat in front of her bowls, tail flicking back and forth, her paw poised to strike her dish once more. She saw me and let out a loud meow that sounded remarkably like *now*.

"Sorry! I wasn't expecting to be on the phone that long," I said, opening up the cupboard where I kept her food. I filled her bowl, and she shoved her face into it, making these purt-growl noises that she only made when really hungry, her tail shaking in happiness. After another minute, I dropped a scoop of wet food into her bowl. If I gave that to her first, she'd never eat the rest of her dinner.

"You should be all set for the evening. See you when I get home." I gave her a quick scratch behind her ears as she continued to gobble her meal. "Don't wait up."

I walked into the living room, heading for the closet by the front door where I kept all my shoes. As I slid into a pair of blue flats, my landline rang once more, sending me back to the kitchen to grab the cordless phone hanging on the wall by the door.

"Hi, Ken," I said after seeing it was him on the caller ID. "I was just getting ready to leave. What's up?"

"Oh, I'm glad I caught you. Listen, Joanie. I hate to do this, but I'm going to have to cancel our date tonight. I'm so sorry it's short notice like this." A concerned tone hung from his words, but it wasn't about me or my reaction to the cancelation.

"Is everything okay?"

"Ivy's sick, so she's not going to be able to go to her friend's sleepover."

"Oh no, it's nothing too serious, is it?" I crossed the living room, stepped out of my shoes, and then pushed them into my open closet with my foot. Turning toward the room, I closed the door behind me and leaned my back against it. Drats.

"I don't think so. Honestly, I think she may have worked herself up about it, thus making herself sick. And as anxious as she had been about it, now she's bummed that she can't go after all, and I'm bummed that she can't go because that means not getting to go out with you."

"Well, I'm glad it's not serious, but I'm sorry she won't get to go." Unslinging my purse from around me, I walked over to the couch and sat down, dropping my bag next to me.

"You're not mad, are you?" This time he did sound concerned about my reaction.

"Mad? No, not at all." How could I be? "You'd both been looking forward to it. I had been too, but we'll get together another time. It's okay."

He sighed. It seemed to be laced with a mix of relief and frustration. "Thanks. And, yes, definitely another time. I am sorry. And I gotta go. I promised we could watch one of her favorite princess movies."

"I'll talk to you later. Tell Ivy I hope she feels better soon."

"I will. Bye, Joanie."

"Bye." I waited to hang up until I he ended the call. For some reason, I'd never wanted to be the first one to hang up on with anyone. What if they had that one more thing to say and I missed it?

I stood from the couch. There was no sense in lounging in my dress and getting cat fur all over it. No doubt there was some just from sitting on the couch. Before heading upstairs, I stopped in the kitchen. Saffy popped her head up from her food, giving me a curious stare as I put the tea kettle on to boil.

"Change of plans, Saf. Looks like all your help picking out the dress went for naught. I'm going to go change. Then it's just you and me tonight."

She dismissed me with a flick of her tail and went back to eating. Right now, she was busy, but soon, she'd be the only one not bummed by the change of plans.

A few minutes later and fully changed, I walked back into the kitchen to pour myself a cup of herbal tea. I loaded my infuser with a hibiscus-citrus blend and set it in the cup to steep. Saffy brushed past my legs on her way to the living room, consoling me over my canceled plans or trying to get as much cat fur on my leggings as she could or both.

Teacup in hand, I followed my sassy calico, nearly tripping over her a few feet into the room. I had fully expected her to be in her spot on the back of the couch by now, waiting to curl up between my legs as I settled into a book. Instead, she stared intently at something.

No. *Someone.*

As I followed her gaze, the grandfatherly lumberjack ghost appeared in the center of the room. Unlike with Kate's hairbrush, I hadn't brought anything connected to him inside the house, and I hadn't invited him in. How had he made it past the wards Gram and Mom had placed at all the entrances? Maybe he knew.

"How are you in my house?"

The ghost looked at me and shrugged.

I'd have to ask Gram about the wards tomorrow when I talked to her for our usual Saturday chat. She could tell me how to strengthen them. I didn't want my home to become a stop for wayward spirits in need of help. Or better yet, maybe she could come do whatever needed to be done for me. After all, she was the witch, *not* me, and it had been too long since I'd seen her. I hadn't seen her since Christmas, one of the few days of the year when the bakery was closed.

"Are you able to talk now?"

Unlike before, he didn't try this time and shook his head instead, frustration obvious as if he'd been trying before he got here.

"Well, perhaps I can get you started on the right track. I believe in the power of names, and I did some digging. Is your name Dale Singer?"

His face brightened, and he nodded enthusiastically. Thank you, Donna and Steph.

"So John is your grandson?"

Again, Dale nodded.

"Are you here because of him, to help him? Does it involve Lily?"

He tilted his head to the side.

"Lily's my baker. I think they might be an excellent match for one another."

He smiled and pointed at me, then tapped his nose. But as he did, his image jumbled as if he were a picture on a staticky old TV screen. He was losing energy fast. Maybe the wards had started to get to him.

We were getting somewhere, but he still needed more energy if he was ever going to be able to talk. "Dale, rest up. Now that I know your name, I know we'll figure this out."

He winked out of sight as if a TV had turned off.

Hopefully he felt more confident in me than I did of myself. Sure, I'd helped Kate and Daniel last month, but could I do it again?

CHAPTER 6

Once again alone in my living room, my stomach growled loudly enough that Saffy turned to look at me from where she'd stayed during Dale's brief visit. She'd been fixated on him, as well as the spot after he disappeared, and it was as if I had awoken her from a trance with the noise.

I was supposed to have eaten with Ken, but with plans canceled, now I needed to find something to make for myself.

Saffy trailed close behind me as I headed into the kitchen, no doubt hoping for more food. She walked to her bowls and sat.

"You just ate," I reminded her as if my saying that had ever prevented her from wanting more food.

She tapped her dish with her paw. It was already empty in her mind, though I could barely make out the bottom poking through in spots. She hit it again.

I caved. "We'll see what I end up making, okay?" I could always give her a treat. She had several of those left. But what did I have?

Without leftovers to eat, I dug through my cupboards. A trip to the grocery store was in my future, but within a few minutes, I'd gathered all the ingredients needed to whip up macaroni and cheese. It was a big meal for one person, however. Too big even after a couple days of leftovers were factored into the mix. For a moment, I considered making some to bring to Matt across the street as a surprise, but then it dawned on me that two other people were also likely lacking dinner tonight thanks to our change of plans.

"Guess I'm going out after all, Saffy."

I swore she gave me the side-eye as she looked at me without turning her head away from her "empty" bowl.

When I reached into the lower cabinet where I kept my spare tote bags usually used to carry groceries, Saffy perked up, tail shaking. It was also where I kept her treats that I gave her when I needed her to give me space to put food from the store away. I pulled out one of my tote bags and the container of treats.

There were only two treats left, so I gave both to Saffy. I thought I had more. Usually I kept better stock of them. "Looks like I'll have to make more this weekend."

I packed up the dinner ingredients in the tote, then slung it onto my shoulder. "I'll see you a little later."

Saffy was too busy chowing down to respond. The baked catnip treats weren't large, but she knew how to savor them.

This time when I opened my closet, I opted for a pair of sneakers. My flats were cute, and they'd fancy up my leggings, but they weren't something I wanted to walk uphill a few blocks in. On the way out the door, I grabbed a sweater from my coat tree for later. As soon as I stepped outside, I was glad I had. May evenings still got cool enough for them.

A short walk later and I had reached Ken and Ivy's front

door. I knocked, fully expecting Ivy to still run to the door and answer it as she always did.

The newly painted yellow door opened.

"Joanie, what are you doing here?" Ken's face was a mix of confusion, relief, and happiness. He stepped aside to let me in, stopping me as I walked through the entrance to give me a quick kiss.

I let the tote bag slide from my shoulder into my hand. "I figured you wouldn't have had much for dinner since you weren't planning for either of you to be home. So since I happened to be free after my date canceled, I thought I'd come by and cook something."

"Now who would do a thing like cancel on you?" Ken fake scoffed, a smile growing wide across his face.

"Doesn't matter. I'd rather hang out with a sick kid and her dad. How's Ivy?"

"Okay. She's snuggled up on her bed. Just restarted her favorite princess movie. I'm not sure how much she'll actually eat of dinner, but I certainly thank you for coming over. You didn't have to."

I crossed the living room and headed into the kitchen. A rolled-up bag of chips lay on the counter.

"Your dinner?" I glanced over my shoulder at Ken, who had followed me into the room.

He shrugged. "It's all I had."

I plopped the tote on the counter and set to work. Soon I had ginger macaroni and cheese baking in the oven.

"I'm not sure if Ivy's going to like that," Ken warned me as cleaned up the scraps of fresh ginger. "She's more of a packet of yellow cheese powder type of girl."

With a knowing grin, I turned to him. "Oh, I have a feeling she'll like this." Over the last few weeks, I'd gotten Ivy to be a bit more adventurous with her eating habits. She'd even found a Chinese food dish she liked. I hadn't tried to get her to eat raisins yet, though. I was still a bit traumatized from the time she'd thought I'd given them to her in a muffin.

Ken held his hands up in surrender, still disbelieving. "Don't say I didn't warn you."

I walked over to him and kissed him on the cheek. "I'm going to go say hi. That has to cook for a while." I headed upstairs and down the hall, coming to a stop at a door with a unicorn poster taped onto it. Quietly, I knocked.

"Yeah?" a small, sleepy voice inside said.

"Can I come in?"

"Joanie?" Her voice had brightened considerably.

I opened the door and poked my head in. "Hey, how are you feeling?"

"Okay . . ." She let out a little sigh.

"Sorry you couldn't go to your friend's house tonight." I approached her on the bed.

Ivy rubbed her eyes. "I ruined your date." The way she said it made me question what she was more upset about—her missing the sleepover or my non-date with her dad.

"Well, about that. I decided to bring the date to you. Dinner is in the oven. Mac and cheese with my own special twist." I winked at her.

"Really?"

"Yep. Won't be done for about an hour, though. What are you watching?"

She pointed at her small TV sitting on her dresser a few feet away.

I peeked over and saw Belle fawning over the Beast's library. My favorite.

After a moment, she scooched over on the bed, and I sat down.

By the time the buzzer sounded in the kitchen telling me

to take the mac and cheese out of the oven, Ivy had restarted the movie. It didn't surprise me, however, when she followed me and sat at the table as I set the baking dish onto a trivet to cool.

Ken walked out of the living room and did a double take at Ivy's presence. He scruffed her hair as he passed behind her to get to the counter, where he pulled out plates and cups from an upper cupboard.

"Smells good," he said as he set the plates down. His gaze darted to the side to land on Ivy before returning to me. Softer, he whispered, "I think I may have underestimated your abilities."

"I have my ways." I giggled, grabbing a spatula from his cooking utensil holder. "Didn't you know I'm a kitchen witch?"

Ken smiled. "I wouldn't be surprised."

I, however, didn't believe it for a moment, even though my gram had been trying to tell me differently for years. She was the witch, not me. My mom too. I was a fabulous baker and great in the kitchen overall, but that meant nothing beyond me having embraced my interests and developing my abilities through continued use. Why did I have to define what I could do by giving myself an additional label? Especially a supernatural one.

"You're not a witch," Ivy chirped.

"Oh yeah? Why's that?" I scooped out two large servings of mac and cheese for Ken and me, then a half portion for Ivy.

Her face grew serious as she answered, "You aren't wicked. You're not afraid of the rain. And you're not green!"

"All solid points." Ken set her dish in front of her and handed her a fork. Then he winked at me. "But what about good witches?"

That seemed to stump her. She thought quietly for a few moments. "Well, I guess you could be a good witch."

As long as she didn't go adding to the rumors around town, I didn't mind what she thought I was. Telling her anything different would only make her dig in her heels, like when she'd refused to believe the blueberries weren't raisins.

I joined Ken and Ivy at the table, and we all dug into our dinners. Ken *mmm*ed about how good it was with each of his first three spoonsful. Ivy asked for seconds, surprising her father, who suggested she take it easy because she hadn't felt good. After a bit of initial protest, and my promise to leave leftovers, she relented.

"You should make this one Monday," Ivy said.

I cocked my head to the side and hurried to swallow a bite to answer her. "Why's that?"

"I think Mattie would like it." My neighbor Matt ruined his dinner at least once a week so he'd have an excuse to eat with me, not that he needed one. Ivy had met him recently and was completely enamored with him.

"That's a great idea. And how about I have you and your dad over again for it too?"

Ivy nodded enthusiastically. "Yes please!"

Ken chuckled. "All right, kiddo, how about you go get cleaned up and finish your movie. I'll come tuck you in at bedtime."

"Okay, Daddy." Ivy picked up her bowl and placed it in the sink before skipping out of the room.

"I'd say she's feeling better," I said, admiring her energy after the inundation of carbs. Me, on the other hand, I was ready for a nap.

"Who'd have thought? Thank you for coming over. You being here had just as much to do with Ivy's spirits as your food did."

A flush rose up my cheeks as I smiled. I tried but failed to hide it, standing from the table and turning to put my dish in the sink. "Anytime." His comment warmed my heart. Ivy and I had come a long way in the last few weeks. She was a great kid.

"Shall we head back into the living room?"

I turned around and nodded, still trying to prevent him from seeing how red I was.

Ken stepped forward and caressed my cheek, turning my face to meet his gaze. "You don't need to hide with me." He let his hand fall and took mine, then led me into the next room. It was a good thing, too, or else I would have melted into a puddle on the floor.

He sat on the couch and pulled me down next to him. "How's it going? Tell me about your day."

I filled him in on everything that had happened with John coming into the shop and the tingling that had me believing he and Lily were meant for one another. He listened, nodding, all the way through my mentioning Dale's multiple appearances. He'd seen Kate and Daniel, so my telling him about another ghost didn't seem to faze him. It felt good to be so open about my abilities with someone.

It wasn't until I told him about what I'd found out from Donna and Holly at the diner that Ken spoke up.

"They seem unlucky. All of them. Maybe this isn't such a good idea."

"What isn't?"

"You inserting yourself into their lives like this. You've identified them as a match, so shouldn't you just let this relationship play out by itself?"

"But that's not how it works." My posture stiffened.

"If they're meant to be, won't they find one another without your help?"

"Maybe. But I'm not sure. I don't think it's a guarantee."

He raised an eyebrow at me. "Have you ever not meddled in the process?"

"*Meddled*? That's what you're calling it? It makes me sound like I drive a van with my Great Dane in the passenger seat."

Ken cracked a bit of a smile at my comment and sighed. "Okay, maybe that's too strong of a word, but maybe you should just let this go and see what happens for a bit."

He'd been a part of my matchmaking with Ashley and Rich firsthand. How could he be telling me to not get involved? That was how I did things. It had been my involvement in their blossoming relationship that caused me to meet him in the first place.

"They haven't even been in the same room together yet. Why not figure out some way to at least introduce them? Dale seems to agree."

"And now you're recruiting Dale?"

"I wouldn't say *recruiting*. As John's grandfather, he's already a part of it. But I think he needs help too. Might as well try to help him too. You saw what happened last time with your grandmother and Daniel."

He rubbed the back of his neck. "Yeah, but—"

I needed to put a stop to this conversation now before one of us said something we couldn't take back. I'd thought he was more okay with this than he was. Had I shared too much too soon?

"I should get going. It's getting late, and I have to be at the bakery early tomorrow for a large order. If you could get the baking dish to me before Monday night, that would be great, just in case I end up using it for dinner." I stood and made my way toward the door.

Ken followed me. "Look, Joanie, I don't want you to get

the wrong idea about things. I think it's great that you have this gift—"

"Then why don't you want me to use it?" I asked, turning toward him.

"I just—be careful, okay?" He reached for my hand and took it in his. "Even I remember hearing the rumors about that family as a kid. And I didn't even grow up here in town."

"You can't believe everything you hear. Sometimes rumors are just that, rumors. I should know. I've certainly had enough swirling through town about me."

"But you don't know John like you did Rich and Ashley when you helped them. Or this ghost."

Thinking better of reminding him that I did know Lily and how I hadn't known Kate or Daniel when I helped them either, I lifted onto my tiptoes and kissed Ken on the cheek. I appreciated his concern, although his way of showing it was growing on my nerves. "I'll be careful. Goodnight, Ken."

He pulled the door open for me, and I stepped outside. "Goodnight."

I spun slowly on my heels and headed away from his house, then waved as I reached the sidewalk as I always did, though it probably lacked its usual oomph. Ken, a gentleman as always, didn't close the door until I had, giving me a small smile before I continued on my way.

The cool night air refreshed my mood somewhat as I walked back to my house, deep in contemplation. If Lily and John were a match—and my senses told me they were—then I was going to see this through. But the doubt about Ken's and my relationship gnawed at my stomach. We'd overcome one hurdle when I'd confessed to being able to see ghosts. I thought him actually seeing Kate and Daniel would have been enough to help him accept everything else I could do, but now I wasn't so sure. Matchmaking was part of me, and I had to help those matches stick especially now that a ghost was involved—again. If Ken didn't think I should do what was in my nature, how much of a chance did we stand?

CHAPTER 7

T he next morning, I stepped out of my house and into the damp air, grateful the mornings were warming up. Sidewalks and roadways were wet, and it smelled like petrichor. I'd thought I'd heard raindrops hitting the window sometime overnight.

"Hi, Joanie," a familiar voice said as I pulled my bike out of my shed. I always kept it locked up—despite the numerous times I'd been told it would be safe if I left in my yard—and I was doubly glad I had now because of the rain. No one liked a wet bike seat.

I glanced up and smiled. "Hey, Alex. What's new in the world?"

He sat on his bike on the sidewalk in front of my house, a messenger bag slung tight at his side full of newspapers. "I just deliver the news, I don't report on it. That's my sister's job." He laughed.

I walked my bike down the short driveway. "Did she tell you I talked to her yesterday?"

The twins had lived together when I moved into the apartment across the hall from them. Even though we'd all since moved, and they no longer shared a place, the two spoke regularly.

He nodded. "She may have bragged about you owing her dinner and wine when we were at our parents' house last night."

"Well, consider yourself invited for dinner. You probably won't want to stay for girls' night, though."

He puckered his face, sticking out his tongue. "Yeah, no. I'll skip the chick flicks, thanks, but you can totally count me in for dinner." He held up the paper. "You want this, or should I toss it onto the porch?"

I hopped on my bike. "Porch, please. I'll read it tonight with tea. Maybe do the crossword puzzle."

"You still do those?" he asked, lobbing the rolled-up newspaper toward my door. It landed on my doormat.

I nodded. "Great shot."

His aim was always perfect. Steph had told me he'd been the star pitcher and quarterback in high school. Could have gone pro with either sport, but he'd taken a job as a gym teacher and football coach here after college. Delivering papers in the morning gave him some extra cash.

"Well, I'll let you get to work. Nice chatting with you. Guess I'll be seeing you again sometime soon."

His comment brought a smile to my face. It had been too long since I'd hung out with him and his sister. "Have a great rest of your day."

I took off and pedaled away as Alex did the same in the opposite direction.

For such an early hour, it never failed to surprise me how many people I would run into on my way to the bakery. Even though it was a Saturday and I was going in a half hour earlier to get a jumpstart on a special order, people—and ghosts—were out and about before dawn.

Gary was unlocking the doors to Leafs and Grounds as I coasted down the hill toward the coffee shop. He waved.

I squeezed my brakes and came to a stop a few feet away. "Little early for you, isn't it?"

He nodded. "I told some the kids they could practice their speeches for the honors ceremony in here since I have the small stage for open mic night. Figured I'd get a jump on my day."

"That's why I'm early too. They ordered a bunch of pastries and scones for their brunch."

"Hey, how about I throw in a tray of marshmallow rice treats?"

"I bet they would love that." So would I. I didn't know what I'd do with myself if I had a full tray of those delicious treats.

"Stop by before you make your delivery. I'll have it packed and ready."

"Great. Thanks, Gary. See you later." I pushed off on my bike and finished the ride to the back of the bakery.

I unlocked the back door for a bleary-eyed Sam and Gina. Lily strode in a minute later, right on time, looking awake and refreshed. I wondered if she was already over her breakup as she pulled her hair back, trying to engage Gina in conversation. Bryan shuffled in not long after, yawning, but the coffee-filled travel mug he held would wake him up soon enough.

Once I'd given everyone their tasks, thanking them all for coming in early, I sidled up to Lily's station.

She glanced up at me as she incorporated butter into sieved flour. Soon it would be a delicious pastry dough. She smiled.

I took that as my opening. "How are you doing this morning?"

"You know? I'm doing good." She added some cold water into the butter-flour mixture.

"I'm glad. After yesterday, I wanted to check in and make sure you were okay."

As she talked, the dough came together into a ball. "Thanks, but really, I'm good. I was frustrated yesterday, but I'm over it now."

I'd seen my fair share of breakups over the years, and I didn't quite believe it. "You sure you're good?"

She shrugged, dusting her work surface with a layer of flour.

"Not everyone can bounce back like that. I'm impressed."

"Yeah. I had a good night's sleep, so things are looking better today." She turned the dough out of the bowl onto her station.

I let Lily continue with her work. She was a key player in getting the pastries ready for the students' brunch. Everyone else was tasked with our regular load, meaning they all had more to do today. I'd have to consider hiring someone else soon, especially once Sam took off for culinary school, preferably sooner so they could get trained while we still had everyone else. At least in the shop, I'd be getting Lauren back to help on a part-time schedule. She had dropped down to Saturdays only until her college classes were over for the semester. She would have been in today, but it was finals week, so I'd told her to stay home and study. Lily had offered to cover the shift in the shop, giving Sarah a much needed and deserved day off since coming to work for me full time.

The town was already bustling with early morning activity as I made my first round of deliveries. I passed the town's jogging club on the way to Double Aitch, and Paul and Walter, who'd helped me with solving Rich and Ashley's problems a few weeks prior, were walking toward Olde Templeton Diner as I was hopping on my bike, so we waved.

When I got back to the bakery, I sent Sam home to get ready for the honors brunch. Sam hadn't wanted to make a big deal about it, but he'd been looking forward to it. He was the hardest-working high schooler I knew. I had no doubt he'd succeed at culinary school.

Bryan, Gina, Lily, and I continued baking until I had to prep the shop for opening. Then we loaded the cases with dozens of cookies, cupcakes, scones, and pastries. They returned to baking—there was still a bit to do because of the special order and now being short-staffed—as I readied the till and gave the bakery a once-over. After a quick dusting over by the window display, I flipped the sign in the door from *closed* to *open*.

Our regular Saturday customers trickled in with a few exceptions missing, but realizing they were all parents of graduating seniors, I expected they were all waiting until the honors brunch for their treats. Their absence was noticeable, though, and the quiet morning seemed to crawl by. As soon as the thought popped into my head, I tried to shove it away. A slow morning could easily leady to a crazy afternoon. The calm before the storm. Today's weather didn't help either. The rain had left a warm humidity in its wake, and the sky was gray.

The ominous feeling nagged me all the way to Leafs and Grounds so I could pick up the marshmallow rice treats, and it continued as I reached the high school, where the gymnasium had been set up for the honors brunch.

"Here, let me get some of that," Sam said from behind me, his footsteps heavy as he approached my bike trailer.

I turned and gave my baker a once-over. "Thanks, Sam. My, don't you look snazzy."

Blushing, he ran a hand through his newly buzzed hair on the side of his head. There was still some length at the top, and he'd slicked it back instead of leaving it shaggy like he usually did.

"I told Todd I'd let him see my hair cut nicely at least once before I left for school. It's what I would have done for prom had we gone." Sam had recently told his family he was gay, but few others knew. I was honored to be among those he'd been comfortable telling.

"Well, I think he's going to love it. It looks great."

"Thanks." He grabbed a few of the boxes in the bike trailer as I grabbed the others, and he led the way to the school's gymnasium.

Another familiar face held the door open for us. "Joanie, it's good to see you again."

"Hey, Rich, you too. Thanks for getting the door." As one of the high school teachers, I'd assumed I'd see him here.

"It's no problem. Let me show you where to set those up." We wound our way across the room, passing two dozen circular tables covered with green tablecloths, over to a large buffet table.

I set my boxes down, and Sam did the same. "Have fun today. You earned it," I told him as I began unpacking the boxes and setting out the pastries on waiting trays.

"Thanks. I'll see you in the morning." He strolled off toward a group of his friends.

I turned to Rich as I broke down one of the yellow pastry boxes. "How are things going between you and Ashley?"

His signature megawatt smile flashed onto his face. "Why don't you ask her yourself?" He cupped his hands around his mouth like a megaphone. "Hey, babe, look who's here!" To me, he added at a normal volume, "She's helping me set up before she goes to the animal shelter to volunteer."

Somehow I'd completely missed Ashley setting up center-pieces when we'd walked by. She looked up, waved, and headed this way. Once she reached us, she wrapped her left arm around Rich's back, and he wrapped his right around hers.

"Hey, Ashley, I was just asking how things were going between you two."

"They're so good. Thanks to you."

I broke down another box. "No more ghosts?"

She shook her head. "Nope, none. Thank goodness." She laughed.

"That's great. I'm really glad. Well"—I stashed the remaining empty boxes under the table in case they had left-overs—"I'd love to stay and chat, but you're still getting ready, and I have to get back to the shop. I'll see you again soon."

"You'll be at the festival next weekend, right?" Ashley asked.

"Absolutely. I'll have a cart full of goodies there." Heart-wood Hollow's annual Love a Tree Day Festival was not to be missed.

CHAPTER 8

Bryan and Gina had already gone home by the time I returned, and as soon as I walked into the shop from the kitchen, I could tell Lily's earlier chipper mood had disappeared. She seemed quiet, reserved, almost brooding. Maybe she wasn't as over Aaron as she'd claimed to be.

"How'd things go?" I asked, slinging a pink apron over my head as I rushed behind the counter.

She shrugged. "It went fine."

"Just fine?" Sarah usually gave me a minute-by-minute update whenever I stepped out. Then again, I think she did it just as much for the gossip potential as anything else. She loved to talk. Lily only offered what was necessary.

"Pretty standard from what Lauren's told me of Saturday shifts."

"Great. So you're sure you're okay?"

"Yeah." She let out a long, hard sigh. "Aaron's a good guy and all, but we weren't meant to be. I get that. Still disappointing, though."

"I understand. How about you head out and grab some

lunch. When you come back, you can start the prep for tomorrow morning."

"Sounds good." She trudged into the kitchen. I hoped food would help give her a boost. After that, she'd be back in her usual environment and wouldn't have to deal with customers. I was grateful for her help today, but interacting with customers exhausted her after too long.

The first half hour felt much like a normal Saturday afternoon. If this was how the time during my deliveries had passed, no wonder Lily had little to report.

All that changed when John Singer entered the bakeshop. This was what I got for thinking it was quiet earlier.

"Hello again," I said in my usual cheerful greeting tone. "How are you today?"

John glanced up and nodded, a hint of a strained smile on his face. He walked over to the pastry case. This was a better reaction than I had gotten the other day, although he still seemed a bit cagey. His gaze roamed the case as often as it did the rest of the shop and the door to the kitchen.

"See anything you like?"

John pointed to an elephant ear with his left hand. His right hadn't left the front pocket of his jeans, and from the bulk, it looked like his hand was clenched into a fist.

"J-just one please," he finally spoke. He had a soft voice, almost pleasant, except it was laced with nervousness I suspected wasn't usual based on what I'd heard about him.

"Coming right up." I reached into the case and grabbed the flakey pastry, then dropped it into a white wax paper bag.

John shuffled over to the counter, and I rang him up. He dug into his back pocket with his left hand and pulled out his wallet. After opening it, he counted out the exact change but put another dollar in the tip jar.

As his eyes darted back to the kitchen door, the tingling

sensation I got when two halves of a perfect match were near started in my toes. The door from the kitchen swung open into the bakery, and Lily walked through. If I had any doubts about Lily being his match, they went away with the knowledge that only she and I were here right now.

"Joanie, I'm back from lunch. I'm going to get started on the—oh, hello." A smile grew across her face as she gave John an appraising once-over. Her shoulders drew straight, and she stuck out one leg with it bent at the knee. Had she put her hands on her hips, I'd have said it was the proper model's pose, but her arms hung loose at her sides.

"H-H-Hi." Considering I hadn't gotten a hello out of him, this was a promising start.

"How are you? Did you find everything you were looking for?"

"Wow," he said on a sigh, still looking at Lily. "Y-Y-Yeah. I did."

Lily's posture changed once more. She relaxed and pushed a stray lock of her pinkish hair behind her ear, momentarily hiding the flush that was creeping up her cheeks.

"I'm Lily." She almost looked as if she wanted to giggle, something I'd never seen her do.

Their first meeting, although awkward, seemed to be going well. The matchmaking tingle I felt had risen up my legs and was taking up residence in my stomach as a swarm of butterflies.

"J-J-John," he answered, drawing his right hand out of his pocket. It was fisted around something, and as he gradually opened his hand, the object glowed brighter and brighter, a pink and yellow to almost a blinding white.

A knife. John had pulled a knife in my shop, but he didn't open the blade, just held it out in his palm, his entire arm shaking. I didn't fear him. If anything, he was the one who was afraid.

"I-I-I," he began, but no other words came out. His hand jerked as if he'd been burned. The knife fell to the floor, landing with a dull thud, and stopped glowing. John glanced at Lily before turning and running out of the bakery.

Placing the pastry bag I still had in my hand onto the counter, I sighed. What was that all about? The tingling remained, but that had to have been the strangest first encounter between a match that I had ever experienced. I needed to call my mom to see what she thought of it. Maybe she had experienced something similar during her years as a matchmaker.

I glanced at Lily. "Are you okay?"

Gone was the flirtatious girl who had been standing by the kitchen door. In her place stood someone completely different. Still Lily, but like with the near giggling, it was a side of her I'd never seen. Her hair had taken on more volume as if it had been windblown, and her expression was cold.

They had a saying here in New England about how if someone didn't like the weather, all they had to do was wait five minutes and it would change. That fit Lily to a *T*. Lily's demeanor changed like the weather. I'd picked up on it when I hired her about three years ago. Cold and blustery outside? Her attitude was brusque and huffy. Warm and bright? She was cheery, smiled all the time, and talked nonstop. The only thing that didn't quite fit was the rain. I'd expected it to make her crabby, but I'd been wrong. She always said it energized her, even those mornings when she came in looking half-drowned after walking in a downpour to the bakery for her shift.

But I'd never seen her so mad as right then. Her mouth set into a firm line, jaw clenched, nostrils flaring. Her breath was audible, coming out in strong, quick bursts, as she marched to the knife and bent to retrieve it. Still crouched, Lily stared at the knife, eyes wide and knuckles white around the handle, her hand shaking. She balled the other into a fist as she watched John's retreating form head toward Main Street.

What was going on?

Lily stood, still vibrating with anger. She flipped open the knife's blade, and that only seemed to enrage her further.

"Lily?"

She glanced over her shoulder at me. "I'm sorry." Then she bolted out the door, following John's path.

CHAPTER 9

This was already proving to be the most complicated match I'd ever had, and it had barely begun. Rich and Ashley's match was tame in comparison, and at times, they'd been under the influence of ghosts.

I ran around the counter and charged out the door, needing to make sure Lily was okay and wouldn't do anything to hurt herself or John.

Two steps past my shop, I barreled into Ken.

He held on to my shoulders out at arm's length and smiled. "Hey, where are you going in such a hurry?"

How had he missed seeing Lily run by? "I'm sorry. I've got to go. It's Lily."

I pushed off against his chest and continued past him onto Main Street.

He didn't follow, and at that moment, I didn't care. I'd call him later to explain. There were more pressing matters to attend to.

It wasn't hard to spot Lily's trail. Many on the sidewalk had stopped to stare down the road in the wake of her path, murmuring something about a knife and asking what's going on. Up ahead, Lily's pink ponytail bounced this way and that as she pursued John.

"Come back here!" she yelled.

John, too, was yelling, but I couldn't understand him.

"Lily, stop! John! Wait!" I called after them. "Someone, grab them!"

That snapped others into action. Carter from Double Aitch Diner sprinted down the steps of the post office and in front of John, blocking his path, mail in hand. Holly from Leafs and Grounds was also coming from the post office. She stepped in front of Lily, grabbed her by her shoulders, and slowed her down. Holly wasn't tiny. She was tall and toned. I regularly saw her at the yoga studio and wouldn't have been surprised if she worked out outside of that too. But even with her muscles, Holly couldn't fully stop Lily. Holly walked backward a few steps, albeit slowly. I hadn't realized Lily was that strong, although maybe she was fueled by adrenaline. Rage was a powerful emotion.

Holly's effort allowed me to catch up to them in several long strides. Panting lightly, I placed my hand on Lily's shoulder. Although I walked or biked almost everywhere, I hated running, and I still had to catch my breath after doing it.

"Please, Lily, let's talk about this."

"There's nothing to talk about." She wouldn't look at me.

Holly whispered something to her, and Lily's shoulders slumped.

"If it were nothing, you wouldn't have taken off from the shop after a customer with a knife in your hands," I said, taking a step back to give her space.

She turned to face me, her eyes welling with tears.

"I'd like to know why you came after me too." John was a few feet away now, Carter right behind him with his arms crossed. A few feet beyond them, Dale stood rapt in the encounter. His eyes were wide open, and he was leaning in as if he wanted to see everything. He didn't seem to realize I was there.

A spark of anger reignited in Lily's eyes. She spun on her heels to face John.

I positioned myself off to the side but between Lily and John to act as a mediator if necessary. It was then that Dale noticed me, and he smiled at me before turning his attention back to the exchange at hand.

"Why did you have this?" Lily cried. She held out the still-open knife in her hand, knuckles white around its handle.

John held up his hands. "It's been in my family for years —decades. I inherited it from my grandfather."

I glanced up at Dale, who nodded, confirming John's statement. Was that how he was still here? Was he anchored to the knife much in the way Kate had been to the hairbrush? But why?

"That's decades too long. Don't you know what it is?" Lily asked, still shaking, though no longer from rage but from holding back her sobs.

"It's a knife..." John said as if it were a trick question. He lowered his hands. "You're upset over a knife? How? It's not like I stole it from you."

The crowd had started to dissipate now that it didn't look like Lily was going to stab John anymore, but several villagers remained, including Holly and Carter. Ken was nowhere in sight. A few others had trickled over to see what was going on, having missed the initial action. They were mostly high schoolers with their parents in nice attire, likely coming back from the honors brunch. This incident was going to be the talk of Heartwood Hollow for some time.

One villager, in particular, caught my eye. Another ghost. I'd never seen her before. Wearing a floral silk blouse with noticeable shoulder pads and beige pants, the woman reminded me of the eighties clothes hiding in the back of Gram's closet that she swore would come back in style one day.

The ghost's stony glare and flaring nostrils were a dead ringer for Lily's, as was her overall build and complexion. Her hair was feathered, a look I'd seen in photos of my mom and aunt, and unless my eyes were playing tricks on me, I'd have sworn her hair was the same color as Lily's too—a light pink. They had to be related. Granddaughter and grandmother perhaps?

But why was she—like Lily—so upset? Was it only because her granddaughter was still so upset, or did it also have something to do with that knife?

Lily strained to rein in her emotions. "It never should have been made."

John raked his fingers across the sides of his head, tugging on the ends of his hair before dropping his hands in front of him, palms up. "I don't get it. It's just a knife."

"It's sacred wood!"

Sacred wood? That was the first time I'd ever heard that phrase. I'd have to ask Gram when I called her later today if she knew what it could be. I studied Lily's grandmother for a reaction. Her insistent nodding told me she was aware of the term. Across the way, Dale shook his head, looking down, the heel of one palm against his forehead. I wondered if he understood what the term meant.

"I don't even know what that is," John said, a hopeless frustration evident in his tone.

Holly scoffed. "Lumberjacks never do," she muttered mostly to Lily. I hadn't realized the two were so close.

"I heard that," John replied. "I'll have you know my company hasn't taken down a tree since its inception."

Both Lily and her grandmother's ghost perked up a bit at that. "Really?" Lily asked.

"Yeah. My grandfather made me swear I wouldn't before his death."

Lily sighed. "Sadly, it came too late for some."

"Look, I'm sorry that this knife upsets you. I don't understand why it does, but I am. I'm sorry that *I* upset you too. But would you mind if I have my knife back? Like I said, my grandfather gave it to me, so it means a great deal."

Lily eased her grip on the handle, slowly opening her fingers until it sat on her palm. Much like it had in the shop, the knife glowed a pinkish-yellow, then flared white before it lifted out of Lily's hands and flew into John's.

The blade was still open, and some in the crowd gasped, likely thinking she'd thrown it at him. Few should have realized what really happened. People tended to accept the easier explanation.

Not me, though. After the hairbrush a few weeks ago, I took things moving on their own in stride. I looked at Dale to see if he had moved it, but he gave me no sign that he had. Had it been John's doing somehow?

Lily crumpled to the ground, her hands buried in her hair. "I need to get out of here."

Holly stooped to lift Lily back to her feet. "Come on, it's going to be okay. Let's go."

With Holly's help, Lily stood, then leaned into Holly for support.

Despite this incident, my matchmaking tingle continued. It wasn't too late for them to find happiness. It just wouldn't be today.

"Lily?" Concern etched my voice. I hated seeing anyone upset, let alone someone I cared about.

She turned toward me, the tears that had been threatening to spill now falling down her cheeks. "I'm sorry, Joanie. I don't think I'm going to be able to finish my shift in the shop today."

"Hey, don't even worry about it." Taking a few steps toward her, I placed my hand on her upper arm and gave her a soft smile. "I just want to make sure you're okay."

"I'll be fine once I get some air. That's all. I'll see you in the morning."

"If you need more time, I'll understand. Text me if you won't make it in."

She nodded. "Thank you."

I let go of her arm, letting mine fall slowly to my side.

Holly wrapped her arm around Lily's back. "I'll take care of her, Joanie. Don't you worry."

"Thanks. If either of you needs anything . . ."

Holly nodded sharply once, then turned Lily around. Together they crossed the street and walked away from Main Street toward the far end of the park. The tingling sensation I'd been feeling lessened with each step they took as physical distance between Lily and John grew.

Needing to get to the shop, I started to head back there as the rest of the crowd dispersed. I'd left in such a hurry so hadn't flipped the sign to *closed* or locked the door. I doubted anyone would have robbed the place while I was gone—Heartwood Hollow wasn't like that—but I didn't like leaving the shop unattended.

"Excuse me?" a voice called from behind me.

I stopped in my tracks and waited for John to catch up.

"I'm sorry for what happened out here and in your shop. I know you don't know me, but that's not like me in the slightest."

"Apology accepted." I pivoted to face him. "That's quite the powerful knife you have there."

John wouldn't look me in the eye. "I don't know what you're talking about." More like he didn't want to talk about it or didn't know how to. Falling under the influence of a not-so-inanimate object was difficult for most to process.

He'd get there eventually. "Well, when you're ready."

"She wasn't really going to stab me if she caught me, right?"

I shook my head. "No, but that knife clearly upset her." I hoped bringing it up again would get him to talk about it, but he didn't take the bait.

He shoved his hands in his pockets. "She's really something, isn't she?"

"She is . . ." What she was, I didn't know, but I wanted to find out.

CHAPTER 10

The last two hours of my day had never been so busy. Word about the incident had traveled faster than I thought it would, and swarms of villagers came to the shop to get my side of the tale.

"Why did Lily have a knife?"

"Was it really John's knife?"

"How did Lily get John's knife?"

"Are you up to your matchmaking ways again?"

With as many times as I answered those questions, I couldn't get anyone to tell me what sacred wood was. A few people knew what it was, however. They clammed up once I asked, then quickly paid for their goods and left. That was the nice thing about Heartwood Hollow's villagers. They always bought something when they were here. John's first trip to the bakery had been the exception.

I followed the last customer to the door fifteen minutes after my usual closing time and locked it behind her. It ended up being my best non-holiday sales day I'd ever had, even after removing the special honors brunch order from the day's totals. Tomorrow's day-old selection was going to feature slim pickings.

My regular nightly cleaning still had to happen, and I had yet to start tomorrow morning's baking prep, let alone finish it since that was supposed to be Lily's task before John walked in and everything else happened.

Heading into the kitchen to grab the broom, I stopped short upon finding the baking trays laid out, croissant dough proofing on the counter, and the dishwasher running. I'd had a ghost turn my fan and stand mixer on before, but this was way more than a single spirit would be able to do.

Not seeing anyone, I called out, "Hello?"

The basement door opened, and Sam walked out with a large bag of flour.

"Joanie, hey." Arms full, he nodded his head in greeting.

"What are you doing here?"

He plopped the bag of flour onto the counter. "I heard what happened and figured you'd need help. Crazy stuff. Someone really pulled a knife on you?"

"Yes and no. He didn't even have the blade open. Everything would have turned out okay had it just been me"—I handed him the scoop we used to dole out portions of flour into smaller containers for each station—"and even with the complications we had, things still worked out."

"I'm glad you're okay."

I walked toward the closet to grab the broom I'd originally come in here for. "Me too. How was brunch?"

"Delicious. The food was so good. I don't know why you bothered to drop off to-go boxes. There was nothing left of your pastries or the rice treats by the end of the event. Good call on those, by the way." Once he'd scooped out the flour for each station, he poured the rest into the big storage container by the industrial stand mixer.

"I'm glad to hear it. Gary thought you'd all like those. Plus, he gave me a couple to take home." I grinned.

Sam laughed. "You do enjoy them. I'd say almost more than any of the treats you sell."

"Well, part of that is because I don't have to make them." My grin widened. "Looks like you're almost done in here. Come into the shop before you go, okay?"

He snapped the lid on the last container. "Sure thing."

I pushed through the swinging door leading from the kitchen back into the bakery. Thank goodness for Sam. If not for him, I'd easily have been here until dark. Now it looked like I only had about an hour's work left to do.

Several minutes later, Sam walked through the door holding the glass cleaner and a couple rags. While I swept, he placed the cleaning supplies on the countertop, then slipped on a pair of gloves and consolidated the partially filled trays of baked goods onto half of one. He covered that, then stacked the other trays before bringing them into the kitchen. Starting the dishwasher for those would be the last thing I'd do before leaving.

"So how did you find out about what happened today?" I asked as I finished sweeping. Sam had come back into the shop and was now at the farthest display case by the window cleaning the glass of the many smudges and finger prints.

"Holly called Lauren to fill her in on what happened. I was over at the house playing video games with Todd." He sprayed the case and began to wipe it down. "I overheard enough to get Lauren to tell me everything. Once she did, I came right over."

"I had no idea you were even here."

"You were swamped when I popped my head in to say hello. No wonder you didn't hear me."

I propped the broom over by the door and emptied the

dustpan into the garbage. "I'm so glad you came. No telling how long I'd have been here finishing everything myself."

He shrugged. "You could have called."

"You had things going on today."

"I don't mind. You know that."

I grabbed a second rag from the countertop and joined him at the next case. "What am I going to do without you when you go to school?"

He gave me a cheesy grin. "I'm kinda irreplaceable."

"You really are. And on that note, do you want a job this summer?"

"I already have a job. You're my boss." He cocked his head to the side and raised an eyebrow. "Did you think I was going to stop working for you just because it was summer and I'm not in school?"

I sprayed the next case and set to work removing my favorite thing to see. Nose prints on cases left by kids trying to get the best view of the treats. "Well, another job. Or rather an expansion of duties that you already do."

"I'm listening."

"How about you sleep in a day or two a week and come work in the shop instead? Then you can see the other side of how the bakery runs."

"Really?" His eyes lit up, and the room grew brighter around us. More and more, I believed it wasn't a coincidence that the shop seemed to react to someone's emotions.

"Of course!"

"Then definitely. That would be wicked awesome." He thought a minute, his hand moving the cloth in a small circle in the same spot as if stuck on something. "But who will take my shifts in the kitchen?"

"I'm going to have to train someone new once you leave, so this would allow me to get a jump on that while still having you around. Then whoever it is will be ready by the time you head to college."

Sam finally started wiping another part of the case. "I might know someone."

"Great, bring them on by sometime."

"I will." He moved to the case on the other side of me.

We chitchatted for several more minutes as we cleaned, mostly about his grandmother, Trudy, whom I had met a few weeks ago. She'd been a big help in solving my last matchmaking quandary. She was a dear and had at one time run a candy store on Main Street.

With the cases and countertop clean, the bakery was as tidy as it was going to get. I grabbed the cleaning supplies then scooted into the kitchen. Sam followed with the broom.

Five minutes and one load of baking trays slid into the dishwasher later, he and I headed out the back door, where we said our goodbyes.

I'd only made it to Main Street before I heard someone calling my name.

CHAPTER 11

I turned toward the caller. Donna waved her hand up in the air. She must have been on her way home from the diner. They did so well there during the morning and afternoon, they didn't run a dinner service.

She trotted over to me. "Joanie! Just the person I was hoping to run into. I heard you were robbed today!"

Her exclamation had turned heads and a few others approached, including Mark, Rachael from the bank's husband.

"Hi Donna, everyone. No, I wasn't robbed today. It was all a misunderstanding."

"A misunderstanding, my behind. Your baker charged John Singer with a knife. Kimmy from the yoga studio saw the whole thing."

I should have known Kimmy was a gossip too. "Well, yes, that did happen, but—"

"Did she stab him?" Greta from the historical society asked.

"No. No one was hurt today."

Greta looked mildly disappointed, which changed my

whole perspective on the elderly woman. She'd always seemed so demure in our previous conversations.

"Shame," she muttered before walking away toward the library.

"I can't believe John would do anything like that," Mark commented. "He's a good guy. A loner, but I've known him and his family since we were kids. My dad used to work with his at the lumber mill."

That piqued my interest. "So do you know what sacred wood is?"

He shook his head. "Can't say that I do, sorry. Anyway, I have to get home to Rachael." He held up a bag from the Dawg Pound. "She was craving cheese fries. Who am I to say no to what she wants to eat. I'm glad she can finally keep things down. Much of it thanks to you, I'm sure."

"Please tell her hello from me. I'm so glad she's feeling better. I'll keep stocking the ginger goodies throughout her pregnancy just in case."

"Thanks, Joanie. Don't know what we would have done without them for those few weeks there. But save me one of those ginger whoopie pies, would you? Rachael won't let me get near them once I bring them home." I promised I would, and Mark took off up the hill. It was a short walk back to his house.

Donna and the remaining three women leaned in. "So what do ya think about the match between John and Lily? A bit explosive, eh?"

I was glad there had been no real explosions. "They're perfect for one another, by my account, but something is getting in the way. You all wouldn't happen to know what sacred wood is, would you?"

They all shook their heads. "No, but we can ask around. Can't we, ladies?"

The other three nodded in response.

"I can ask my husband. He worked as a driver for the lumberyard before it closed," one of them added.

"Thank you," I replied. "If you hear anything, please let me know down at the bakery. There's a free pastry in it for you." Their eyes lit up at the promise of free treats.

"We'll get this mystery solved soon enough, Joanie," Donna added. "Your matches are never wrong, so we need to do all we can to get this one on the right track after today."

The three ladies all nodded again.

I bid everyone a good evening, knowing that Donna would keep me at the diner for the "real" scoop in the morning no matter how long I talked to her right now. But it was time for my dinner, and Saffy would be waiting for me to give her hers too. There was nothing like an impatient calico being kept from eating, and I was already late. She'd be getting a treat tonight for sure once I made them.

The rest of my walk back home was peaceful, with no one else around to stop me, human or ghost. I wondered if ghosts gossiped the way we did, at least the ones who seemed to carry on with their everyday lives even after death. I'd never asked, partly because I didn't want to draw attention to the fact I could see them. Maybe I'd ask Arthur Miller, not that I expected him to answer. We'd never spoken.

Saffy jumped down from the couch with a loud thud as soon as I inserted the key into the lock of the door. My being late had apparently negated her greeting me like she usually did. I caught sight of her round bottom and shaking tail scampering into the kitchen as I stepped inside.

"Sorry, Saf," I called after her, kicking off my shoes. I slung my bag off my shoulder before sliding into my slippers and following her into the kitchen.

She meowed loudly at her empty bowl, her tail flicking

back and forth. Now dominated by her hunger, she refused to look at me.

"I know, I know," I began as I opened the cabinet where I stored her food. As she tapped her bowl to tell me I was taking too long, I proceeded to tell her all about my day. My tale continued even after I fed her and got my own dinner ready to cook. Once she had something to eat, all seemed forgiven about my being late. Occasionally, she'd look up at me as I talked, her mouth open as if in shock—food falling back into her bowl, but she made no sound other than the crunching of her food.

That left one other person to call to explain what happened. Well, two, I still needed to call Gram like I did every Saturday, but I still had time for that. Oh, and I had to call my mom, too.

I picked up the phone and dialed Ken. After four rings, it went to voicemail. "Hey, Ken. It's Joanie. I wanted to apologize for leaving in such a hurry after bumping into you today. Not sure how fast word travels to the hospital, but it was quite the afternoon in the shop and on Main Street. I'd love to tell you about it. Call me back or stop by the shop tomorrow. Tell Ivy hello for me. All right, talk to you soon."

I hung the phone back on the receiver, then put the kettle on the stove to boil. Today required an additional half scoop of chamomile to my tea infuser. Although everything had been fine in the end, all the hubbub had wound me up, and I'd need the extra to calm down.

Once the water was ready, I poured myself a large cup to steep, then headed upstairs to get comfortable. It was a yoga pants and oversized sweatshirt kind of night.

By the time I walked back downstairs, my dinner had finished cooking. I set it out on the counter to cool a moment as I took a slow sip of tea. Saffy rubbed up the side of my legs before disappearing into the living room. Now that her appetite had been satisfied, she could probably sense I needed a few more minutes of alone time and had left me to eat my dinner in peace.

After a delightful meal of taco-stuffed peppers, I ventured into the other room with a second cup of tea and the phone. I could probably sneak in a chapter of my book before calling Gram.

I stopped short as I looked across the room. Someone was sitting on my couch. Saffy lay just behind her, completely unaware she was there. Based on recent experience, this was not her usual reaction to ghosts. I needed Gram to come visit to help me with the wards on the doors. Wait, help me? No. So she could do them. She was the witch, not me. Maybe Mom would be able to come too.

The ghost glanced up, and we made eye contact.

"My, my. Look how much you've grown! It's been years. How are you, Joanie?"

Did I know her? She obviously knew me.

The ghost remained quiet as I studied her, squinting to look past her age to see if I could remember her from my childhood. If I added more dark brown to the white in her hair, made it shoulder length, and gave her brighter red lipstick to make her green eyes pop . . .

My gaze grew wide with the realization of who it was.

"Miss Susan?" I took another step closer. One of Gram's oldest friends, she'd been a regular presence during my childhood. She'd had a magnificent garden, and I loved to smell all the pretty blooms whenever I visited with Gram. Always knew just what to put in a cup of tea to suit one's day too. I was sure she was the reason why Gram, Mom, and I drank so much loose-leaf. Miss Susan dried it fresh and always sent us home with some along with a beautiful bouquet for the kitchen table.

"I knew you'd get it eventually, dear. I had all the time in the world for you to figure it out." She smiled at her attempt at a joke.

If she was here, that only meant one thing. "I'm sorry. I didn't realize you had died."

"Oh, that's all right. A recent affliction, I'm afraid." She patted the cushion next to her. Saffy failed to react. Had Miss Susan put a spell on my cat? If Gram was a witch, Miss Susan had to be one too.

I sat. Finally Saffy stirred, paying no mind to our visitor. She stood, turned around in a circle three times, then lay back down.

"Does my gram know?"

Miss Susan nodded. "I'm sure she'll tell you herself when you talk to her later." At my questioning look, she clarified, "I know all about your Saturday chats. You're quite the topic of your grandmother's conversations with the ladies. She's real proud of you and your abilities, even if you won't acknowledge them."

She patted me on the leg. Her hand felt solid, real. The sensation always threw me. Even though ghosts appeared as whole human beings, part of me always expected them to pass right through me the way they did in movies. Just like with walking through objects, they could do the same with people if they wanted to—and usually if they were surprised by the contact, it happened—but it wasn't the norm.

"So you know about what I can do?"

"Sure do. I'm here, aren't I?"

She had a good point. "Why are you here?"

"Well, to be honest, I wasn't sure I was heading toward you until I saw your cat. Your gram has photos you've sent with her in them on her wall. I felt pulled this way. And once I realized where I was going, I received a message for you."

"A message? Who'd want to send me a message?"

Miss Susan shrugged.

"What is it?"

"You are the convergence of multiple cursed blessings. At least one is the matchmaking, and another is your ghost-seeing ability. Not only do you see people who are meant to be together, you see those matches that can only be healed through ghostly interference. And not only matches but individual people too. You're a bridge to happiness both here and, well, on the other side."

"What's a cursed blessing?" It seemed I had another mystery to solve, this time one about me.

"That's all I was told. Seems like a lot of responsibility to shoulder if you ask me," she said with another shrug, then sighed. "Now, it seems that since I have delivered the message, my time here grows short. So let's chat until I drift away."

If that's what Miss Susan wanted, that's what we'd do. We talked for a while, her telling me stories about her childhood and about Gram. Even had a few about my mom that I'm sure Mom would have preferred to go with Miss Susan and never be spoken of again.

She yawned. "My time is almost up, dear."

"I hate for you to go. This was nice, even if under these circumstances. Why do you have to leave? I've seen some of the same ghosts around here for years."

"They're all here for their own reasons. Nothing's keeping me here now that I've delivered my message, but something's keeping them. They'll all get to where I'm going eventually. Maybe you'll help them with that." She patted my leg again. "Now, stand up and give this old lady a hug."

It was something she used to say to me when I was little before either of us would go. I gave her the response I always did. "You're not old, just older than me."

We stood, and she wrapped me in her arms. I put mine around her tall frame. Even though I'd grown since the last time we'd done this, she still had a couple inches on me.

"Oh, before you go . . ." Just like how Gram called me a kitchen witch, I'd grown up with her calling Miss Susan a *green witch*. Perhaps she'd know the answer to my current mystery. I should have thought to ask sooner.

"Hmm?"

"Do you know what sacred wood is?"

Her embrace faded, and when I pulled back, she was gone.

CHAPTER 12

Saffy popped her head up at that moment, as if noticing the change in the atmosphere. It was subtle but there. A comforting warmth, no doubt from Miss Susan, had left as if a light blanket had been pulled off one's legs. It wasn't enough to make someone uncomfortable, but it was enough of a change to recognize it. Had that been it? Had Miss Susan's presence added a blanket-like comfort to Saffy's already comfortable spot, sending her into a deeper rest as she dozed after dinner?

My calico cat glanced around the room.

"No one's here, Saf," I said, sitting back down on the couch.

She looked at the spot where Miss Susan had been.

"Not anymore anyway."

I needed a moment to collect myself before I called Gram. There'd be no reading, not right now. My mind was abuzz. Miss Susan was dead. I was a cursed blessing. And what sacred wood was still eluded me.

Saffy shifted behind me, and a moment later, she bonked the back of my head with hers.

Reaching up to scratch her neck, I remembered my promise to her. "Said I'd make you some more treats, huh."

She headbutted me once more before hopping down to the floor and scampering into the kitchen. Guess that was her answer. Not that I minded. A promise was a promise, and it would keep me busy.

Cooking and baking always gave my hands something to do when my mind was too occupied for much else. I knew Saffy's treat recipe by heart and could probably make them in my sleep.

Saffy sat on one of the kitchen chairs, watching me as I gathered the ingredients. As excited as she was to get treats fresh from the oven, she knew they wouldn't bake any faster than the recipe called for. I'd told her that enough times as a kitten. Now, treat baking was probably the one time she was patient about food. She gave me plenty of room to work, and didn't even sit in front of her bowl, nevermind tap it impatiently like she did when demanding dinner. It was almost as if she worried I would change my mind about making them if she were impolite.

As I pulled my hand mixer out of the cabinet, I thought back to Saffy's first encounter with the one I had shortly after I got her. She was still a kitten and I'd made these treats for her then. Between the tuna draining and the freshly chopped catnip, the allure of what I was doing must have been too much for her. She'd hopped onto the counter despite my protests—listening was never her strong suit when it came to food—and even after I'd moved the most tempting ingredients, she'd come back to investigate. The egg whites in the bowl probably weren't appealing on their own, she hadn't gone after them before, but as part of this recipe, they *had* to be good. I'd warned her the noise was coming. Even put her back down on the floor. But then, and now, she was insistent.

So I did what I had to do. I turned on the hand mixer, and no sooner had I done so than she sprang back a foot, half missed her landing, and scrambled to get back onto the counter. Only then did she realize that she didn't want to be on the counter near the mixer, which I had turned off as soon as I saw her reaction, and she took off. Once I knew she was okay, though hiding under my bed, I resumed my mixing. She didn't come out until the treats were in the oven.

Did she get a lot of treats that night? Yes, yes she did.

For some time, she avoided the kitchen whenever she saw the hand mixer come out, but over the years, she'd gotten used to it. I used it often enough. Now she didn't bat an eye. Although she maybe licked her lips in anticipation of what was coming.

Once the treats were in the oven and the bowls wiped out, I picked up the phone and dialed Gram. I had twenty-five minutes until the treats were done and thus had twenty-five minutes in which I needed to occupy my mind.

"Hello?" the voice asked on the other end of the line. It was not Gram.

"Mom?"

"Oh, Joanie." She sounded a little caught off guard by my call.

"Where's Gram?"

"Now's not the best time."

"I always call at this time."

There were muffled voices in the background as Mom didn't respond right away. "Something's come up and Gram—"

"I know about Miss Susan," I blurted.

"Oh." More muffled voices. Then the line cleared for a moment.

"Joanie, dear." *Gram.* She sniffled.

"I'm so sorry about Miss Susan."

"Thank you." Her voice cracked and she sniffed again. "But how did you know?"

"I saw her. Here. In my living room."

"You did?" She sounded excited. "Did she say who killed her?"

"Killed her? You mean Miss Susan was murdered?" I stood from the table, startling Saffy who was still in her chair. "Gram, what's going on?"

"I'll take that as a no."

"No. She didn't tell me. She came with a message for me."

"A message? Tell me everything."

For the next several minutes, I recounted my entire meeting with Miss Susan, from her unexpected appearance to what she'd been sent to give me. She only had to shush Mom twice during the process.

"Hmm…" Gram said once I was done. "I can't say I know what to make of that."

"It's okay. I know you have a lot going on right now. I really am sorry. Do you want me to come home and help do something?"

"No, no, dear. You and that sassy cat have your own mystery on your hands. I'll be able to handle this one."

She had a point. "Well, if you're sure. But please call if you need anything."

"I will. Is there anything else you need to chat about?"

"Just one thing real quick. Do you know what sacred wood is? It's something to do with my latest match."

More mumbling with the phone covered. She sounded distracted when she came back to the line, and I wondered if she'd even heard me properly. Not that I could blame her given what had happened. "No, sorry. Not your mom either."

"That's okay. I'll let you go.

"Love you, Joanie."

"Love you too, Gram. Does Mom want to talk to me at all?"

Muffled voices again. "She says she'll talk to you soon dear, but she loves you." That didn't surprise me. Mom wasn't a big phone talker. And I knew she was busy. They both were. But if Gram said she could handle it, I had no doubt she would, even if that meant her solving her friend's murder.

We hung up the phone just as Saffy's treats were coming out of the oven.

Gram's call had been a good distraction for the time we were talking, but unfortunately, the thoughts remained clogging my brain for the rest of the evening. Gram was right, though. I had a mystery on my hands, and only solving it would answer my questions.

CHAPTER 13

The next morning, the bakery kitchen bustled with the noise of getting treats ready for the day. But that was the only noise. No one talked. The five of us all ignored what had happened in the shop yesterday. After Lily had made it clear she still wasn't in a mood to talk about it, I wasn't going to press her. She needed time to process whatever had upset her so much. At least she was here.

I'd added another few batches of baked goods to the normal Sunday workload. I expected tons of foot traffic in the shop above and beyond what was already one of the busiest days of the week. By now, everyone in Heartwood Hollow would have heard what happened, and many would know I was seeking an answer to what sacred wood was. They'd soon all be stopping in to get my side of things or to try and help solve this next mystery.

As soon as the muffins for the two diners were boxed up, I raced to deliver them on my bike, hoping either Carter or Donna would have information for me. Carter because he'd been there, and Donna, well, because she was Donna.

Usually not a chatty man, Carter was waiting for me at the back door to Double Aitch Diner, arms crossed.

"Two things before you head out on your way," he started as I walked in.

"Sure thing." I dropped the two boxes of muffins onto the counter where I always put them.

He led me to his tiny closet-like office. I hadn't been in here in the four years since we first discussed the terms of my bringing him muffins in the morning.

I closed the door behind me as he sat at his desk. His entire kitchen staff didn't need to hear what he had to say. Figuring it best to get it out of the way, I started the conversation. "Thank you for your help yesterday."

He motioned for me to sit across from him. "Glad I was there to help. John and I went to high school together. We were on the track team, and he could have kept running. Distance runner. Lucky for you, I also played football and could still stop a linebacker if needed."

Carter's comment about football didn't surprise me in the slightest. He was all muscle.

He sat up straight. "So what happened yesterday?"

"You saw the most of it. Started when John pulled that knife out in my shop."

"That doesn't sound like him at all." His brows furrowed.

"So I've been told. But he didn't threaten me. Didn't even open it. His hand was shaking, and he took off after dropping the knife on the floor. Lily is the one who opened the blade and charged after him. *Why* is a mystery. Do you happen to know what sacred wood is?"

Carter thought for a moment. "Can't say that I do, but it's gotta be something with the lumber company or the woods they cut down." He chuckled. "Maybe Lily worships trees or something. That tree love festival is coming up this weekend.

That's been going on for longer than I've been alive. How are you doing with your prep?"

Just like that, he'd changed the subject. But what if he was onto something without knowing it? Gram hadn't known what sacred wood was either when I'd asked her last night, but she'd said others in her circle gathered energy from the trees and their wood. Maybe Lily was a witch like Gram. If that was the case, would Lily open up to me if I told her about my family history?

"Need to grab my cart out of my garage and clean it up a bit, but other than that, I'm ready."

"If you need any help moving it up to the clearing, just let me know. I'll have my guys tow it out there for you." His *guys*, as he called them, were his younger brothers. They were as big as he was and ran the town's towing company. It was a family business. I'd seen Carter in one of the company trucks a time or two, hauling cars out of snowbanks in winter or towing tourists' cars when they were illegally parked.

"Thanks, I will."

"And on that note, here's your check for the week's muffins. After this week, I'd like to up my order for the summer season. Same as last year."

I headed out from Double Aitch a few minutes later, biking toward Olde Templeton Diner, where Donna would be waiting for me. Maybe Walter and Paul would already be there since my conversation with Carter had put me a few minutes behind my normal schedule.

Through the front window, I smiled at my coffee waiting for me at my spot at the counter. Donna was refilling the sugar pourers as slowly as possible, likely hoping I'd show up soon.

The chime above the door jingled as I entered, and Donna looked up, a broad smile on her face. "'Bout time!"

"Sorry, I was chatting with Carter at Double Aitch."

"He have any news for you?"

I lifted myself up onto the stool. "Nothing concrete, but he thinks that sacred wood might have something to do with tree worship of some kind. Know anything of it?"

"We've got a lot of nature lovers here, but"—she shook her head—"I've not heard anything about that."

"Said maybe it was tied to the festival."

"Pish!" She waved a dismissive hand. "Festival was my great-granddad's idea. Once the eastern grove was clear cut, there was suddenly this great big open space for us to do things in. Mind you, this was before the park came about. But we carry on the tradition by having the festival in that spot every year."

The bell chimed again, but I continued talking. "So the village decided to celebrate trees in an area that had been stripped of them?"

Donna shrugged, then screwed the caps back onto the sugar pourers. "Didn't say it made sense. Maybe it was to give thanks to them? That wood helped build a lot of homes up here."

"Besides," Paul said, sitting down next to me as Walter sat on his other side, "we started planting trees there again to give us shade at the festivals. It's not so bare now." He had a point. The clearing where the event took place was surrounded by a bunch of new growth forest.

"Do you know what sacred wood is?" I asked the two men.

They both shook their heads.

"This about John Singer and your baker? You playing matchmaker again?" Walter asked.

"Yes to both. Lily mentioned the term, so I'm trying to figure out what it means."

"Maybe something to do with the north woods." Paul gave Walter and Donna a knowing look that I didn't understand. "You know the stories that come from up there."

"I wouldn't call them *sacred*," Donna started. "More like the opposite. Those woods always gave me the creeps. Weird noises. Things moving around."

"Let's not forget the disappearances," Paul added.

"I'd rather not think about it." Donna shivered, then grabbed the pourers and began distributing them at the few tables around the room.

I'd never heard about this part of Heartwood Hollow's history. "Disappearances?"

"Oh, that's right," Walter said. "You fit in so well here I sometimes forget you're new."

Given how long I'd been here, *new* was a relative term. I wasn't sure he was right on the whole fitting in aspect either.

"Right when the lumber company started cutting the north woods, people started disappearing up there," Walter explained. "Thought was they'd gone up to protest, that was the thing to do back then, but then they never came back."

"Was there ever an investigation?" Did the sacredness of the wood have to do with the fact it was the last place these villagers were known to have been before they disappeared? Had Lily's grandmother been one of them?

Walter nodded. "Oh sure, sure. Nothing ever came about it, though. Said they'd left on their own. Maybe some did."

"You done talking about that cursed forest?" Donna asked as she came back around the counter. She ducked into the kitchen and returned with Walter and Paul's breakfasts, which must have been cooking before they even got here. They got the same thing every morning.

"Yeah, not much more to tell," Paul said. Both of the old men helped themselves to a muffin straight out of the box.

"Good, 'cause that's enough of that." Donna removed the rest of the muffins from their boxes and set to work displaying them on cake stands she'd put on the back counter. She'd place glass vitrines over them to keep the muffins fresh.

I glanced at the clock behind her. "Oh, goodness. I need to get going." I was running behind by at least fifteen minutes. Sliding off my stool, I bid my goodbyes to the three of them.

The kitchen was still void of all talking when I got back to the bakery, but the silence had lent everyone an efficiency I hadn't seen before. Trays of cookies sat ready to go into the oven once the pastries came out. Two more batches of everything and we'd have enough to last us through the busy day. I quickly apologized for being later than usual, then hopped right in to help with the baking until it was time to prep the shop for opening.

When Sarah came in, I joined her out front, sliding a clean pink apron over my head after taking off the yellow one I'd been baking in.

"What happened yesterday? Why didn't you call me?" It didn't surprise me that she'd immediately want to know what happened. She liked to gossip as much as Donna did.

"You had the day off, and I was going to respect that no matter what. I had it handled." Though Sam's help in the kitchen and during cleanup had been tremendous.

Sarah crossed her arms. "That doesn't tell me what happened."

"Given who was involved, I'll fill you in later. I'd like to respect the fact she's in the other room."

Sarah busied herself with her opening duties, made all the faster by our busy day yesterday that depleted our usual day-old selection. She hadn't done more than nod in response to my comment, but she appeared ready to burst from wanting to know the details. Although I'd been doing a fair share of it,

I didn't like to gossip, and if it could have been avoided, I wouldn't discuss it at all. But if I didn't, Sarah would hear some wild versions of it, more so than what I was sure she'd heard already, and because she worked here, it was best she knew the real story. Maybe this time, she could help put the rumors to bed.

Right at nine, we flipped the sign from *closed* to *open*, and within thirty seconds, we had our first three customers walk through the door. Once again, customers asked the same questions as yesterday, and that trend continued right into lunchtime.

"Why did Lily have a knife?"

"Was it really John's knife?"

"How did Lily get John's knife?"

"What is sacred wood?"

"Did John know it was sacred wood?"

After lunch, the tone of the conversation had changed, taking on an eerie feel as the topic shifted to focus not on what had happened but the meaning behind Lily's phrase sacred wood. Many concurred with the idea that it had something to do with the north woods. Seemed everyone had a tale to tell about this last tract of forest where the lumber company harvested trees for a short time before going out of business.

"Those woods are cursed."

"People go up there and never come back."

"Something's hunting them."

But when I asked who disappeared and what they thought was up there, the details grew sparse. No one could name anyone who had disappeared within the last fifteen years, although I got several names from before then that I'd have to check out. Theories on what could have taken or hunted those people ranged from a very smart bear to Bigfoot to aliens. Some villagers talked about creatures with large glowing eyes and others mentioned beings that could camouflage into the tree branches and drop down behind a person so they'd never see what was coming for them. After a while, it sounded like people were competing in a contest about creating the scariest boogie monster.

Around three, the door to the shop opened, and in walked Nathan and his father, George. My backyard neighbors, they rarely visited the shop, instead benefitting from my experimenting with new flavors in my kitchen at home.

"Hello, you two, what a pleasant surprise."

"Hello, dear," George said as he walked toward the case with the pastries.

"How are you doing, darling?" I asked, using the term of endearment I always called him. Even without his answer, I could tell the elderly man was having a good day.

He tapped on the case. "We're always getting cookies or cupcakes from you, but we never get pastry. It's been ages since I've had a good strawberry éclair, so I convinced Nathan to bring me here after my doctor's appointment on account of good behavior." He smiled mischievously at his son.

That explained why Nathan was home. George usually spent his days at the senior center while Nathan was at work.

Nathan looked to the ceiling and shook his head. "More like demanded it." He glanced at his father as he approached the counter. "But pastry isn't the only reason you insisted we come. Remember?"

George gave his son a blank stare. A moment later, the fog lifted and he brightened. "Right. Show her the newspaper article. You didn't forget it, did you?"

"Have it right here, Dad." Nathan took his wallet from his back pants pocket, then opened it and removed a folded piece of newsprint. He placed the paper on the countertop and flattened it, making the article he revealed easier to read.

George pointed at the headline.

Sixth Disappearance in North Woods Spells Additional Trouble for Lumber Company's Latest Endeavor

"Heard you were looking for information on the forest up there," George said.

Wow, everyone in town really was talking about this.

"I picked Dad up at lunchtime," Nathan started, "and he was all in a tizzy, talking about curses and the woods. Thought he was having one of his episodes, but when we got home, he ran and got this clipping from a box he had in his closet."

I lifted the clipping off the counter and read: *Fern McOsker, 57, is the latest in a string of strange disappearances since the Singer Lumber Company opened up a new tract of forest for logging six months ago.*

So at least the disappearances were true.

"Used to be your mom's," George told Nathan. To me, he added, "Her best friend is the missing person mentioned in this article."

"Thank you for bringing this in. Did they ever find her?"

"Naw, the investigation said all of them had run off for one reason or another. But Fern never would have done that. She'd been friends with my Isabelle since childhood. She'd never leave without saying goodbye or saying where she was going. It's all funny business if you ask me. Six people. Come on, really?"

I nodded and set my lips into a tight line, unable to help but agree. To conclude that all six people had disappeared from the same place under their own volition? The investigation—or lack thereof—seemed just as suspicious as those woods.

"Well, let's get you that éclair, darling. On the house to thank you for bringing me that article. If you wouldn't mind leaving it for me to look at, I can bring it back to your house later." I shuffled down to the pastry case, then pulled out the cream and strawberry-jelly-filled treat for George, one that had a little more filling than the rest. His eyes widened with anticipation as I handed him the bag. "Nathan, do you want anything?"

He held up a hand. "Ah, no. It's all right. I prefer your cookies and cupcakes from over the fence." He smiled shyly, a hint of pink coloring the tips of his ears.

"Boy, I'm getting out of here cheap," George quipped.

Nathan's face morphed to one of amusement. I wondered if it was something George used to say when Nathan and his siblings were little. Since the mooning incident a few weeks back, I hadn't seen George beyond a quick wave through windows. It was nice to see him doing well today. I could only imagine how Nathan felt on George's good days.

The shop door opened, and three more customers walked in, making a beeline toward the cookies.

"Well, we should get going, Dad, and leave Joanie to the paying customers."

"All right, all right," George said as Nathan guided him toward the door. Before they reached the exit, he called over his shoulder, "Goodbye, dear."

"Goodbye, darling. It was lovely to see you both. And thank you so much for the article." I couldn't wait to finish reading it when I got home.

The two left, and the three ladies flocked to the counter, simultaneously ordering several cookies and providing their thoughts as to what happened up in the north woods. Like the cackling of gulls that sometimes found their way up the river from the coast, it was hard to follow as they spoke over one another. I was grateful just to get their order correct. But from what I could tell, as with many others I'd heard, there was little substance to their spooky stories.

The rest of the afternoon was spent much in the same fashion. After the long day and so many people parading into the bakery to provide their theories, there was one noticeable absence. It felt like the only person who hadn't stopped by was Ken. Even with the possibility of him having forgotten to check his voicemail, there was no way he hadn't heard something about yesterday. I'd assumed he would come to at least say hello, but maybe he was busy with Ivy.

Then again, he'd told me not to get involved between John and Lily. Was he upset because I hadn't listened? What was I supposed to do—not go after Lily when she tore out of the bakery with a knife?

This was who I was. He'd either have to accept me and what I could do... or else I wasn't the right one for him.

I pushed all thoughts of Ken aside as I walked home from the bakery that evening. Things would happen with him however they were meant to. I couldn't do anything about that, but I could do something about John and Lily's match.

First I needed to get Lily to talk to me. But how?

CHAPTER 14

My bakers filed in one by one on Monday morning. First Sam, then Gina, then Bryan. For the second time ever, Lily was late. But she had texted me to say she wouldn't be in on time. Given recent events, I'd have worried otherwise. Regularly the first one to the bakery, Lily would often spend a couple minutes talking with me before the others showed up. It was obvious she was trying to avoid being alone with me to prevent us from being able to discuss what had happened and why.

I wasn't the only one who had picked up on it either.

"She really should talk to you," Sam said as he stamped his cookie cutter into the dough he'd already rolled flat.

"You should get her alone," Bryan suggested. "She can't avoid you if you are the only two people around."

Gina shot him a look. "Does that work for you?"

He stared at her blankly.

"You do realize how that sounds, right?" she asked. "Get her alone?"

It dawned on him after a moment, a horrified look

coming over his face. "I didn't mean it like that! I'd never do that. I'm not some creep who can't take a hint when someone doesn't want to talk to me."

I didn't doubt his statement in the slightest. Although he had a quick wit and was pleasant to chat with, Bryan was a quiet guy overall. Affable and easygoing, it had honestly surprised me when I learned he was single. He was a catch, and I hoped he'd find someone soon—with or without my involvement. Not everyone needed a matchmaker.

"All I was saying," he continued, "was that if we weren't here, we wouldn't be a buffer between Lily and Joanie. They'd have to talk to one another. There'd be no one else around to distract her."

"That's not a bad idea," Sam said, sprinkling a cinnamon-sugar mixture onto the scrap dough after he'd cut out all the cookies he could. He'd turn these into spirals. "Joanie, why don't you have her help you make that last-minute birthday cake order that came in? I can keep working on the cookies instead. You'll have time to deliver it if I don't start on it now, right?"

I glanced at the clock hanging above the sink. It could work.

"As long as she comes in by the time I get back from making my deliveries, that should be fine."

Gina sighed, molding her scones into a large circular shape before cutting it down to individual pieces. "It's a little strange when you think about it."

The others turned to look at her as I asked, "What do you mean?" With everything that had happened, *strange* could apply to a lot of things.

"Finding a good guy is all she's ever wanted. Who'd have thought the guy would be someone who she chased down the street with a knife." She cracked a smile as she looked toward the ceiling. "You've got your work cut out for you, Joanie, but you can do it."

"It will be quite the story to tell their kids one day, that's for sure," Sam added.

Everyone laughed. I appreciated their unwavering faith in my abilities, even if they didn't know they were a little more than normal.

By the time I'd come back from my morning rounds, Lily had arrived and was already prepping the cake batter.

"Morning, Lily," I said as I usually did, making her appearance no big deal. I didn't want to set her on edge by giving her too much attention or draw the rest of the team's thoughts away from what they were doing. A lot of baking still needed to get done before they could leave, and I couldn't have anyone be distracted thinking about what would happen when they all left. "Did Sam show you the preliminary sketches for the cake?"

"Yeah, it's a sweet idea." The honeycombs and bumble-bees for the little girl's birthday were sure to delight her when she came home from kindergarten.

"Feel free to put your own spin on it. It was a homemade cake disaster from the message I received, so I think they'll be happy with anything at this point."

"You got it." She turned back to the batter and said no more.

A few minutes later, Sam left for school, mouthing "good luck" as he pointed to Lily on his way out the door. She fortu-nately didn't catch it, either too absorbed in pouring the batter into the three round baking pans or still avoiding us all as much as she could.

Gina hopped on Sam's station to finish up the last of the cookies while Bryan continued with his muffins. He had one more flavor to do before he'd switch over to cupcakes. I got to work cutting pastry flour into strips so I could create raspberry twists.

When Sarah came in, I ducked out of the kitchen to brief her on what we had going on today but didn't tell her my plans for talking to Lily. She didn't need to be listening in from the other side of the door like she'd done in the past. Plus, she was terrible at hiding the fact she knew a secret. Although her contact with Lily was minimal while they were here, I felt better knowing Sarah couldn't tip her off in any way that something was up.

Turns out, I needn't have worried. Gina and Bryan helped Sarah and me load the cases while Lily worked on rolling out fondant for most of the birthday cake decorations. She needed all the time she could get with the cake.

Once the shop was ready to go for the day, and with Lily on the special order, I jumped back to pastry duty, taking care of what was one of her regular duties. Gina joined me after finishing the last of the cookies. I always made sure everyone could do someone else's job, but they all had their favorite foods to work with.

An hour and a half later, I headed out to make my delivery to Riverwood Inn, and by the time I came back, Gina and Bryan were ready to be on their way. I had enough cookies, cupcakes, and scones to last me the rest of the day. All that needed to be done were a few more pastries, which I could handle with Sarah up front, and the bumblebee cake Lily was still working on. The layers of the cake had been stacked and a crumb coat applied. Things appeared to be going well, and Lily was softly humming as she sculpted small beehives out of fondant and modeling chocolate. Now was as good a time as any to talk to her.

"So I wanted to touch base with you about the other day and make sure you're okay," I said from my station, hoping to keep this casual. There was no need to approach her station and make her think she was in trouble.

"Yeah, about that. I'm sorry for how I behaved. I can't believe I ran out of here like that and made you leave the store." Lily sighed, sounding half like a groan. "I'm so embarrassed. It won't happen again."

"You're okay now?" I folded whipped cream into pastry cream with a spatula, glancing at her from the corner of my eyes.

Lily nodded but wouldn't look at me.

"You were clearly upset," I pushed. "And I'm having trouble understanding why since you'd only met John a few minutes before."

"It doesn't matter."

I put the spatula into the bowl of cream and faced her. "Surely it does, given what happened."

"Joanie, please." She squeezed one of the fondant honeycombs a bit too hard, then rolled it into a ball to start over again.

I didn't want her to shut down on me, so I tried a different tactic. "Could you tell me one thing, though?" Although I had many more questions, maybe she'd answer if she believed one thing was all I had left to ask. Depending on how she responded, we could go from there.

"What's that?"

"What is sacred wood? No one I've asked seems to know."

She looked up at me then. "It's um . . ." She paused, then said no more.

"Do you worship trees? Is that why the wood is sacred?" Before Lily could answer, I rephrased, "Sorry, that didn't come out right. I'm new at this. I mean, are you what they'd call a green witch?"

Lily's lips pursed and her brow scrunched as she studied me, her hands working the fondant back into a domed shape.

I put my hands up. "It's okay if you are. My gram is a witch, though I'm not sure the kind. And I guess I sort of am one too. A kitchen witch if you couldn't figure that one out." Part trying to lighten the mood and part out of nervousness from what I'd confessed and what her reaction might be, I chuckled. I hadn't expected to tell her I was a witch. I'd barely admitted it myself yet.

Her eyebrow ticked up.

Might as well tell her everything, especially if the ghost who looked like her was related to her somehow. "You already know about my matchmaking ability, and don't even get me started on the ghosts."

"Ghosts?"

I took a deep breath, and my next few sentences came out in a rush. "Yeah, I can see them. Sometimes I help them. It's something I've been able to do since I was a kid. Only a handful of people know, and I'd appreciate more not finding out."

She looked down at the fondant, nodded, and placed it on her station. "Oh, um, sure." She grabbed another hunk of fondant and rolled it into a ball.

She'd taken that easier than I'd have thought. Last time I'd told someone, I had to prove it. Maybe it was because she understood. "So are you a witch?"

"A witch? No." The way she said it made me think there

was more she wasn't telling me. So perhaps she wasn't a witch, but she was something.

"You don't see ghosts too, do you?"

"No, nothing like that."

She tried to smile as if she thought this was all amusing to her, but I couldn't press her for much longer. I had one last thing to ask.

"Does it have anything to do with the north woods?"

Lily froze. "What? Why would you think that?"

"I've heard things."

She scoffed. "From your ghosts?"

"Surprisingly, no. They're not usually that forthcoming with information." I thought of Miss Susan and her message for me. Her appearance had only left me with more questions. Just once, I'd like to get straightforward information from a ghost. Though right now, I'd take a straightforward answer from Lily. "I know about the disappearances that happened several years back. Are you connected to it somehow?"

The ball of fondant fell from Lily's hands and landed with a *thunk* on her station, the metal surface gently rattling the sculpting tools sitting on it.

I'd simultaneously stumbled over the line and hit the nail on the head. But how was she tied to the forest? Did she know someone who had disappeared?

"I . . . I . . . I need to go." Lily removed her apron and tossed it in the bin with the other dirty ones I'd have to take home to wash tonight.

She scooted behind me and toward the back door. As she pulled it open, she looked back over her shoulder. "I'm sorry."

The door closed behind her, and a heavy silence fell over the kitchen.

I sighed and wiped my brow, smearing whipped cream across my face.

At that moment, Sarah popped her head into the kitchen. "Hey, we just had an order come in for an afternoon pickup." I walked over and took the slip from her, then she ducked back into the shop. I was grateful Sarah hadn't seemed to notice Lily's absence. No doubt there would have been questions, and I didn't know the answers to them.

Reading the order slip, I turned back around. It wasn't a large order, but it also wasn't the only thing I had left to do back here. As I surveyed the kitchen, one thing was clear. I couldn't finish this alone.

"Drats," I muttered to myself as I shuffled to the phone on the wall. I picked it up and dialed. "Hey, Gina, it's Joanie. Are you doing anything right now?"

"I was going to make lunch and take a nap. What's up?"

"Is there any way you could come back in?"

"Things not go so well with Lily?"

"You could say that. And now I am flying solo trying to finish this cake, and we just had another order come in, and—"

"Say no more," she said through a stifled yawn, making me feel a bit guilty. "I'll text Bryan, and at least I will be right over."

"Thanks, G. You're a lifesaver." I didn't mean to sound melodramatic, but this was the closest I'd come to not finishing something on time since my cheese soufflé deflated during my savory bakes class in culinary school.

Knowing help was on the way, I quickly folded the rest of the cream together and then popped that into the fridge. Gina could finish the pastries for me. I approached the fondant decorations at Lily's station—several beehives, a pile of bee bodies, and wings that still needed piping. It would be tight, but I'd get it done.

This attempt at getting Lily to talk hadn't worked, and I'd divulged my biggest secret in the process. I had run out of ideas, but the mystery of the north woods and Lily's probable connection to it remained. How was I going to get her to confide in me?

CHAPTER 15

"I'm here, I'm here," Gina called as she bustled into the kitchen and over to me.

"Oh, thank goodness." Although she had said she'd come back when I'd spoken to her by phone, seeing her washed a wave of relief over me.

I scooted to the side as she dumped a lump of pastry dough onto the stainless-steel counter. "I got this. You go make the bees. Bryan's on his way."

"Pastry cream is in the fridge," I told her as I darted into the bathroom to get flour off my hands and wipe the smudge of whipped cream from my eyebrow and forehead. The splash of cold water against my face reenergized me, and as I walked back out of the bathroom, Bryan was pushing his way through the back door into the kitchen.

"What do you need me to do?"

"The order slip is at your station."

He saluted me. "Say no more."

Neither of them questioned me about my failed talk with Lily as I piped lacey patterns onto the bee wings and attached them to round black and yellow striped bodies. Either they had no more ideas on how to get Lily to talk or they realized now wasn't the time. We had things to do. Once Gina slid the last pastry tray into the oven, I told her to cover the layers of cake with fondant and stack them.

Everything came together quickly after that, and with Bryan's baked goods ready to go in the oven, he and I switched to putting decorations on the cake as Gina finished making the last of the beehives.

Finally, everything was done and we had the cake loaded into the trunk. I wiped my forehead with the back of my hand and leaned against the door that led to the bathroom, likely getting more flour on my face and perhaps a bit of food coloring from the dye used in the fondant.

"Thank you both so much for coming back to bail me out."

Gina removed her purple apron and then dropped it into the bin. "Anytime. I mean, we would have been done a while ago had we not left to give you and Lily some privacy. I'm sorry that didn't work out."

"Me too," Bryan added, balling up his apron and tossing it on top of Gina's. "You'll figure something out. You always do."

"Don't worry about it," I said with a shrug. "It was for a good reason that you left. And even though I didn't find out everything I was hoping to, I know more than I did."

Gina headed for the door. "Good. Well, we'll see you on Wednesday. Do yourself a favor and actually take tomorrow off, okay?"

I laughed. "I make no promises, but I'll try." Gina's advice was sound, but I had to figure out Lily's connection to the forest, so I wasn't going to have much downtime. If nothing else, it would be a day off from the bakery.

Bryan opened the back door for Gina, and she stepped

outside. As he followed her out, he called goodbye over his shoulder.

From my position against the door, I surveyed the mess of a kitchen. It wasn't dirty, but it wasn't up to my usual standard. Thank goodness the cleaning crew was coming in tomorrow for the bakery's weekly deep clean. Although we gave it a good scrub once baking at the end of every day, the cleaning crew did more than one or two of us could on a daily basis.

I had one thing left to do before I could join Sarah in the shop for the rest of the day, so I pulled myself from the door and popped my head into the bakery.

"Back in a few. I gotta go deliver the honeybee cake." Even I could hear how tired I was.

Sarah turned and took one look at me. "And get us both some coffee."

I stuck out my bottom lip and blew out hard, causing the wisps of hair too short to pull into a ponytail tickle my forehead. "That bad, huh?"

She nodded, her lips pursed and one eyebrow raised. "Better make yours a large. I'll take a medium."

"Oof. Worse than I thought. Coffee it is." Ducking into the kitchen, I took off my apron, grabbed my purse from the closet, then left out the back. I slid into the driver's seat of my station wagon, grateful for once for not needing to ride my bike to make a delivery. The humidity had yet to break, and the last thing I needed after this morning was to have the cake get ruined from the excess moisture in the air. I'd outfitted my trunk to securely hold cake bases and boxes, and with the car's air conditioning, this was the best mode of transportation for the cake.

The drive across town took only a few minutes. I pulled up to a small Cape Cod house with yellow and black balloons tied to the mailbox. A flag in the shape of a bee flew next to the front door. Even if I hadn't had the address, there would have been no doubt this was the place.

The inner wood door opened as I stepped onto the walkway, cake in hand. No doubt someone had been on the lookout for my arrival.

"Joanie, that looks adorable! Let me get the door." A brunette woman with her hair tied up into a messy bun stepped onto the front steps, pulling the metal storm door wide open. "If you don't mind bringing it to the kitchen, that would be great. It's to your right when you walk into the living room."

"Not a problem, Natalie." I walked into the house, entering the cutest party setup. Bunches of yellow and black balloons were placed all around the living room, and a tea set —complete with a honey bear and sugar cubes in a little jar— was laid out on the coffee table. Several presents sat in front of a rocking chair in the corner.

"This is adorable!" I half squealed as Natalie followed me through the room and into the kitchen.

"Glad you think so. I hope Betty loves it." She tapped a spot on the kitchen table with her hand.

I set the cake down where she indicated and stepped back. "She absolutely will." There might come a time when she'd grow out of the theme, but Betty, short for Beatrice, would always have the bee theme following her. Did Lily always get lilies when people bought her flowers?

"I'd ask if you wanted to stay for some tea or lemonade, but I know you have to get back to the bakery." Natalie dug into her purse on the counter before handing me a check. "Thank you so much for the cake. I won't even show you the disaster that mine was. My husband took a picture to send to one of those online sites about cake fails or something like that. How embarrassing!" She led me back through the living room.

"I'm sure Betty would have loved that one too."

"Oh, no. It was really that terrible," she said, giving her head a tight shake back and forth, a disgusted look on her face.

I did my best to stifle a giggle.

"I swear"—she crossed her heart—"no more cake baking for me. I'm coming to you from now on. Should have from the start."

"Well, I'm glad we could make something for you. Please tell Betty happy birthday for me. Next time you bring her in, a cookie is on me."

"She will love that. Thank you."

I stepped out onto the front steps, then headed back to my car.

Next stop, coffee.

Fifteen minutes later, I had two drinks in hand, a marshmallow rice treat in my purse, and was mostly ready to get back to the bakery and finish the day.

I had barely stepped foot into the shop when Sarah sent me away.

"Okay, now go sit outside and drink your coffee," she ordered when she saw me, "and don't come back in until you have a bit more pep in your step."

"But what about your lunch?"

She waved me off. "I snacked on a chocolate peanut butter whoopie pie while you were gone. Don't worry about it. You need the time more than I do today."

I wasn't going to argue. I marched myself out of the bakery and to Founder's Park next door, where I collapsed onto the bench with a loud sigh. Thank goodness for Sarah.

I'd be lost without her. She was destined for better things, that I knew, but for now, she and I made a great team.

"Running a little behind your normal schedule, aren't you, Miss Joanie?" a voice called from behind me.

I jumped and whipped my head around to find the source. There, on his normal bench, sat Arthur Miller with his dachshund. "I didn't even see you. I'm sorry. Would have waved like I always do."

"Aw, it's all right. You look like you have a lot going on in that head of yours."

"Now *that* is a fact," I said with a chuckle.

The man in the fedora and trench coat stood, and he and his dachshund walked over. "Need to lighten the load a little?"

I studied the ghost and his spectral companion, curious about why he was talking to me now for the first time since realizing I could see him a few years back. But everything happened when it did for a reason, so I scooted over, and he sat down as his dog sniffed my feet.

"What do you know of the north woods?" I asked.

"Well, now. That is quite the heavy topic on your mind. Though I had an idea that's what you wanted to talk about. The ghosts talk, same as the living."

I'd suspected as much at times, not that they talked to me until recently. "You were here then, right? Alive, I mean."

"I was. Lost a good member of the cheerleading squad up there."

"Any insight from the other side as to what may have happened?"

He studied me from over his thick black-rimmed glasses. "The forest isn't haunted if that's what you're asking."

"But there has to be something more to it than they all just up and left, ran away, or what have you."

"None of them left."

I tilted my head as I looked at him. "Then where did they all go?"

"They died."

My mouth dropped open. "So Heartwood Hollow had a serial killer? Is the killer still alive? Do we have something to be worried about? Do—"

He held up his hand to silence me, and I took a sip of my coffee to stop myself from talking as he spoke. "No, nothing like that. It's complicated and more than I'm able to explain. But all parties involved are gone now even if some are like me."

"You mean some are still around?"

He nodded. "Believe you've already come across two of them." He had to have been talking about Dale and the ghost connected to Lily.

"Why do you stay?" I asked, switching topics.

"I like it here." He bent over to scratch behind his dog's ears.

"I'm sure it's nice over there too."

"Bet it is, but the football team hasn't won a championship since I died, and I'd like to see them win one more time. I have high hopes in their coach now." He quirked a grin.

"You were his coach, weren't you?" If Alex knew about my abilities, he'd have been happy to hear about Coach Miller's assessment of him.

He nodded. "Sure was. Alex had a lot of potential. Still does."

At that moment, my phone rang. I glanced into my purse to see the lit-up screen. Ken.

"I'll let you get that. It was good talking to you." He stood and tilted his fedora forward in a manner of farewell.

"Wait, before you go, what's your dog's name?"

"Bardi."

They left the park side by side as I answered my phone.

For the next few minutes, Ken and I chatted as I sipped my coffee, energy slowly creeping back into my body. Whether that energy came from the caffeine or the thoughts running through my head, I wasn't sure. Arthur had filled in a few blanks for me, but others were still gaping holes. If it wasn't a serial killer who had killed them, who or what had killed those six people in the north woods? Why weren't their bodies found? Was there more in Heartwood Hollow than the ghosts I knew about?

I needed to find out, but it could wait until my day off tomorrow because I had the rest of the afternoon to get through and Ken and I had just confirmed a dinner date for tonight.

CHAPTER 16

I met Ken at Founder's Fresco, a new restaurant down one of Heartwood Hollow's alleyways off Main Street. Chelsea and David had spoken highly of it when I'd shown them potential wedding cake designs a couple weeks back.

Ken gave me a quick kiss on the cheek as we said hello at the hostess stand.

"It's good to see you."

He agreed. "It's been crazy lately."

"Tell me about it."

"You first. What really happened the other day? I've heard multiple variations of what went down." He said that last part with a hint of laughter as the hostess sat us down at a table off to the side of the room.

With the way gossip spread through town, especially when there'd been time for the stories to grow, I wondered what crazy versions he must have heard.

After we ordered our food, I told him everything I'd witnessed. His face grew more concerned by the minute as he heard about the people and ghosts involved.

"And you think these two still belong together?" he asked as the waiter set down our appetizer.

I pulled one of the zucchini fritters onto my plate. "I do."

"Couldn't that be a little dangerous? Lily charged after him with a knife."

"Lily can get a bit feisty, but she's not dangerous." I blew on the fritter. "It was all a misunderstanding."

"And this John fellow? He pulled a knife out at your bakery. Why didn't you press charges?"

"It wasn't open, and he wasn't going to use it." I shrugged and popped the fritter into my mouth. "If anything, he needed help."

He raised his eyebrow. "And you're just the person to help him?"

"Well, partially. Lily will do most of it. You'll see. They'll be okay once they get together."

"John sounds like he needs a therapist. Not a girlfriend." Ken scrubbed at his face with both hands, up his cheeks and then down. "Joanie, look, my mom was what one would call a busybody. It drove me crazy growing up . . ."

I didn't like where this was going and grabbed another fritter, unable to look him in the eye. As I avoided his gaze, someone standing at the back of the restaurant waved and caught my attention. She pointed at me and then down the side hall to where the bathrooms were before disappearing behind a wall.

". . . And I worry that you're putting your nose where it doesn't belong just like she would. They're grown adults, and they don't need you to get in their business and solve their problems."

"I'm sorry, can you excuse me for a minute? I want to run to the restroom before our main course arrives."

"Oh, yeah, sure, okay." He cracked a small smile. "But

don't think this is going to stop us from talking about this. I'm concerned about you."

With a small smile and a nod, I said, "I'll be just a minute, and then we can continue this conversation," that I didn't want to have. I stood from the chair and pushed it in as I stepped away from the table, then weaved my way through the restaurant to the side hallway. Its tin-stamped walls had a slight geometric-floral pattern that led me to the restrooms. I entered the ladies' room and locked the door behind me. Thank goodness it was only made for one. There wouldn't be anyone walking in on me talking to myself.

The ghost stood by the counter, leaning over the sink and peering at herself in the mirror. "My eyes were greener once," she began.

"Hello?" I gave her an awkward wave of my fingers as she caught sight of me in the reflection.

She spun to face me. "Oh, good. You're here."

What was with ghosts being suddenly able to talk to me? Dale had been struggling for days to speak, and we'd still had no luck. And Rosa—Kate—a few weeks ago couldn't talk to me either, not until Rich, Ashley, and I performed our first séance, and even then, she didn't say much until after the second time. Daniel too.

But first Arthur this afternoon and now this young woman. Ghosts had talked to me when I was younger, but nothing for years until Miss Susan. Had she somehow enabled me to talk to them when she appeared to me the other night?

"You wished to speak with me?"

"Coach Miller sent me."

"He did?" I hadn't realized ghosts had that capability, although I shouldn't have been surprised. She must have been the cheerleader he mentioned.

"My name's Chrysanthemum, but you can call me Chrys."

"It's nice to meet you. I'm Joanie."

She nodded. "I know." She spread her arms out wide and turned in a circle. "We *all* know."

I wasn't sure how to feel about that. Since moving here, I'd tried to keep a low profile with the ghost population. Usually that meant ignoring them completely so they couldn't realize I'd seen them. I'd slipped a few times over the years, like with Arthur, but we all seemed to have an unspoken agreement to go about our business without disturbing one another.

Chrys cleared her throat. How long had I been lost in thought? "Arthur said something about you wanting information about the north woods in town. He was alive back then, so he'd heard about the disappearances, but he was human, so it's not like he understood what was going on."

"But you do?"

She put her hands on her hips. "Well, considering I'm one of the six who died up there, yes."

My mouth dropped open slightly. "So you were all killed? But Arthur said you weren't murdered."

"Well, not in the traditional sense of the word. But we were."

"What does that mean? I don't understand. How were you killed if not by someone or something?"

"It's all tied to the trees."

A knock on the door interrupted us from continuing.

"Just a minute," I called out to whoever was waiting. "I should go. My date must be wondering what's taking so long." Drats, if we'd been at home, I'd have no worries about how long she and I were talking. But Ken was already worried about my involvement. I couldn't explain my absence by saying I was doing exactly what he was telling me not to do.

She waved me off in a small shooing motion. "Come back

at the end of your date. I'll be here." She poofed out of sight. I could only hope she was right. Chrys was the closest I'd come to any answers.

I unlocked the bathroom door, and exited the room, passing the woman who was waiting to use it.

Wait, had Chrys said *human* as in she wasn't?

CHAPTER 17

Our waiter was just coming out of the kitchen as I turned the corner from the side hallway. Still wrapping my head around what Chrys could have meant, I was grateful for spotting him when I did. The last thing either of us needed was a run-in and the resulting mess.

Urging me in front of him, likely so I wouldn't bump into him from behind, he followed me to the table where Ken sat waiting patiently.

"Sorry about that," I said as I plopped into the chair.

"It's all right. Looks like you had perfect timing. You okay?"

The concern in his voice made me suspect I'd been in the bathroom longer than I'd realized. "Yes, thanks."

"One House Burger with sweet potato wedges," the waiter said putting the plate in front of Ken. "And one chicken cordon bleu sandwich with the garlic parm fries." He set the large square plate down on my placemat. It didn't dawn on me until that moment that I'd ordered garlic. No kissing for me tonight. Then again, it wasn't like Ken was a vampire, so maybe he wouldn't mind. Vampires weren't human—was that what Chrys meant? No way. That would be ridiculous.

"This looks delicious," I stated as I popped a fry into my mouth. The mellow herbaceous flavor of the cooked garlic blended perfectly with the nutty parmesan "Oh, that was divine."

"It does look good. You'll have to thank your friend for the recommendation."

"I will. Have you met Chelsea yet? She teaches swim lessons at the gym, amongst other things."

"No, I haven't. I didn't realize the gym had swimming lessons. Should probably sign Ivy up for some. She'd love it."

"I bet." Any activity was a good activity as far as Ivy was concerned. "She's feeling better, I hope."

Ken nodded emphatically as he quickly chewed a bite of his burger. He swallowed. "Much. She was fine the next day, although she already wants more of your macaroni and cheese. Not sure I'll get her to eat it from the box ever again."

"I was intending to make it again tonight for us all until you asked me out. I hope she's not disappointed. Though tomorrow's an option. It would just be the three of us. Matt's getting a pizza from the place that just opened tonight, and he said it should last him a few days."

He shook his head, and we chatted about Ivy for several minutes, but I could tell our earlier conversation was weighing on him. I was hoping to avoid returning to the topic, but unfortunately, it wasn't meant to be.

"Look, about what I was saying earlier—"

"I really appreciate your concern, but this is what I do. I help people find who they are meant to be with."

"I thought you were a baker."

"That too, but I thought you realized I was more when you saw what I can do." Could I fault him if he didn't? It had taken me seeing what I could do to realize I was more than a baker with a knack for matchmaking... and the ability to see ghosts. Perfectly normal.

"Joanie, this could be dangerous."

"I've had plenty of experience. I've been matchmaking since high school and dealing with ghosts since before that."

"Has anyone else pulled a knife on you?"

"John didn't pull a knife on me."

"Whether the blade was folded in or not, he still took a knife out in your shop." He took a sip of his drink. "And that knife may be possessed since you said it flew back to John's hand. I don't like it."

"You don't have to like it. I just want you to understand."

"I don't know if I can do that. Putting your nose in other people's love lives isn't a good thing. Let what's supposed to happen, you know, happen."

I grabbed a semi-cold fry as I collected my thoughts. I didn't want to say anything I would regret. Ken was a great guy, but I wasn't going to abandon Lily, and what was I supposed to do, let the ghosts wander Heartwood Hollow until they found someone else who could help them? Unless they ran into my great-aunt Pegee, who was the only other person I knew of with this ability, they could be stuck here for a while. And who knew where she was—if she wasn't on the other side herself. Hadn't the ghosts been here long enough? It wasn't fair to them if I stopped any more than it would be to Lily and John's love life. When two people who were meant to be together weren't, part of them would always be missing without the other to bring it out in them even if their lives were happy and complete in every other way.

"Well, I'm sorry you feel like that, but this is who I am."

"And I'm sorry too. You're an amazing woman, Joanie. What you can do is incredible, but I have Ivy to think about, and what if things go south? What if you try to help someone who wants to hurt you? I can't have that near my daughter." He sighed long and hard. I knew what was coming before he opened his mouth. "Maybe it would be best if we take a break. A pause. I like you, but I need to dig deep and really decide if this is something I can do."

"It's okay. I understand. But you have to realize I would never do anything to hurt Ivy or put her in harm's way. If I ever felt in danger, I would walk away. That's not the case here. I'm fine, and everything else will turn out fine too." I tried to give him a reassuring smile but ultimately failed, unable to muster more than pulling my lips back into a thin line.

Ken stood and dug out his wallet. He pulled out two twenty-dollar bills and placed them on the table. "This should cover dinner tonight. I asked you out, the least I could do is still pay for your meal."

"You don't have to."

"Please let me."

I nodded. "Take care, Ken."

"You too." He walked around the table and placed a hand on my shoulder before bending down and kissing the top of my head. "Please."

I nodded again, now at a loss for words.

Ken gave my shoulder a small squeeze before walking away. I didn't watch him go but felt the shift in the air as his serious and disappointed demeanor left the restaurant. Had this been the bakery, no doubt the lights would have brightened.

The waiter came by to clear our plates, and I asked for the check. He returned a moment later with it, and I put Ken's forty dollars and another six from me into the billfold. I took a sip of my water, then stood and walked toward the restroom, where I hoped Chrys would still be waiting. If she was anything like Arthur, who seemed like he had enough energy to be out and about for as long as he desired, she'd be there.

I breathed in deeply as I walked in, locking the door behind me. "Chrys?"

"I'm sorry about your date."

I glanced at the mirror and saw her sitting on the closed toilet seat. "Thanks. I hope he comes around."

"He will if it's meant to be. Must stink to not be able to use your powers on yourself."

I barked out a laugh. "You're telling me." It was ironic that matchmakers couldn't use their own power on themselves. I wondered if Mom could match me and vice versa. I'd never asked, and she'd never offered that information. Whether because she couldn't or because she hadn't ever found a match for me, I wasn't sure. I'd not found one for her either.

"Okay, so you had to deal with a lot out there, but did you have time to think over what I said at all?"

"You said it all had to do with the trees. Do you mean the species of trees like maple or oak or pine?"

"Not really, but sort of."

"And what did you mean by saying Arthur was human? Are you trying to say you aren't? You look pretty human to me. You're not like a vampire or something, are you? I should warn you, I've had garlic."

Quirking a grin, she stood, then came toward me. "Have you ever heard of dryads?"

"Dry-whats?"

"Dryads. Tree people."

I shook my head. "Can't say that I have. Tree people? Do they live in trees?"

Now it was her turn to laugh. "That's one way to put it.

But the north woods is where they lived when everything happened. They don't now. Look, I'd love to make this easy on you and just tell you everything, but my time here is short. So you're going to have to do some research. It will probably be more beneficial for you to absorb it all that way anyway."

"You mean you can't stay here for as long as you want?"

"Not me. I have to go back and recharge, shall we say. Arthur's different. He draws his energy from his routines and exists here almost all the time. I'm more crossed over than not but can come and go since all my business hasn't fully resolved itself. But now having met you, I'm thinking that might change soon. You're affecting way more than just the people you think you are by doing this. I'm glad you didn't back down when your date asked you to stop. Keep putting up the good fight." She gave me a salute followed by a peace sign as she faded from sight, leaving me alone in the bathroom.

She had left me with my biggest piece of information yet.

Tree people. Dryads.

Now I needed to figure out what it meant.

CHAPTER 18

A normal Tuesday would have seen me in my pajamas until noontime, several cups of tea consumed, and at least one book read while Saffy slept on my feet at the end of the couch. This, however, was not a normal Tuesday, and Saffy wasn't happy.

Fully dressed, minus my shoes, I steeped maple earl grey tea in a travel mug, standing in the kitchen as my cat eyed me from a chair at the kitchen table. She'd learned long ago that she wasn't allowed on the table or the counter. I always tried to keep my kitchen clean, and cat paws were not something I wanted on surfaces where food went even with a good sanitizing before I started prepping anything. She'd get whatever was safe for her to have if I was cooking. Or she'd get some other morsel if she couldn't eat what I was making. The only thing that tempted her to get on my counters now was the presence of fresh flowers. She could never stay away, which was why they lived on the refrigerator out of reach when I had them.

"I'm heading out to the library," I told her in an attempt at appeasement. She knew that meant I was getting another book to read and would be back soon. It was nothing new.

Saffy flicked her tail at me. She saw I had only partially read the book I'd started this morning as I waited for the library to open. It sat on my coffee table with a bookmark tucked inside it. I should have put it in my bag to keep up appearances.

"I know, I know. But I really am going there. I have to figure out what a dryad is and find out their connection to the north woods. You wouldn't happen to know, would you?"

Saffy cocked her head to the side and lifted a paw, licked it, and began cleaning her face.

It seemed she didn't know and didn't care. My desire to know was apparently not a good enough reason for me to be leaving the house and disrupting her routine.

"I'll bring you back a treat," I promised, drawing out the *E* sound in *treat*. Great. Now I was bargaining with my cat. Again. I really was a crazy cat lady, and it had only taken one cat.

Saffy perked up at this and jumped off the chair. She scampered to her food bowl and meowed at me.

"Okay, okay." I walked over to the cupboard where I kept her treats. There was really no telling her no at this point. "You can have something now." Thank goodness I still had some left over from the other day.

She wriggled her bum and sat, watching me the whole time as I pulled the container out from where I stored her homemade cat treats. I grabbed out two and dropped both into her bowl before snapping the lid back on. Saffy munched greedily as if I hadn't fed her in days. It had been four hours. By no means was she starving, although she acted like it whenever food was near.

I removed the tea bag from my travel mug, then screwed on the lid.

"Back as soon as I can, Saf. I miss my normal Tuesdays as much as you do when I don't get them."

Still eating, she ignored me as I slipped out of the kitchen. At the front door, I slid my shoes on and grabbed my tote bag that had been sitting on the small bench portion of my coat tree. I slung the bag over my shoulder and opened the door,.

The morning was already warm. I was used to stepping out into the cooler pre-dawn mornings, but hours had passed since then, and without a cloud in the sky, the day had already had the time to heat up. At least the air was significantly less humid than it had been these last few days. It had rained overnight again, and I hoped it would make for a better day. The first warm snap of the season had been getting to us all.

I walked to the library, it was too nice not to, and arrived just as Pete was unlocking the door.

He held it open for me. "Morning, Joanie."

"Morning, Pete. How are you?" I hadn't seen him in a couple weeks.

I followed him through the lobby and toward the circulation desk as he answered, "Oh, the usual. Thanks for that birthday cake you made for me. It was wicked good."

Emily had already told me it was a hit, but it was nice to hear it straight from him. "You're welcome. I'm glad you liked it."

"It wasn't easy turning forty, but having a cake like that, well, I would have many more birthdays if I could keep getting one." He turned on his computer, and the screen flared to life a moment later.

I laughed. "That's one way to flatter your baker. I can make cakes for more than birthdays too. Anniversaries, weddings, book launches. Whatever you need. Even if you don't need it but want it."

Now it was his turn to laugh. "I might just hold you to that. Do you sell by the slice?"

I shook my head. "But I make cupcakes."

A smile spread across his face. "So what can I do for you?" he asked as he typed something short into the computer, likely a password. "Let me guess. It's Tuesday, so you're here to return a book."

"No, actually. I'm here to find one."

"Well, you've come to the right place. Looking for something specific?"

I took a deep breath. "I need to find out what dryads are."

Pete blinked rapidly a few times as if surprised to hear that answer. Finally, he spoke. "You mean you don't know?"

"Am I supposed to?"

"With all of those fantasy books you've read?" He sighed. "You must not be reading the right ones."

There was nothing worse than disappointment from a librarian.

"I've been told they live in trees."

"They're people who live in the trees because they *are* the trees." He wrote something down on a piece of paper, typed into the computer, wrote something else down, then handed the paper to me. "Here. This should have what you're looking for."

The title of a book and its call number. "Thanks, I'll go grab it."

"It's a good one."

I headed over to the fantasy section and pulled out the book. Within the first few pages of skimming, I knew this was talking about what he'd described. But people who could turn into trees were fantasy creatures. People didn't do that in real life.

Then again, I spoke to ghosts and at least half the town probably thought I was a witch. *Real life* had a different meaning for me. Who was to say reality didn't have a different meaning for these dryads as well?

I closed the book, then clutched it against my chest. Next on my list to check out was the non-fiction section where, a few weeks ago, I had found some books on supernatural versions of witches as well as the history and practice of witchcraft and Wicca. There, I spotted two reference books on mythological creatures, so I grabbed each one to peruse them. Each had entries for dryads, chronicling their history in literature all the way back to Greek and Roman mythology. But they were short enough to read here, and beyond some paintings of women in flowy dresses with branches coming out of their heads, they weren't going to be useful enough to check out from the library. I placed both back on the shelf and returned to Peter at the front desk.

He glanced up at me, pausing his scanning of books from the overnight return bin. "Ah, you found it."

"Not sure what it will tell me, but it looks good, so I figured I would make it my next read." I fished out my library card from my wallet and handed it to him.

"The other books on your TBR won't be happy you have a list jumper." He took the book and scanned the barcode on the back along with my library card before returning both to me.

"I think they'll understand," I said with a laugh. "Thanks for the recommendation."

"Anytime. You know, you could have looked up what a dryad is on the internet, right?"

I nodded. "I never think to check there first, though."

He quirked an eyebrow at me. It was a look I'd gotten several times before whenever I said something similar.

"Would it make more sense if I said I didn't have a computer until I went away to college?"

"You can't be serious. I'm older than you are, and I had one before high school."

"My mom didn't like them, so she never got one for the house. She still doesn't have one at home, although she uses one at work all the time."

"But that still leaves you with having one now and not using it."

I shrugged. "Old habits." He didn't need to hear about how I couldn't get the Wi-Fi to work in my house. Much like with the inability to get a cell signal inside my house, I blamed the lack of Wi-Fi on something my mom and Gram had done when I moved in. Without the ability to connect, I rarely used the computer at all. Or my cellphone.

Pete nodded slowly, studying me as I placed my library card back into its designated slot in my wallet.

I slipped both the book and my wallet into my bag. "I'll see you around."

As soon as my feet hit the sidewalk outside, my cell phone rang. Had it not been for the vibration against the library book, I might not have realized what the noise was. I grabbed it from my purse and looked at the screen, momentarily hoping Ken had called to say he'd changed his mind about our break.

But no.

I accepted the call and brought the phone to my ear, starting toward home. "Hey, Libby. How are you?" It was rare for her to call my cell. Rare for anyone. The last time she had called, it was during a major freak-out about a high tea she was having. The governor had RSVPed to it, so everything had to be perfect. She changed her scone order at the last minute to include the governor's favorite fruit flavor. Thank goodness it had been in season.

"Joanie, I was thinking about what we talked about yesterday during your delivery, and I remember my grandmother used to tell me stories about how the wood used to make some of the earliest buildings in town was alive." She paused as if she expected me to chime in, but I waited to hear more. "Now, I know what you're thinking. You're thinking, Libby, of course the wood was alive. That's because trees are alive. But that's not what I mean. I really think she meant *alive*, alive. As if the trees were people who could walk around like you or me."

"That is quite the story, Libby." Had she told me at any point before now, I'd have said such things were impossible. Now her grandmother's story fit right in with everything I'd been hearing over the past few days. It couldn't be a coincidence. Maybe dryads were real after all.

"I know it all sounds crazy, and I'm sure it was nothing more than a tall tale she told me to creep me out as a child, but those woods are freaky, especially when you add in the disappearances. Anyway, I thought you'd like to know just in case. So there you have it."

If Libby believed it was a story, I wasn't going to be the one to tell her the possibility about it being otherwise—especially not over the phone. These sorts of things were hard enough to tell people in person.

I switched the phone from one ear to the other. "Thanks for telling me."

"You're welcome. I'm sure it's nothing, but I'd hate to not have told you if it could help." She sighed. "Okay, well, I won't keep you from your Tuesday routine."

"You're not keeping me. I'm walking back home from the library."

"Oh. Well, in that case . . ." Libby didn't want to say outright she had a request for me, but I knew she did. She had told me numerous times that she hated being a bother. It was why she usually let me choose what flavors to bring her for teas.

"Want to put in a special order of anything for tomorrow?"

"Since you mentioned it, yes."

I turned onto the far end of my street as Libby rattled off a few flavors she'd been thinking about lately. One would require a trip to the grocery store, but the rest weren't anything out of the ordinary. I could go to the store later. It wouldn't be long now before I was inside and could sink into this new book after changing back into my pajamas. Saffy would be glad to see me. Barely an hour had passed, but she'd likely demand an early lunch out of my absence. It wouldn't take much to whip up a little something with leftover chicken I had as an extra special treat for her and save the rest for a light lunch.

"J-Joanie, Joanie!" a man's voice shouted—one I didn't recognize.

Turning, hope swelled in my chest when I saw who it was.

CHAPTER 19

No wonder I hadn't recognized the voice. I'd never heard him speak before. Guess he had finally found his voice. Dale waved at me from my neighbor's yard. As much as I wanted to drop the phone and run to him, I couldn't do that to Libby. I held up a finger to tell him one minute as I veered toward him and waited for a pause in the conversation on the other end of the line. It didn't take long.

"Okay, Libby, I've made it home. I'm going to let you go now, okay? For whatever reason, the signal drops as soon as I get inside." That last part was true. I'd had a technician come check it out shortly after I moved in, but he couldn't figure it out. Although I had a sneaking suspicion Gram was to blame, she had never confirmed it. She'd never liked the idea of cell phones, said they messed with our personal energy fields.

"Oh, sure, sure," she said in a way that made me think she was waving me off as if I was standing there getting ready to get on my bike. "Good talking to you. I'll see you tomorrow. Think you'll be able to stay for tea?"

"Not tomorrow, but I promise it will be soon. Once I

figure out what's going on with the whole Lily and John thing."

"All right, well, good luck with it all." She hung up.

"Dale, was that you yelling for me?"

He nodded, a broad smile across his face. Then he opened his mouth to speak, and nothing came out. Drats. His neck stiffened and his face tensed. I could understand his frustration.

"You're making progress," I said, trying to sound encouraging. "That's something. Keep working at it. Is there something I can help you with?"

Dale took a deep breath to calm down before nodding again. He turned away from me and headed toward the sidewalk, waving at me from over his shoulder to follow him. I glanced at my house. Saffy was in the window on the back of the couch. As far as I knew, she hadn't looked up to see me, but she no doubt sensed my presence. She wasn't going to be happy with my leaving again before I could give her a snack, but I couldn't worry about her not-empty tummy. Dale was the priority. If just saying my name had drained him of so much energy he couldn't continue to talk, then I didn't know how long his energy would hold. The last thing I wanted was for him to disappear before he was able to show me whatever he needed to. That wouldn't help solve anything.

I rushed to catch up with him halfway around the corner. The whole time he kept urging me on as if what he was leading me to was of vast importance. How long had he been trying to get my attention?

We turned at the next street and again at the next, weaving our way back toward Main Street then past it as we approached the block of houses between Main and River Streets. I was familiar with this area, having dropped Lauren off before at her house down the road. Lily lived around here as well.

Dale stopped short, causing me to nearly walk into him. Or rather, through him. Although ghosts looked solid, and at times were, it was still possible for them to go through things or have things go through them, especially unintentionally. It had happened to me before, and the sensation was not one I wanted to repeat. It was cold, and emotions that weren't yours momentarily took hold of your own. If you didn't know what to do with them, strong emotions from ghosts could linger. Although it had been years since it happened—before Gram banished the bad spirits from being able to reach me— I'd never forgotten the feeling.

Shaking away the memory, grateful it was only a memory, I turned around in a circle. "I don't see anything." Nothing but houses on a quiet street at least.

Dale pointed at something up over my head behind me.

I turned to see where he was directing my gaze. Up on a fire escape of the apartment building on the corner of Main Street stood John, looking this way. I tried waving, but he didn't spot me. What was he watching so intently?

"You want me to talk to John?"

Dale smiled and nodded.

At least he could tell me that easily enough without needing to speak.

I marched toward the fire escape and used an overturned milk crate to get up on the ladder. A few minutes later, I stood on the landing below the one John was sitting on.

"What in the world are you doing up here?"

John jumped. How could he be so focused that he hadn't heard me on this rickety piece of metal? He cast a quick glance my way, but he didn't otherwise turn to look at me. "You scared me half to death! What are you doing up here?"

"I should ask the same about you." I climbed another three stairs until I was tall enough to see over John's shoulder and get a better idea of what he was looking at.

Or *who*.

Down below, diagonally across the street, Lily worked in her backyard garden, crouched over a bed of, what else, lilies. How long had he been up here staring at her? How did he go from having just met her the other day to following her and knowing where she lived?

"John, this is getting a little creepy." Maybe Ken had been right. I glanced back down at Dale, and he nodded once firmly, steeling my resolve. "Why are you watching Lily?"

"I . . . I . . . I can't help it. I know this is making me come off as some crazy stalker, but I can't help it."

"Why can't you?"

"It's this knife."

That's when I realized he had a white-knuckle grip on the closed knife, just like Friday in the shop before it started to glow.

"Tell me about this knife, John. It's special, isn't it?"

He nodded. "My grandfather gave it to me."

"Dale?"

For the first time since I'd gotten here, he tore his gaze from Lily to study me. "How do you know my grandfather's name? He's been dead for years. What did you do, look into my family or something?"

"Well, yes, I did that too, but I know Dale. Not well, but I've met him."

His brows pinched in confusion. "How? You aren't from around here."

"I could almost say the same for you, considering I'd never seen you in until last week. You don't get out much, do you?

"I try to avoid town. It's hard being among people who

had their lives upturned when your family business closed. I'm the only one left for them to take their anger out on."

"You think they're angry?"

"I know it."

This was news to me. Heartwood Hollow was a vibrant, thriving community. It wasn't down on its luck as if there had been no other industry to turn to when the lumber mill closed. There was plenty here, but things could have been different then.

"So you obviously haven't heard the rumors about me," I said, getting us back on topic.

John shook his head. "What rumors?"

"That I'm a witch."

He scoffed and rolled his eyes.

For quite a long time, that would have been my reaction too, but perhaps it was time to embrace who I was. It was who Gram was. And Mom too. Telling Lily hadn't worked, but maybe it would with John.

"But they're not rumors. They're true. Oh, and I can see dead people too."

"Isn't that a line from a movie?"

"Close." I'd seen it once when it first came out, and that was enough for me. I had a lot of empathy for that kid since I'd gone through the same thing. "But it doesn't make the statement any less true. It's how I know Dale."

"Prove it."

I always had to prove it somehow and had learned to expect it. "Okay, well, he wears pretty much the same thing you were wearing on Friday. The buffalo check shirt, the jeans, the work boots."

"Yeah, him and how many other lumberjacks?"

"Fair enough." I glanced down at Dale, still waiting on the

sidewalk. "How about the ring on a silver chain around his neck or the blue knit hat stuffed into his back pocket?"

He squinted at me a moment, scrutinizing me, then said, "That's better."

"Would telling you it's not his ring be enough? His is on his finger. This one is your grandmother's." The last part had been a guess, but it wasn't a man's ring.

That seemed to convince him at least. "So where is he?"

"Right below us. He's the one who led me here. How else would I have found you? Do you think I randomly climb fire escapes or something?"

He raised his hands up in surrender, his grip still tight around his knife. "Okay, okay. You have a point. I can't imagine you found me by mistake."

"He's worried about you and this whole situation."

"*I'm* worried about me and this whole situation. I can't stop thinking about Lily, and I keep ending up wherever she is or somewhere close to it. It's like the other day. The knife pulled me into your shop. I really had no control over it. Today I found myself in front of her house. I saw her through the window and then climbed up here." He rubbed his eyes with the palms of his hands. "Ugh. That really makes me sound like a stalker. But I'm telling you, if ghosts are real, then this knife must be possessed or something, because when I hold it, I feel as if it's pulling me to her.

"Have you tried talking to Lily since the other day?"

He reared his head back, and his eyes widened. This reaction was more along the lines of what I had been expecting when I told him I could see ghosts. "What, are you crazy? She hates me. Why would I go do a thing like that?"

"I don't know, maybe because that's the normal thing to do as opposed to following her around without her knowledge?"

He let out a long sigh. "Please? Just a little longer. At least this way I get to see her."

"You're coming off a bit creepy again." It had been a long time since I had heard someone sound so heartsick. I had to do something. "I have an idea. Let's go."

CHAPTER 20

John didn't move.

"Come on," I insisted. "She's already gone back inside anyway." I turned and stepped down the first flight of stairs, stopping at the middle landing to wait for him. When he still hadn't moved, I crossed my arms and faced him. "Don't you want this problem to get solved? That won't happen if you don't follow me."

"Okay, okay." He stood and met me on the landing. "What are we doing?"

Refusing to answer that question until he and I were both off the fire escape, I continued down to the next landing. I let myself hang from the lower rung of the ladder and then let go, dropping to the ground with a light thump as my feet hit the pavement.

John landed with an even larger thud, nearly falling as he jumped from the last rail. "Now are you going to tell me what we're doing?"

"Not yet." I crossed the street and strode over to Lily's house.

John stopped in his tracks in the middle of the street. "Joanie, I don't know about this."

"Trust me. The only way either of you is going to get answers and the only way this pulling feeling is going to stop is if you two talk." I climbed the first step to her door. "What's the worst that can happen?" I stepped onto the second, and this time John followed me, reaching the sidewalk. He gazed back across the street.

"You've come this far. Don't think about turning around."

"Oh, I'm not going to run. Considering how fast you caught up to Lily and me the other day, I expect you'd be able to catch me and haul me back." He smiled for the first time since I'd met him. "I was looking to see if I could see my grandpa."

I glanced at Dale who was standing next to John, a hand on John's shoulder.

"He's right next to you," I answered, lifting my hand and pointing at John's side. "He followed you across. I don't think he would have let you run off either. Whatever is happening between you and Lily with this knife, he wants it solved too."

John looked to his left, and for a moment it seemed as if the two men were able to see one another as their gazes met. The illusion was broken soon after when John sighed. "I'm kind of envious of your gift right now. I'd love to see him again."

"You will. When the time is right." I walked onto the top step in front of Lily's door. "Ready?"

"No, but I don't think that bothers you in the slightest, does it?"

I knocked three times. "Not really."

A moment later, Lily opened the door.

"Joanie? What are you doing here? It's Tuesday."

"Mind if we come in?"

"We?" She opened the door a bit wider, spotted John, and her face flared red. But at the same time, the butterflies that signaled a nearby match rushed up my toes and zoomed into my chest. There was no doubt in my mind these two were meant for one another.

Lily pulled the door closed, but before she could shut it all the way, leaving us standing here empty-handed, I stuck my foot in at the bottom, preventing her from her goal. It had worked when Ashley needed to stop Millie from shutting us out of her cabin a few weeks back, and I hoped it would have the same effect here.

"Please? How about just long enough for a cup of tea. Then we'll go. But I think we could all benefit from talking with one another to sort this out."

Lily sighed loudly, but much of it was for dramatic flair. I'd heard her sighs of true disapproval before, usually due to the boys' antics in the kitchen, and this one wasn't even close to what those sounded like. Despite her anger, part of her was putting on a show for John. She was still interested. There was hope.

"Fine," she said as she let go of the door and let it swing open. "Come on in. But one cup, Joanie, that's it. If I don't like where this is going, you're both gone."

"Deal." I took a step forward, crossing the threshold to her house. John remained standing on the sidewalk, prompting me to clear my throat. "Coming, John?"

Dale gave him a quick slap on the back, and he snapped out of whatever trance he'd been lost in. John bounded up the steps, then pulled the door closed behind him.

As we entered the living room, I glanced out the narrow window to the left of the door in time to see Dale disappear. I wondered if he'd run out of energy or left because he had decided he'd done his job. Or maybe he couldn't come in.

Lily's house could have been warded like mine was. Well, at least until I broke them.

I stopped short as I turned toward the living room to take in the view. If anyone said they lived in a tree and then showed me a photograph of this room, I would have believed them. No way would I have expected an interior to look like this even if it was the home of a suspected dryad. Wood paneling lined the walls, but it wasn't like any regular wood paneling from the sixties and seventies. This was natural tree bark panels of different widths and shades. What wasn't paneled had been painted in various green hues.

A large window seat made from a thick slab of a purple wood I didn't realize existed featured green pillows with a leaf pattern that matched the couch sitting across from the window. The blanket on the couch was a color similar to the purple wood.

Tree saplings sprung from pots in every corner of the room, some reaching five and six feet tall. The coffee and end tables, as well as the wood mantle above the fireplace, were dotted with small pink flowers that reminded me of budding trees. The banister leading upstairs was made from birch branches, its white and black bark a stark contrast to the rest of the room.

"Wow, this is quite the decor," I said for a lack of anything else to say as Lily continued walking into the kitchen. "I don't think I've ever seen a room that felt more like being outside than this one."

"Thanks, Holly and I find it energizing," Lily answered from somewhere the kitchen. I couldn't see her from where I stood, but I could hear her filling up a kettle with water from the sink.

"Oh, you live with Holly?"

"Sure do. We go way back. We're cousins."

No wonder Holly had been so protective of Lily that day on Main Street. I let out a small "Huh."

"Please, sit. It's weird to have you both still standing in my doorway."

That was John's cue to beeline over to the coffee table to inspect it. He ran his hand along its surface. "This is amazing walnut wood. Barely any knots at all. Where did you get it?"

She poked her head through the open doorway and smiled knowingly before coming back into the room. She leaned on one leg and placed a hand on her hip, popping the opposite one out—her ultimate flirtation stance. "You didn't think you were the only one who could build furniture in town, did you?"

John's mouth dropped open. "You did this?"

Lily beamed with pride. "A couple years back."

John turned toward me. "No offense, but her talent is being wasted in your kitchen."

I couldn't disagree. Lily was full of surprises today.

"Man, I'd hire you in a heartbeat for my furniture company if you wanted," John said, returning his gaze to Lily, a hopeful smile across his face. "Do you have any more pieces in here that you've made?"

"I have some stuff in the kitchen. One of the chairs. Mostly bowls and kitchen tools. I made my headboard too."

I quickly got lost as the two talked about wood graining and something called a *burl*, but it warmed my heart with how easily the conversation flowed between the two of them. Anyone could see—and hear—they were perfect for one another. The matchmaking tingle continued throughout their discussion, working its way up my legs and settling in my chest.

Lily's woodworking talent both impressed and confused me. If she was connected to the supposed dryads of the north woods, possibly to the extent of being one herself—and given her strong reaction to the wood on John's knife—then how was she okay with all of this wood around her? Was all wood sacred? Or just some of it? And what was the difference?

I found my opening to reinsert myself into their conversation during a lull, the two of them "making eyes" at one another as Gram would say.

"I had no idea you could make all of this, Lily. Wow, just wow. I should get you to build some new displays for the shop. I've been looking to make some upgrades."

The teapot whistled as the water hit boiling point. Lily stood, then walked back into the kitchen to turn the burner off. "I'd be happy to do it. Let me know when you'd like to talk," she called, "and I can either come in before you close up for the day or stay later in the morning to go over some things."

"That would be great, and of course I would pay you," I replied loudly enough so she could hear me as she rummaged around in her cupboards, the clanking of cups audible.

"Do either of you take milk or sugar?" she asked.

I glanced at John, and he shook his head. "Do you have honey?"

"Sure do. Be right back out."

A minute later, Lily returned carrying a sheet pan holding three coffee mugs, a honey bear, and sugar. Below it, hanging from two of her fingers, was a half-full quart of milk. She set it all down on the coffee table, which John was still admiring.

"Where did you get this wood?"

"I have my sources," she said in a way that was flirtatious but held a hint of hesitation.

He didn't pick up on the shift in demeanor. "Any way you could put me in touch with them?"

"Maybe."

The atmosphere in the room had lightened considerably since we'd entered even with her slight reluctance in answering his questions. Fully expecting it to sour Lily's mood, I almost didn't want to address what we'd come here for. Unfortunately, I didn't see other options.

"Lily, I wouldn't have pictured this much wood in your home after what happened on Friday. I'm sorry, but I have to ask. Is this sacred wood?"

Her face fell as she sat down on her brown leather chair next to the couch. "Please, sit."

John moved to the window seat, and I took a spot on the couch. I reached in front of me and grabbed one of the tea mugs. Lily did the same, then dropped in a spoon of sugar and a drop of milk. I stirred a spoon of honey into mine.

"No, not all wood is sacred," Lily continued. "It's all in the type of wood, and I don't mean whether it's oak or pine. Sacred wood is wood that was once alive. From Dryads."

"You believe in that?" John asked as if trying to hide his skepticism.

"Don't you? That's where all of this stems from. All of your family's problems. The way some of the old-timers here must look at you."

So John hadn't been completely wrong about people's opinions of him.

John leaned forward. "But my dad said they're just stories."

"I've done a lot of thinking since yesterday when you tried to talk to me, Joanie. Gotta give you credit. It was clever getting us alone to talk. I'd never have said anything in front of the others. But you shared your secret, and now I want to tell you mine."

She was quiet a moment as she took a long sip of her tea as if steeling herself for what was to come.

"The stories of dryads aren't just stories," she finally said. "Considering I am one, I should know."

"I wondered," I confessed.

"I knew you were close to figuring something out when I heard you were looking into the north woods specifically. Holly and I talked. She trusts you with this, and so do I."

"But why aren't you a tree?" John asked. "Or part tree or whatever." He was taking the news remarkably well, almost better than he had when I told him I saw ghosts. How many stories of dryads had he grown up with?

"We don't always have to be trees." Lily lifted her hand and held it out. Her skin started to harden and take on a darker hue as it became bark-like. I glanced at John. His mouth hung open slightly, a look of awe on his face. "And I don't just suddenly take root wherever I'm standing in case you were wondering. I've heard that before. I merge with trees. Particularly the one out back."

I followed the line of thought. "So is the tree out there sacred?

She nodded before taking another sip of her tea. "Those trees capable of being merged with are sacred. It wasn't always like that, though. At one point in time, it was one tree to one dryad except for our elders. Historically, we spent much more time merged with our tree too. But that caused many problems as time went on."

John reached into his pocket and pulled out his knife. "So this sacred wood once was a dryad's home?"

Lily's grip on her mug tightened and her nostrils flared. "Worse."

John frowned. "I'm not sure if you heard me when I tried telling you on Friday. This came from my grandfather. He gave it to me before he died. I didn't know it was sacred. Still don't know what that means. Not really. Why is this knife's wood worse than others?"

"This was heartwood."

Maybe it was another woodworking term I didn't know because John seemed to understand. "Heartwood? What's that?" I asked, hoping she'd explain.

"Remember how I just said merging with just one tree caused problems?"

Both John and I nodded.

"When you merge with a single tree and that tree is cut down, you get sick and die. When you merge with a tree and that tree is cut down with you in it . . . well, you die right away."

All the dots connected for me at that moment. "So the disappearances in the north woods a couple decades back . . ."

"Weren't disappearances at all." Her gaze remained fixed on John. "The dryads who went missing were killed when they merged with the tree and your family cut them down. I'm sure you'll find many incidents of people who were otherwise healthy getting sick and dying around that time too. Someone cut my grandmother down. That knife of yours was made out of her heartwood. Part of her is still in that wood. Even just sitting here looking at the knife, I can feel her."

So it was Lily's grandmother in the knife, not Dale like I had thought. So what tied Dale here? Was he like Daniel, just a lonely ghost who followed his grandson around because he felt he couldn't move on?

"I didn't know." John's voice shook as he held the knife out in his hand, gazing at it reverently. "It's not much, but do you want it? Please take it."

"No. I couldn't bear it. As much as I want to be close to her. It can't be like that. I can barely look at it without getting angry. It disgusts me. They tried telling your family what was up there, you know. To get them to stop. But they didn't. Not until it was too late. I have no doubt that you'll find it had something to do with the downfall of the lumber business."

I blew across my mug of tea. "You're both innocent in this matter. John, you were just a boy when all this happened. Lily, you too. You both lost so much when this happened. But it isn't John's fault that he has the knife."

Lily looked up at me, tears threatening to spill from her eyes. "I know," she said glumly. "But she was there and then she just wasn't."

The couch cushion next to me shifted, and I looked to my right. Sitting by my side was the female ghost I had seen in the crowd when Lily confronted John.

"Lily, what was your grandmother's name?"

"Juniper. Why?"

"She's still looking out for you." I smiled warmly.

Lily's gaze darted around, seeking out her grandmother.

"Next to me on the couch."

Her voice broke as she said, "I can't see her."

Juniper stood, walked to her granddaughter, and then wrapped Lily in a big hug.

"But you feel her, don't you?"

Lily nodded, her tears now falling. "I miss her so much."

"She misses you too."

"What about your parents?"

"They uprooted like the rest of us. But they went away. I couldn't leave. This is my home. Holly's family took me in. That's why we're all scattered throughout the town and elsewhere now. Me and Holly in the backyard. Others in the park. Some are still in the woods, but no one goes up to the north woods anymore. Not the dryads anyway. It's the site of a tragedy."

Her shoulders fell. "But now we don't merge with just one

tree. The elders taught us all how to merge with multiple trees so that something like this can never happen again. If one tree goes down, the rest won't, and so we won't die. We can just go to another tree."

"I have so many questions, but now isn't the time. I think I need to process the whole idea that there is more to Heartwood Hollow than just its ghosts that only I can see."

"Well, now you know you're not the only one who's different. I'm not sure about the whole ghost seeing thing or the matchmaking thing, but there are other witches here too."

That was news to me. What else called Heartwood Hollow home?

I glanced at Juniper, who returned to her spot on the couch. She smiled at me. "Lily, I don't want to take up too much of your afternoon, and I have some things to look into now because of all this, but how about you and John talk a bit more. Not necessarily about the past and what happened or the knife that has somehow decided now is the time to bring you two together. Take this as an opportunity to learn more about one another. You have plenty in common." I looked at John. "She likes ice cream, and the place on Main Street just opened for the season. Why don't you both go get some?"

"I'd love to. I mean"—his gaze traveled to Lily—"if you'd like to go out with me."

"I think I'd enjoy that. Can you leave the knife at home, though?"

"Sure can." He slipped it back into his pocket.

"I'll leave you two alone to figure out your date. I'll see you tomorrow, Lily. John, good to see you too. Have fun." I cast a look back at Juniper on the couch next to me. She gave me a broad grin and nodded once before disappearing from sight. Her approval of the two made me happy, although if she had been the one pulling the knife toward her granddaughter, it only made sense. I hoped Dale, wherever he was, was just as satisfied with the outcome of today's meeting. Part of me hoped I would see them both again, but the other part of me realized that if all I'd had to do to was get these two together and talking for both spirits to be satisfied, then they wouldn't appear again.

Lily saw me to the door. As I reached the sidewalk, I turned toward the house. Lily had joined John on the window seat. She pulled her knee up onto the seat so she could face him. Both were smiling, and the tingles coursed through my body as the match started to root more firmly, the two of them finally meeting under good terms.

CHAPTER 21

I t was well past lunch by the time I reached Main Street, and most of the restaurants were either closed for a short break between the lunch and dinner services or closed for the day entirely. That left me few options to pick up a quick bite on my way back home, the idea of cooking for lunch long abandoned. Dinner, however, was another story. I grabbed my phone from my purse and dialed.

"Hey, Steph," I said once she'd picked up. "It's short notice, but how about that girls' night tonight?"

"You realize it's a Tuesday, right? You have to work in the morning."

"I know, I know. But I could use the girl time." I sucked in a breath. "Ken dumped me—"

"Say no more. I'll be over after work."

"Plus, I could use your help with something."

"So what your saying is, is you're going to owe me another girls' night after this anyway."

I laughed. "Yes, that's exactly what I'm saying."

"So what do you need me to look into?"

"Remember how I was looking into the north woods disappearances?

"Yeah . . ." she said, a hint of hesitation in her voice.

"I would like information on Juniper Albero and Chrysanthemum I don't think I ever learned her last name."

"They're two of the people who disappeared," she stated plainly. "What about them?"

"Well, you're not going to believe this, but I think they may have been dryads." So much for my not talking about this sort of thing on the phone.

"Oh, that."

"You don't sound surprised at all."

"Joanie," Steph said in a way that made me stop in the middle of the sidewalk. "I am one. Alex and I both."

"Why did you never tell me?"

"Would you have believed me if I had told you before now? Besides, it's not like you've come out and said you're a witch."

"Oh, well, I'm a witch." I quickly looked around me to make sure no one had heard. I didn't need to go causing brand new rumors about myself that would actually be true.

"About time."

I laughed. "So dinner tonight?"

Sure. "I'll call Alex and tell him. He mentioned you running into him."

"I'll call some of the other girls. Unless you'd rather me not because of what we might be talking about."

"Go right ahead. They might surprise you. Besides, we'll spend most of tonight talking about how much we hate Ken."

"But we don't hate Ken."

"Tonight we do. It's a rite of passage. One that is high time you go through. Now, go pick up some wine, get something to make for dinner, and warn Saffy. You know how she doesn't like to be surprised with lots of people."

"All right, I'll talk to you later." I hung up the phone and continued down the street toward the coffee shop, hoping I could grab something to hold me over until dinner.

"Joanie!" Gary called as I walked into Leafs and Grounds. "What can I do for you? Wait, wait. Don't tell me." He marched behind the counter and pulled a marshmallow treat from under a shelf. He tossed it at me.

"How did you know?"

"I had a feeling you'd be in at some point today," he answered with a grin on his face that he was trying to keep steady.

"You have special powers you want to tell me about too?"

He cocked his head to the side, his eyebrow raised slightly. "Actually, Holly saw you walking around earlier, so I figured I'd save one for you in case you stopped in. You know how we're usually out by lunchtime."

"Well, thanks. I'll take it. Is Holly here?" I looked around the shop and peered into the back but didn't see her.

"Nah, sent her home after lunch. We hit a lull during the weekdays until school lets out, and that's nothing Duke and I can't handle without her."

I nodded, fully understanding. I always had a small after-school rush at the shop too.

"So just this today?" He walked to the register and began keying it in.

"Yep. Need something to hold me over until dinner." I handed him three dollars.

He dropped the change into his tip jar when I refused to take the few coins from him. "Thanks. Whatcha making?"

With a shrug, I said, "I'll think of something on the way to the grocery store."

"And I bet it will be delicious. You have a good rest of your day. See you soon."

"Thanks. You too."

As I walked to the store, I texted Ashley to see if she wanted to come over. She wouldn't get back to me until class was out for the day. Then I called Courtney at her office. She squealed in delight as I asked her. It had been way too long since our last girls' night, and she'd always liked hanging out with Steph and Alex. I considered messaging Sarah, but we'd never hung out socially before. Not for a girls' night. Who would want to hang out with their boss on the one day off they had?

When I finally reached my porch a short time later, arms now full of dinner supplies, Saffy picked her head up to glare at me through the window. She waited until I'd made it inside before she nonchalantly jumped off the couch and sauntered toward the kitchen. Then she threw a look over her shoulder as she reached the doorway as if to say, "you better be coming."

There were times when I thought she could talk—actually talk—but so far in the six years I'd had her, she'd not said a thing. She did a fine job communicating without words. There were moments like now when I still wondered if she could talk and simply wasn't going to unless she had to.

I swapped my shoes for my slippers, then followed her to the kitchen, grocery bags in hand. Saffy refused to look at me, but she'd forgive me for her not getting a bonus meal at lunchtime today once she realized what she had coming. I placed the bags on the counter and reached into the one that had her present.

Her head popped up as soon as she heard me crack the lid on the container. She scampered to my feet as I opened the drawer that had her empty stuffed mouse in it. I pulled it out, then loaded up the catnip before sealing the toy and dropping it in front of her. She pounced and flopped over on her side, the mouse still between her feet. She had me pinned against the counter, kicking at the tiny toy with her back paws. After a moment, she flipped it up into the air and batted it, sending it toward the living room. She chased after it, giving me space to put everything that I didn't need for dinner away.

I hoped the girls liked pasta with chicken sausage. Pineapple bacon was a new flavor combination for me, and I had to try it. If it was a winner, I'd have to figure out a way to put it into a baked good. Then again, bacon crossed into the savory territory, which put it on the no-can-bake list without express permission from Zeke, owner of The Corner Bakery, the other bakery in town. He didn't make sweets, which was the only way I had been permitted to open when I first moved to Heartwood Hollow. I had to agree to the terms put forth by the town council that I wouldn't try to compete. Zeke made all sorts of breads, rolls, and pizza doughs. He also sold deli sandwiches and things like Stromboli and calzones that you could take home and heat up. Maybe someday I'd be able to expand into baking savory items but not right now.

After I put the pasta bake into the oven, I went in search of my cat. Saffy was stretched out in some afternoon sunshine in the middle of the floor, her catnip mouse under her head. She was trying to lick it, but her tongue wasn't long enough with the way her head was positioned.

"I also wanted to tell you I'm having some people over."

That seemed to snap her out of her catatonic state. She rolled over onto her stomach and stared at me, head up straight. Her eyes were wide and still a bit buggy, but I had her full attention.

"Don't worry, Ivy's not one of them."

She plopped her head back down onto the mouse, which

set off another round of mad licking. Ivy's enthusiasm toward Saffy was not met in-kind. Saffy much preferred to hide under my bed when Ivy was around to not be subjected to the squealing in delight and the loud thumping of feet. She'd gotten better about it, but her initial reaction was always the same.

"Ivy probably won't be coming around here again anyway," I admitted. Saffy's ears twitched in response. "Ken and I broke up, so you won't have to worry about it."

Saffy stood and clumsily walked over to me, bonking her head into my shin before rubbing up against the side of my leg as if to say she was sorry.

"That's partially why I'm having people over. It's a girls' night, so you're welcome to stay. Ashley is coming. I know how much you like her." Ashley had found Saffy's special spot the last time she was over and had my cat in a purring puddle after a few minutes of petting.

Saffy rubbed her face on my leg again before returning to her mouse.

"She's bringing her roommate, who you haven't met yet, but she's nice." She'd asked when she texted me on a break. "Steph, Courtney, and Alex are also coming."

At the mention of Alex's name, Saffy tilted her head.

"I know, I know. Alex is a guy. He's coming for dinner. He'll leave before the movie starts."

Saffy nodded, or at least it looked like she did, then grabbed her catnip mouse and brought it up to her spot on the back of the couch. She licked it repeatedly, the sound of her rough tongue against the burlap-like fabric mouse audible a few feet away.

That would keep her entertained until everyone showed up, so I went back into the kitchen to prepare the salad. No bagged salad for us. I cut a head of lettuce, shredded a carrot, chopped a red pepper, then cut cherry tomatoes in half so no one would have an errant cherry tomato hop out of their bowl when they tried to stab it. That had happened once at a dinner party back when I was in high school during my town's library fundraiser, and from then on, I always made sure mine were cut. It was funny when it happened, but I remember the night more for the tomato hitting the chandelier and landing in the centerpiece than I do for the speech my mom made to ask for donations. The croutons were from a bag, though. They took longer to make than I had time for tonight. Plus, the pasta bake already occupied the oven, and they didn't cook at the same temperature. With everything ready, well, almost ready, all I had to do was wait.

No, first, I had to make dessert.

What would girls' night be without that?

CHAPTER 22

Steph and Alex arrived first, Steph with a bottle of wine in hand and Alex with some fancy flavored water. He'd never been a drinker. One time I'd asked him about it, genuinely curious about his beverage choice—I was never one for sparkling water—and he'd gone into a whole discussion about the filtration of alcohol from his system and how it affected his sports playing. His being a dryad added on a whole other meaning to that filtration aspect. How did trees do with alcohol? Then again, it never seemed to bother Steph. Steph ducked into the kitchen and headed for the drawer where I kept my bottle openers. She tossed one to Alex and then hooked the rabbit ears over her wine bottle to pop the cork.

"Glasses still in the same place?"

Nodding, I pointed to the cupboard over the sink. "Me too please."

Alex flipped the cap off one of his bottles and placed the rest of the six-pack into the refrigerator. "What's on the menu for tonight?"

I'd just finished telling them when Courtney walked in.

"Seth is going to be so jealous when I tell him you were here, Alex."

"Tell Seth he can come next time. I owed Alex dinner. He's not staying."

"Yeah," Alex began after taking a swig of his water, "I don't need those girly movies to ruin my cred."

Steph and I threw our heads back in laughter. "Your cred?" Steph asked. "I'm pretty sure that disappeared the time you cried while watching—"

"La-la-la-la-la!" Alex shouted to drown out his sister, but I knew exactly where she'd been going with that line of thought. I had been there to witness it. Courtney looked on in amusement.

"Okay, okay," Alex said at a normal volume. "I admit I like them. But I'm not staying because this is girls' night, and I respect that."

Courtney laughed. "Well, Seth's home by himself if you want to keep him company. I'm sure he could use a second player in one of his games."

"Nah, I'll go home and hop on the network to play with him. It's easier. None of that split-screen stuff to deal with."

"He'd probably smell Joanie's cooking on you anyway."

"I'll send you home with a doggie bag, then, since he'll smell it on you too," I offered her.

Courtney laughed again, a loud and infectious sound that set us all off on a giggling fit. "He'd like that," she said once she'd calmed down enough.

Steph grabbed another wine glass from the cupboard, still giggling. "If there's any left, that is."

"Did I hear something about a doggie bag?" Ashley said from the front door. "Rich is going to want one too."

Within the few minutes people had been here, I'd decided I needed to have girls' nights at least biweekly. It was good for the soul. With all the guys in our lives, however, dinner parties would have to be a regular thing too. I'd make it a potluck so I wouldn't have to worry about making everything, though. That could be fun.

The timer on the oven buzzed as Ashley stepped into the kitchen, a bag slung over her shoulder with two bottles of wine poking out. Emily followed with one of her own. Added to the bottle I'd bought, Steph's bottle, and Courtney's, we were well stocked for the evening.

I pulled out the pasta bake to *oohs* and *ahhs*. They were humoring me, but I let them. I placed the glass baking dish on a trivet at the center of the table so everyone could serve themselves, then grabbed the salad bowl and set it next to the pasta. Courtney dug out the salad dressings—I didn't make one of those this time, either, because everyone preferred something different—and Steph topped off everyone's glasses of wine.

We chatted for several minutes about our day, but conversation turned to what had happened in the bakery on Friday. Lily and John were still the talk of the town. When they pressed for more details, I deflected instead, having done no more than confirm I was on the case of another match and that things were looking up.

"It's all so romantic," Ashley said. Recently matched herself, she was enamored by the whole idea and fascinated by what it could entail. She was in love and wanted everyone else to be in love.

"Isn't it?" Courtney agreed.

"I'm glad you all think so," I said, a hint of uncertainty in my voice.

"Who wouldn't be for love?" Ashley asked.

Steph scoffed. "You should ask the hot doc."

"Wait. What? What did my cousin do?" Ashley said, clearly confused why Ken had been brought up.

I had yet to fill her in on the whole story. "He broke up with me last night—"

"He did what!" Ashley's mouth dropped.

"Said I was a busybody or compared me to his mother who was a busybody or something like that. Either way, he told me not to get involved with what was going on between John and Lily, and when I told him I couldn't do that, he said we had to stop seeing one another."

"Joanie, I'm sorry," Ashley said, frowning, her eyebrows drawn down in concern. "You know I haven't known him long, and I can't speak to his mom's behavior at all, but seriously? I thought he understood everything."

"But doesn't he get that's who you are?" Courtney asked.

"I thought he did," I said, answering them both, "but I guess not."

"My cousin is an idiot. He just let go of a fantastic person."

"Why do guys do that?" Emily asked.

"I don't know," Steph replied as she turned to her brother. "Why *do* guys do that?"

"Hey, don't ask me," Alex said through a mouth half-full of pasta. "I haven't had a date in two years." He shoved another forkful in his mouth to discourage any follow-up questions.

If anyone deserved to find a match, it was Alex.

"So that's why we're having girls' night tonight?" Ashley asked.

I nodded.

"Say no more. I know he's my cousin, but ugh."

Despite my attempts to redirect it a few times, the conversation turned to a mini-bash Ken session. He didn't deserve it, though. Ken wasn't a bad guy. What I could do was just too much for him. He'd find someone eventually, as would I, but it would be someone who didn't mind my getting involved in my matches' lives.

As we wrapped up dinner, I pulled the dessert I'd made out from the fridge and wrapped some up in a container to send home with Alex. The rest of us would dig in while we watched the movie. He said his goodbyes to everyone, telling his sister to call him if she needed someone to come get her and walk her home. I offered her my couch, but she waved me off, saying she'd be good after some time outside. Did merging with a tree allow her to shake off however inebriated she was? I'd always wondered how she'd drink more than me when we lived in the same building and bounce back without a problem, whereas I needed a bit more time to recover.

I walked Alex to the door, and he gave me a big hug, nearly lifting me off the ground. "He's stupid for letting you go," he mumbled so the others cleaning up in the kitchen wouldn't hear. "He'll either realize that or it's his loss. I don't know him, so I can't say if he's a good guy or not, but maybe he just needs time to wrap his head around everything. It's an adjustment being with someone who's . . . different."

He opened the door, then stepped outside and bounded down my steps to the walkway before turning around to face me.

"Maybe I'll see you in the morning. Although I'm thinking you're gonna need an extra few minutes to get ready." He gave me a cheeky grin. "I hear aspirin and water help."

I laughed. I'd only had two glasses plus a little more from Steph topping me off once before my cup was empty. "Don't worry. I'm cutting myself off and making some tea, but thank you."

"Have a good night, Joanie."

"You too."

I turned to find Steph in the doorway between the kitchen and living room, a sly grin on her face. "What was that?"

"What was what?"

"Alex hugging you."

I shrugged. "He's always hugged me."

"But what was he whispering?"

"That Ken is stupid."

"You are not allowed to date my brother," Steph said, giggling.

"I'm not going to date your brother." I didn't see Alex that way. He was almost like a brother to me in the way he'd taken me under his wing when I moved to town, the same way Steph had. Alex was a great guy, but he wasn't for me. I hoped I could set him up with someone great soon.

"What did I miss?" Courtney asked as she scooted past Steph and walked toward the couch, her bottle of rosé tucked under her arm, a wine glass in one hand, and a bowl of dessert in her other. Saffy sniffed her head as she sat down. "Oops! Sorry to disturb you."

"Oh, just Steph telling me I couldn't date Alex."

"What?" Ashley shrieked. "You and Alex? That would be cute! We could double date. He and Rich get along great."

This fact didn't surprise me since they both coached at the high school. "I'm not dating Alex. She was joking."

"It would be cute," Courtney agreed.

"Does anyone want tea?" I asked, trying to change the subject before I got flustered by their attention. "I'm going to go make some."

"No thanks," Emily said quietly as I darted past Steph and Ashley.

I grabbed the kettle, then filled it up at the sink before

placing it back on the stove. As I walked to my cupboard where my loose-leaf teas were, I looked back at my friends.

"Tea?" I asked again since only Emily had answered.

Still in the doorway, Steph and Ashley shook their heads. Courtney called out, "I'm good."

Ashley headed into the living room, but Steph walked back over to me as I scooped tea leaves into an infuser. "We're just teasing. I hope you realize that."

I nodded.

"It's just we've never been in this situation with you before. It's about time with how often you've had to help cheer us up over guy things." She placed a hand on my shoulder. "I would be okay with it, though. You and Alex."

"Thanks. I know." It was sweet how much she cared. I was glad to have such good friends.

"Now hurry up and get your tea. We have a movie to watch!" She opened my fridge and grabbed out her other bottle of wine, then darted into the living room. Based on the squealing from two of the others, she'd either hopped on top of them or was trying to wriggle her way between them.

Once the water had boiled, I made my tea, then joined the girls in the other room, settling on a pillow on the floor next to Steph since there was no more room on the couch. Ashley and Courtney had spread out, and Emily had taken the armchair.

Midway through the movie, we paused it to make popcorn, but aside from that, we all watched the rom-com with minor commentary from Steph. There was no more talk of Ken, and the subjects of ghosts, witches, and dryads never came up.

All in all, it was a normal girls' night.

When the movie ended, the four left with promises to make this a more regular occurrence. They also all agreed a potluck dinner sometime would be fun. Courtney offered to make her famous chili, which was one of my favorites.

Although I headed to bed once they'd left, I forced myself to stay awake until they all texted to say they'd made it home. Ashley's message came first since she lived the closest, followed by Steph's, then Courtney's. I remained reading until I hit the end of the chapter, then fell asleep with Saffy between my knees, her catnip mouse beneath her head. She'd carried it upstairs as I got ready for bed. In the morning, it would go back in the drawer until the next special occasion.

Tomorrow was another day, and it would start bright and early.

CHAPTER 23

T he next morning was a bit of a slow one, but it was nothing a little bit of caffeine couldn't fix. Saffy dragged herself out of bed behind me, a rarity as she usually sped to her food bowl. An afternoon with her catnip mouse followed by an evening cuddling with Ashley had apparently worn her out. Or maybe she had wanted a last few minutes with her mouse, which she plopped by my feet on her way to her dish.

She waited by her actually empty food bowl as I switched the burner on for tea, but I fed her before grabbing a Monday muffin that I'd been saving for myself from two days ago. Walter and Paul had told me there was something special about them the last time I'd talked to them at the Old Templeton Diner, and since then, I'd kept them on hand for myself. I wasn't entirely sure, but they might have been on to something. Monday muffins left me with a bit more pep in my step and a cheerier attitude. But maybe it was all just the power of suggestion. Saffy had yet to tell me if she thought it made me any different.

My newspaper was waiting for me at my door when I

finally stepped outside. Alex must have been here early. Or I was moving slower than I thought, though the muffin was kicking in. I tossed the paper onto the bench portion of my coat tree to read later, then closed the door behind me.

I breathed in deeply. The outside air was warm but dry. A gorgeous start to a mid-week day in May. Despite my tiredness from last night's fun, this was one of my favorite times of day. Being one of a few people awake, passing numerous houses still dark with sleep, enjoying the quiet slumber of town before the hubbub.

With three days left until the Love a Tree Day Festival, Heartwood Hollow was seeing its first wave of summer visitors and tourists. We'd need to up our baking quota to accommodate them. Everyone stopped by on vacation for special treats. That plus the fact Suncraft Bakery would be running a booth at the festival, which we still had to prep for, meant we had a busy few days ahead of us in the kitchen.

Feeling fully awake by the time I reached the bakery, I unlocked the door to the kitchen, then stepped inside and flicked on the lights. There was something about the morning after the cleaning crew had been here. The stainless-steel fixtures shined and were smudge free for the next few minutes, the floors were mopped and reflected the light from above, and not an errant speck of flour could be found anywhere. As I stood in the corner by the sinks drinking my tea, waiting for my bakers to come in, I told myself to remember this quiet moment as things got progressively crazier through the festival weekend and the summer as a whole.

Lily walked in right on time, back to her usual routine. A broad smile spanned her face, and her pinkish hair seemed to glow. Then I realized the pink had streaks of pale, almost-white yellow in it, giving it that appearance.

"You look utterly radiant. I take it the date went well?"

Lily spun in a circle, her arms rising slightly away from her side as she did. "It was amazing. Then I spent the night in a tree by the river, and the warm breeze coming off the water was exactly what I needed to clear my head and find my center. It was such a lovely evening followed by a perfect night."

"I'm so happy to hear that. So what did you two do?"

She told me all about how they went to Nick and Etta's, where she had a delicious eggplant parm, before catching a movie at the one-screen theater in town. Then they went for a stroll in the park, which was how Lily had gotten the idea to return there for the evening even after John had walked her all the way home before saying goodnight.

I tried not to let the similarities between Lily's first date with John and my first date with Ken get to me. Nick and Etta's was the perfect first-date location with its homestyle Italian food, and the park was a beautiful backdrop to any date.

She restarted her story as Gina walked in, then again when Sam and Bryan did. Lily's cheerful attitude spread to the rest of the kitchen, the lights brightened, and we all became a lively animated unit as we took to our tasks. Inspired by dinner last night, I had a few new pastries to try, all featuring pineapple cream. After a taste test, where I explained the sausage I'd had, everyone told me I needed to try something with both pineapple and bacon in it. They were all aware of my agreement with the town council, but they convinced me it was worth the risk, especially if we used candied bacon to tilt things toward the sweeter side of savory.

"Roll it out for the tree festival," Sam urged. "Zeke's going to be so busy with sandwiches that he's not going to care if there's bacon in some of the scones." He had a point. Zeke only brought pre-made sandwiches to the festival.

I'd probably have the biggest food variety there aside from the food trucks that came with their full menus. Double Aitch only brought soups. Donna didn't set up a stand at all for Old Templeton Diner, preferring to enjoy the festival as an attendee instead. I brought everything I could, knowing I could do business the entire time we were there. It didn't mean we wouldn't enjoy ourselves, though. We all rotated shifts throughout the day.

Soon it was time for me to make my delivery run to the two diners. Donna kept me over as she usually did at least once a week, figuring that today would be the last day I'd have any time to spare with the upcoming festivities. After getting such a glowing report on Lily's date, it was good to tell Donna that things might finally be settling down. She almost seemed disappointed that there wasn't something juicier to tell. Things being fine didn't make for good gossip, so I avoided talking about the one thing that wasn't. My breakup. She didn't question me about it either, so she definitely hadn't heard Ken and I had broken up or else she would have. By the time I left, however, she probably suspected something based on my deflections.

Once I returned to the bakery, I jumped right back into the fray. Libby had wanted special scone flavors, which meant more to do because, in order to be special, they couldn't be repeated here in the shop. At least not until after she reported how she, Billy, and her guests liked them. It wasn't anything we couldn't handle, though, and by the time I was ready to make my delivery to Riverview Inn, the team had mostly finished up what we needed to get done. Lily had already switched to working on fondant decorations for the cupcakes

I'd be bringing with me to the festival. Thank goodness those could be made in advance.

Libby waved to me from the porch of Riverview Inn as I pedaled up on my bike, two boxes full of cookies and scones in the trailer behind me.

"Morning, Joanie."

"Hi, Libby," I said as I hopped off my bike. I grabbed the two boxes and made my way to the side kitchen entrance. I placed the boxes side by side on the table and began unpacking the first one.

Libby joined me and opened the second box. "Busy today? I'm sure things are gearing up for the festival. We're booked solid through Monday."

"That's great. Will you have time to sneak away and enjoy the tree fest at all?"

"Oh sure. Billy will run things down here. I decided to set up a table for the first time so I can have some teas available to advertise my tea services to not just the tourists but to the townspeople too. They forget that it's open to everyone, not just those who have booked a room."

"I'll be sure to stop by and say hello."

"And have something to drink, I hope. Maybe that will convince you to come to a tea again. It's been too long. Like I said, bring that man of yours."

Unable to help myself, I sighed.

"Uh oh."

"Yeah. He's not my man anymore." I explained the whole non-date with Ken to her. Unlike with Donna, or even Sarah, I didn't worry about her telling anyone.

"Well, shame on him for not seeing how great you are."

She turned the tiered tray around to continue loading cookies onto it. I had already begun arranging scones on the other display. I had a feeling Libby would tweak things after I left, but loading it up at least gave her a start.

"So did that story help you any?" she asked, referring to the wood used to build Heartwood Hollow's oldest buildings having been alive.

"You know? It actually might have."

"Really? Don't tell me you believe in trees that walk around."

"No, nothing like that." I'd already learned the trees themselves didn't move—it was the dryads who merged with them—but I didn't need to tell her that. "But I have to ask you, did your grandparents ever tell you other stories about weird things going on in Heartwood Hollow's early days?"

She thought for a moment, her lips drawn to the side. "There were a couple about the trees. My grandparents also said we used to have a wolf problem. I don't know about you, but I've never seen a wolf in these parts. A coyote or several, sure, but never a wolf. But my grandfather swore he and his brother shot one."

There was always the possibility that early hunters had driven wolves from the area. I'd always thought the region was more known for its beavers, though. Moose too. Still, there was nothing necessarily paranormal about that.

"Then my grandma swore there were things living in the river. 'Yeah, fish,' I used to tell her. But no, she'd tell me, people. But you don't see mermaids in rivers. Astoria claims to have a lake monster." Libby shook her head. "They were talented storytellers, but that's just what they were. Stories. Why the interest?"

"Well, after you told me about the dryads, I got to

wondering what other types of creatures we had up here according to the stories."

"Dryads?"

"That's apparently what they call people who live in trees."

"Oh . . ." She nodded slowly, eyeing me skeptically as if she thought I was taking this a bit too seriously.

"Anyway, I loved hearing about all those sorts of stories from where I grew up when I was a kid. I'm going to have to have to see if the library has any books like that for here."

"Bet you a lot of it will be about these dryads with Heartwood Hollow's logging history. I know you're not from here, but you know that's how this town started, right? The inn used to be the town founder's home. He built the first mill here and started the logging operation." She paused. "Oh, who am I kidding? Of course you know all that. With the amount you read and try to find out about people, you've obviously come across all of that information before. Especially when you were looking into John Singer. His family got the mill straight from the Dunmore family. Should have just left it alone if you ask me. Nothing good came about that mill once they got ahold of it. Would have been better to close it after the Dunmores and let everyone go than make promises they couldn't deliver on and abruptly close after one failure too many."

I'd never heard Libby talk this way before. It sounded a lot like what John had been talking about with people still looking at him like he was guilty for what his family had done with the mill.

"Was your family involved with the mill?

"Sure was. How else would my grandfather have claimed the wood was alive? Billy's family too. Nearly broke both our parents when the mill closed. Thank goodness

Mama had gotten a job as a teacher once we got a little older. She carried the family until my dad got a job at the hospital as a janitor. Billy's dad wasn't as bad off since he drove trucks and hopped straight to another company as a driver."

"It's good both of your families came out okay."

She nodded in broad motions as she spoke. "Not everyone was as lucky, mind you. Took a long time for some of us to come out of the holes that got dug by the Singers' empty promises."

"I'm glad we have other places like the hospital that can always use the help."

"Me too. The hospital was a saving grace at the time. Then the town developed the tourism board, creating new opportunities for people. Glad I can do my part now too."

I glanced around the kitchen. "You really have something special here. This is what, your fifteenth year in business?"

"Sure is." Libby placed the last of her cookies on her second display stand, then clapped. "Well, that should just about do it. Thank you so much for bringing these and adding in those few extra flavors I asked for. I hate to be a bother."

"You're no bother, Libby. Let me know how you like them. Oh, and these here"—I pointed to the few pastry cream puffs I'd brought—"are pineapple."

"Don't tell Billy. They'll never make it to the table if he finds out. He loves pineapple on everything. Even pizza." She made a face.

A laugh escaped me before I could clamp my mouth shut. "My lips are sealed," I promised, running my thumb and finger pressed together across my lips. I sided with Billy on the pineapple on pizza debate, but I wouldn't tell Libby that.

She picked a cream puff off the tray and set it aside, then rearranged the tier a little to make it look like she hadn't taken anything. "However, I'll never hear the end of it if he finds out I didn't save him one. So he can have that later."

"I'll remember how much he likes them next time. I'll make him one special."

"He'd love that." She made a shooing motion. "Okay, now get. You have a lot to do before the festival starts on Saturday. I'm not even going to ask you to stay today. I already know you can't."

"It was great talking with you," I called over my shoulder as she rushed me out the door. "I'll see you Friday."

"Same thing for next time unless I call saying otherwise. I trust your baking, but I want to make sure they're well received before I commit."

I turned to close the door. "Sounds good."

The door opened back up behind me as I walked down the driveway toward my bike. I spun on my heels to face Libby.

"But seriously, Joanie, shame on him. You're such a nice girl. After all the people you've gotten together in town, you deserve someone of your own."

"Thanks again," I said with a wave, then walked my bike in a semi-circle to turn it around before hopping on.

I couldn't think about me and my relationship, or lack thereof, right now. There was a festival to prepare for and a match to make sure would stick. Lily and John's first date had been a success, but until I knew for sure the ghosts were gone, I'd be keeping an eye out for them.

CHAPTER 24

After a quick bite of leftovers from last night's dinner party, I scooted into the shop to join Sarah for the rest of the afternoon while Lily and Gina worked on decorations in the back. Bryan was at my house cleaning the bakery's vendor cart and making sure it was good to go for the festival. We'd put him in charge of the cart two years ago when we realized he could pull the thing out of my garage on his own. Although Wednesday was normally our slowest day, the increase in customers was noticeable, no doubt already thanks to the tree fest.

During the usual after-school rush, the last person I'd expected to see walked into the bakery.

"Joanie!" Ivy squealed as she ran over to the end of the counter.

I walked over to her, and she gave me a great big hug, throwing her arms around me.

"How are you doing? How was school?"

"I had a test today."

"You did! And you must have done well if you're coming

in for . . . let me guess"—I rubbed my chin—"a cookie. No, you want a palmier today. Cinnamon and sugar sound good?"

She bounced up and down.

"That okay, Ken?" Mustering up the courage, I glanced up at him as I walked to the pastry case.

"Can't be any worse sugar-wise than one of your huge cookies. Go for it."

He might rethink that statement after she had the palmier. I grabbed a piece of tissue paper, then reached in for the biggest one I could find. Before handing it to Ivy, I slipped it into a pastry bag. I'd learned not to give her baked goods directly if I didn't want crumbs everywhere. This was true no matter where we were, although it was only a worry here now. I didn't anticipate any more baking sessions together at either of our houses.

"Ivy, why don't you run and go eat this in the park next door? Daddy wants to talk to Joanie for a minute."

Sarah picked her head up at that statement and widened her eyes at me. I hadn't told her about the breakup, and she hadn't asked. I shrugged at her and mouthed "later."

"Okay, Daddy! Bye, Sarah. Bye, Joanie!" Ivy scampered out of the bakery and turned toward Founder's Park.

"Hey," Sarah began. "I'm going to head into the back and start packing up the decorations the girls have been working on." She ducked into the kitchen faster than I could respond to say it sounded like a good idea.

When the door between the shop and the kitchen had closed, Ken gave me a small smile, one that lacked genuine happiness. "How are you?"

"I'm fine. You didn't need to come check up on me if that's what you're doing. I'm a big girl and can handle a breakup."

"Actually, I wanted to come by and apologize again for the

other night. I hadn't gone into it with the idea that what happened would, well, happen. It's just, my mom and I didn't really get along as I got older. She was always butting in and trying to insert her opinion into everything I or people around me did. Questioning their every move. Even the neighbors. 'Oh, why's so and so trimming the bushes like that? They're going to be all bare on that one side now,'" he said in a nasally feminine voice meant to imitate his mom. "I loved her, and she loved Ivy, but I dreaded bringing her to visit because Mom was always on my case about something. Usually Kelly."

I wanted to interrupt, to say that wasn't like me at all since he had compared me to her during our date, but decided against it. He needed to get this off his chest.

He laughed sardonically. "Thing is, Mom was right all along about Kelly. I should have done a bit more listening to my mom than getting defensive about whatever it was she was saying. Might have saved a bit of heartache in the process for Ivy and me both."

He seemed done, so I said, "I'm sorry you regularly had to deal with that. That's not an easy personality to get along with. Especially when you have to live with them." Many of the gossipers who came into the bakery sounded just like that, but as soon as they walked out the door, I didn't have to think about them again. And I certainly didn't have to go home to them. Saffy must have had her opinions on things, particularly the neighbors with as much staring out the window as she did, but she mostly kept them to herself when they didn't involve her stomach.

"Anyway," Ken said, sticking his hands in his pants pockets, "I shouldn't have taken it out on you like that."

"You know I'm not like your mom, right? I don't nitpick over the neighbors' bushes, and I don't needle people to be any different than they are. I'm not trying to change people. I'm just trying to help them be with who their meant to be with. Lily and John are a perfect match. I have no doubt about it, and they had a marvelous date last night. Now I'll admit sometimes matches need a bit of gentle coaxing if they get off to a bumpy start, like it did with these two, but I don't force anything. If it felt forced, it wouldn't be meant to be."

Ken nodded slowly. "I don't know if I'm meant to be with anyone. You don't happen to see a match out there for me, do you?" He looked up at me then, his lips pursed to the side.

I drew my bottom lip over the top slightly as I shook my head. "It doesn't work on command, and it's not like that either. There's no invisible string connecting you to someone else."

His shoulders sagged. "If someone is out there for me."

I understood the feeling, but I wasn't going to tell him that. It felt too much like rubbing salt in the wound after the breakup, which he was remorseful for but not taking back. He wasn't ready yet, and I didn't know if he ever would be. Maybe I'd have to invite my mom and have her walk around town with me to see if she'd pick up on anything between me and someone else. Then again, if she didn't feel a match, did that mean I was destined to be alone? How ironic was that? A matchmaker who was single all her life. At least Mom had my dad for a while before I was born. Okay, she wasn't the greatest example either. Were we all doomed to be alone?

"Anyway, I best be going. Don't need Ivy to get lost chasing after a squirrel or anything like that. I'll see you around."

"Have a good afternoon, Ken."

He left the shop so quietly Sarah didn't notice or immediately rush back into the shop demanding answers about what had happened between the two of us. It took her five minutes before she reentered the shop.

"Okay, spill," she ordered.

And I did. I told her everything. Well, everything that didn't involve ghosts, dryads, or being a witch, but enough for her to get the gist of what happened. She, like everyone else so far, told me it was his loss.

I wanted to agree. But after seeing Ken again, it felt like my loss too.

With an hour to go until the end of the day, I sent Sarah home since it was my Wednesday to clean and close solo. She took off after giving me another pep talk about Ken. The cleaning would hopefully drown out my thoughts about him. I quickly checked in on Lily and Gina as I grabbed the broom and dustpan from the kitchen closet. They had just a few more things to wrap up before heading out but had made great headway on decorations.

When I stepped back into the shop, the front door opened. I smiled and set the broom against the counter. "Hi, John. What can I do for you today?"

"Hey, is Lily here? I already tried her house, and she wasn't there." That was odd to me. Since the first day he'd entered the bakery, John's knife had been like a homing pigeon focused on its nest—in this case, Lily. But maybe now they were together, the knife was just a knife again. Nothing possessed about it. I took it as a good sign.

"Yeah, she's in back. Let me pop in and grab her."

"Thanks." He stood swaying front to back, from his heels to the balls of his feet. He patted his jeans pockets repeatedly. Was he nervous? I wasn't getting any weird vibes from him like I had the last two times he'd come in here, but something was going on.

I poked my head into the kitchen. "Lily, you have a gentleman caller in the shop who would like to say hi."

Her face brightened, and the lights did too. She wiped her hands on her apron.

I held the door for her as she stepped into the shop.

"John, this is a pleasant surprise."

"Hey, Lily." His unease lessened momentarily but not enough.

Lily tilted her head to the side. She could sense something was going on too. "Is everything okay?"

He shook his head. "The knife is gone."

CHAPTER 25

L ily's eyes widened. "Gone? What do you mean *gone*?" Overhead, the lights flickered, no doubt reacting to the sudden shift of her attitude.

"I can't find the knife anywhere." John's hands were at his sides, empty palms facing out. "I tore my whole house up looking for it. You didn't take it, did you?"

"No, of course not. Like I said, I don't even want to see it, let alone handle it."

He sighed. "Okay. I didn't think you would have, based on your reaction to it the other day, but I had to ask. It was the only other thing I could think of."

"Where could it have gone?"

"I swear I put it away before our date just like you asked, but when I got home, it wasn't there. Then I started doubting myself over having left it. I carry it with me everywhere, so it may have been something I grabbed without even thinking. But it wasn't in my pockets either. Or in the jeans I wore yesterday before the date."

"Well, where do you think you put it?" I asked, wondering if the ghosts could have done something to it.

"Right behind my wallet on the dresser where I always put it at night."

"Could it have fallen behind your dresser and gotten stuck?" Lily suggested.

He shook his head. "I pulled it away from the wall and everything."

"I'm really sorry to hear about that," Lily said, sadness clear in her voice. "I don't like the thing, someone had to cut down my grandmother in order to make it, but it meant a lot to you. I'd never want something bad to happen to it." She reached out and touched his upper arm.

"Man, I don't want to be responsible for losing part of your grandmother."

I was still having a hard time wrapping my head around the fact that a piece of wood could be part of someone's grandma. Fortunately, the gravity of the mood in the room helped tamp down my reaction to what would have been a funny statement if I had heard it out of context.

John turned to me. "What are your thoughts on this? You said that the knife had been leading me to Lily. That maybe my grandfather had been possessing it. Could he have done something?"

"Or my grandmother?" Lily added.

"Truth is, I don't know who might be inhabiting the knife. It could be either one of them or both. Maybe they took the knife because it finally brought you two together. I can't be sure."

John reached for Lily's hand and took it in his. "If that's the case, I'm grateful that it did what it was supposed to do, but I've had that knife for years. I don't want it to be gone for good. It's almost like it's a part of me now for as long as I've carried it around in my pocket. It's worn the material down in some of my pants."

"I can try to contact Dale or Juniper." Though I was unsure if it would work, as John stood there worrying with Lily beside him, I couldn't not offer to do something.

John sighed with relief. "Thank you. Can I help you at all?"

"Can *we* help you at all?" Lily corrected.

I shook my head. "Lily, you have done more than enough today. You've been here as long as I have. Go on home. Or how about you two go on a date since you're already together."

Lily blushed as she glanced up at John. "I like the sound of that."

John smiled warmly at her and squeezed her hand. "Me too. I know just the place."

I clapped my hands. "Great! Well, while you two have fun tonight, I'll see what I can do about finding that knife. It couldn't have gotten far," I said with more certainty than I felt. The hairbrush Kate had inhabited could go upstairs in my house and float across my living room. Had it got outside, I believed it would have made it back to Ashley's house. In reality, the knife could have gone anywhere.

"Okay, well, let me just clean up, and I'll be ready to go," Lily said. She dropped John's hand and then hurried into the kitchen. She was back moments later, hair neatly pulled up without a speck of flour or fondant on her. I admired her ability to freshen up so quickly. Seemed no matter what I did, I was always covered in something. Hopefully tonight I wouldn't end up doused with flour like the last time I'd tried to summon a ghost by myself.

"See you tomorrow," I called to the two of them as they left the shop. Then I grabbed the broom and rushed through the sweeping, doubly grateful there'd been no cookie crumb mishaps today in the store. Next came cleaning the exteriors of the glass cases. The nose prints were my favorite. Left behind by kids eager to have a treat, they reminded me of how the lower half of the picture window in the living room had Saffy's nose prints all over it.

Right at five o'clock, I switched the sign on the door from *open* to *closed*. Thoughts of where the knife could have disappeared to swirled through my head. I hoped either of the ghosts would have an answer for me. I could probably reach out to Chrys if I had to. She'd been the only one with enough energy to speak to me aside from Dale's calling my name the one time. She seemed fully capable of moving a knife around. But why would she have gone to John's home to do that? No. It was much more likely Dale's or Juniper's doing.

In a way, I was grateful for the missing knife. It gave me something to focus on other than Ken's appearance in the shop today. He'd seemed almost remorseful when he arrived. More so than just for making me feel bad. Was he regretting what had happened? Did he want to get back together? Did I want that? I wasn't ready to think about it. My love life, which seemed to be in stasis once again, could wait.

John and Lily's love life, however, was just starting out, and I didn't want this lost knife to come between them. Not when it was what had brought them together.

I locked up the bakery, and instead of going home after making my bank deposit like I did every Wednesday, I walked to the library. It would be closing soon, but I hoped I'd have enough time to continue my dryad research.

Emily smiled and waved as I walked in. "Not your usual time to be coming in here. Do you need the next book in that series you're reading? It's a good one."

She knew me well, and I thought of my latest read moved to the bench of my coat tree, pushed aside for the book Pete had recommended and then again with girls' night. "Not this time. I can't believe I'm asking this, but where is your local history section?"

Emily hopped off her chair. "Curious choice for you but follow me." She led me around a corner and down a short hallway. "We keep it a bit out of the way so not just anyone can stumble upon it. Sort of a you have to know where to go type of thing. A lot of the books are older and more delicate than what we keep out in circulation, so we have them a bit more under wraps.

"Do I need to wear gloves or anything?"

"Oh goddess, no."

I didn't miss the phrase I'd commonly heard Gram and Mom utter. Was Emily a witch too? Or was she saying it in jest because of my researching Wicca and witchcraft a few weeks ago? She never had seemed the joking type before, but I didn't want to ask her to clarify. That would be weird. Maybe now that she'd come to girls' night, she felt more comfortable around me.

"Just make sure your hands are clean and dry. It's actually worse to hold old paper with gloves because you lose some of the dexterity in your fingers, so ripping the paper becomes a bigger problem."

She turned as she reached an open doorway and then threw her hand to the side toward the room in a displaying motion. "That's probably more than you wanted to know."

I laughed. "Perhaps it will come in handy at trivia night sometime." The pub in town sponsored weekly trivia nights during the winter to occupy the townspeople when tourist season was over.

"Oh, don't get me started. We just finished winter. I don't want to start thinking about it again already. I'll leave you to it, but you only have about a half hour before I need to lock up."

"Not a problem."

She left, her footsteps growing quieter as she walked down the hallway. I wandered around the large wooden table at the center of the room. Had it once been alive? Was there a way to tell? Part of me expected to see faces in the wood grain, but there were none there.

Books filled the room from waist high to ceiling on all four walls, the only breaks in the shelving for the two windows on one wall and the door I'd come through on another. I scanned the titles, hoping something would jump out at me. As much as I liked to read, research wasn't my forte unless it was in an old recipe book. Nothing stuck out amidst the books, some made for the bicentennial, others for the centennial, and even more labeled as early accounts of Dunmore Falls. I reached for one, then perused the first few pages. Dunmore Falls had been the town's name before it became Heartwood Hollow. Until now, I'd only known Dunmore Falls to be the waterfall that had once powered the water wheel at the lumber mill. I hadn't even realized it was natural, always thought it was created through damming the river.

The area closest to the mill had been populated by a tent village. Aside from the mill, the first three permanent buildings were constructed on what became Founder Street using wood from the trees they cut down as well as some fieldstones that were numerous here. From the old photo in the book, I could tell one building was the pub next to Leafs and Grounds, another the art studio on the other side of that, and a third that was no longer standing but had been next to the studio.

I would bet these were the buildings Libby's grandfather had told her were alive. As the oldest buildings in town, it made sense.

As more buildings were built, and more land forested, the lumbermen's wives moved to the area. I scanned the list of early villagers' names on another page, recognizing those of Donna Templeton's family as well as the Barretts—who later built the hospital—and the Singers. I hadn't realized they were original, thinking them newer and opportunistic to the Dunmores ending their stake in the lumber business.

There was nothing on the idea of trees coming to life or people living in the trees. Had the dryads always lived in the north woods, undisturbed until the Singers began logging there, or did they move in like the rest of Heartwood Hollow's residents once the village was in operation?

"Hey Joanie," Emily said, startling me. "It's time to go. Did you find anything?"

I stood and gathered the books I'd been perusing. "Maybe, but I'm thinking I'll need to come back tomorrow."

"We're open later on Thursdays, so that should work out better for you." Noticing me with the books, she added, "Leave them on the cart in the corner. We'll shelve them in the morning."

"Great, thanks." I did as she said, then followed her out of the room and back down the hallway. The lights throughout the building were already off, the computers powered down. "Thanks for giving me as much time as possible."

"Of course. What are friends for?" We left the library together, and Emily locked up behind us. "Thanks for letting me crash girls' night yesterday."

"Anytime. What are friends for?" I chuckled at my repeating her question.

"That pasta bake you made was fantastic. I was tempted to steal Rich's doggie bag for my lunch today." She laughed. "But I wouldn't have done that to him even though he's stealing my roommate soon. He's a good guy."

"They're going to move in together?"

"As soon as his lease is up in the place he's sharing with Tim. He doesn't want to leave him in the lurch after all the time they've lived together, and we're not doing some roommate swap with me trading places with him. I found our house, and I'm staying in it. Looks like I'll be the only original left. At least Rachael is still across the street."

"She seems to be doing well," I said of the friendly business window bank teller. She'd had horrible morning sickness a few weeks back and could only eat the ginger scones, whoopie pies, and cookies that I'd been making for her.

"Much better. She's showing now."

I smiled. "Aww, how wonderful."

"It really is. She's wanted kids for years and is going to be such a great mom. And Mark a great dad too. You find me one like him, okay?"

"I'll put my best people on it."

We chatted a few minutes while our path home was the same, and then she turned down her street, walking backward a few paces so she could wave goodnight. I continued to my house, hoping I could summon either Dale or Juniper to my kitchen table by myself.

Saffy popped up from her spot on the couch as soon as she heard the key in the door but barely glanced out the window at me. Once again, I'd get no greeting from her at the arm of the couch. Her thump to the floor was audible from where I stood. By the time I got the door open, she was nowhere to be seen.

"Sorry I'm late, Saffy," I called as I kicked off my shoes and got into my slipper. "I stopped at the library to get some information, but I'm not sure how useful it was."

Unsurprisingly, she was at her bowl when I stepped into the kitchen. She took a step back as I reached into the cupboard where I kept her crunchy food so I could pour some for her. She'd get wet food after. If she got it before, she'd never eat anything else.

"I'll have to go back again tomorrow. At least I know what dryads are now." I said as I put the bag of food away.

Rather than dive headfirst into her bowl, she turned her head toward me. If she could have lifted an eyebrow, she would have at that moment.

"Remember me asking you yesterday?"

She shook her head and started eating.

I laughed at her perfect timing. "Well, they're tree people."

As I reheated the last of the pasta bake from the night before, I gathered what I needed for the summoning. Silver candlesticks from my cupboard, then a black candle and a white candle from my drawer. After using them multiple times in the last few weeks, I'd have to buy new ones for the bakery's holiday decorations. Then I grabbed the stick of blue sage that had finally arrived from its box hidden in the storage bench of the coat tree.

Once I had everything set up, I lit the candles. Immediately, the energy in the room shifted. Saffy, who had been cleaning her face after finishing her dinner, took off. In recent weeks, she'd encountered several ghosts, some multiple times. She was still getting used to their presence in the house —as was I—and I never knew how she'd react to spiritual energy. She chased one and batted at its anchor only to become friends with the ghost, participated in a summoning where she saw two, ignored one, and had been surprised by the next.

"Dale? Are you there?"

After a few minutes, there was still no response.

"Juniper? What about you? Can you come forth and speak with me?

Nothing.

"Chrysanthemum, I ask for you to show yourself and help me once again."

I waited and, again, nothing.

I glanced to my left and right. The candle flames stood at attention, barely flickering. Drats. Despite the earlier energy shift, there was nothing here. Saffy's reappearance confirmed that for me. She'd jumped onto the chair across the table from me.

"Maybe I'm not strong enough on my own yet," I said with a sigh. I thought about calling the ghosts forth again with Saffy sitting here, but unless she leaned against me like last time, I wouldn't. Using her energy wouldn't be fair to her. It wasn't like she could tell me it was fine. "Maybe I need the knife like I needed the hairbrush. Or maybe the ghosts are just gone because the problem's resolved, meaning they're not around to summon. I wish I knew."

As I blew out the candles, Saffy climbed down from the chair and headed back into the living room, leaving me alone with my thoughts while I continued to clean up. I still had questions, but I didn't think there was anything else I could do alone to find out the answers.

I had to recruit help.

Luckily I knew just who to ask.

CHAPTER 26

L ily came into the kitchen the next day conflicted. She'd had a great date, but the loss of the knife still weighed on her.

"I'm doing everything I can to find it. The ghosts weren't cooperative last night, but I'll be back at it once we close up for the evening. Please don't worry. It will turn up." I refocused her attention back to her date. "Now, tell me what you did last night."

John and Lily had driven a half hour away to Snowhaven where John had a few contacts for wood he used to make furniture.

"And we drove to this place that was kind of like an antique store, but nearly everything was busted. They take everything, though, all kinds of architectural features. Mantels, windows, even huge things like barn doors. John's only used reclaimed or naturally felled wood since he founded his company, did you know that?"

John had said something similar to everyone standing around watching the encounter between him and Lily after she chased him. I didn't want to remind her of that, though. "I thought I'd heard something about that. It's wonderful."

"It's *amazing*. And do you know how much harder that makes his job? Trying to find enough matching pieces to put together all of that furniture?"

"I can't say that I'd ever thought about it before. It's impressive." No wonder the furniture cost so much. I appreciated handcraftsmanship like the next person, but this added a whole other layer of understanding to the mix. I'd have to reconsider that expensive reading chair after all.

A smile crept across my face with the thought of how well things were going. "When's your next date?"

"Tonight. We picked out a huge old door and a fireplace mantel, and we're going to work on something together. Either a nightstand or side table. Maybe a small kitchen table depending on how much useable wood we have once we take the existing pieces apart."

As Lily beamed, the lights above her brightened too.

"That sounds wonderful!" If anyone had doubted they belonged together, I hoped hearing about this date and their project would change their mind. It was a perfect activity for the two of them and would hopefully bring them even closer together. I momentarily wondered if Lily's days in the bakery were numbered. If they continued down this path, would they end up in business together? The dryad furniture maker and the descendant of lumberjacks. Who would have guessed?

"Not my thing," Gina said with a shrug, "but do whatever makes you happy."

Lily turned to Gina. "What's your ideal date, G?" And just like that, the conversation shifted, and all thoughts of the missing knife were forgotten for the time being. It was better that way because nothing could be done right now. We had no clues, and for all we knew, this had been part of the greater plan all along.

"Joanie, would you mind if I stayed a little late to make John something special for my date?" Lily asked.

"Not at all, what are you thinking?"

"Not sure yet, but we rarely keep sweets in the house, including ingredients. Holly says she'd eat it all. So I have nothing to make anything with, and she'd kill me if I brought stuff home to make anything because then I'd be able to make more."

Bryan laughed. "It would serve her right for living with a baker." Everyone agreed.

Chuckling along with him, I said, "No worries, I totally understand. I get enough of it here so don't keep anything in the house either. If you need any help coming up with something, let me know."

Lily ended up making a batch of cupcakes to test the arrangement of the various decorations she'd been making for the festival. The pine trees stood proudly in the pale mint-green icing with tiny yellow flowers surrounding the trunks. On other cupcakes, larger yellow flowers bloomed from chocolate icing.

Overall, the day ran smoothly and without interruption. However, that left me with plenty of time to think about that knife and where it could have gone. As soon as I'd flipped the sign on the door to *closed*, I called Steph.

"Hey, Steph . . ."

"I can hear the hesitation in your voice that tells me you're going to be adding another girls' night to what you already owe me," she teased. "What's up?"

I filled her in on the knife, everything I had meant to tell her the other day but had gotten sidetracked when she revealed that she, too, was a dryad. How the knife's handle was made from sacred wood, and how either Dale or Juniper was at least partially anchored to it, and how it had seemingly disappeared on its own.

"Have you ever heard of something like that happening?" I asked her as I walked toward the library. If I found nothing there this time, I'd ask Rich for help. As the high school history teacher, he loved research and had known exactly where to go for information during the mystery surrounding his grandfather. I bet this would be right up his alley.

"I can't say that I have, although it isn't unheard of for sacred wood to retain some imprint of the dryad who had once resided in it." She grew quiet, enough so I thought the call had dropped out, before adding, "especially if it had been cut down while they were still in it."

"That's what happened in the north woods, wasn't it? That's why they thought the villagers had left?"

"Yeah," she said somberly. "There's no real walking away from that. And trees take a while to fully turn brown and dry once they're felled, so it isn't fast. At least that's what we've been told. It's even longer for some coniferous trees."

"Those are the ones that don't lose their leaves, right? Like pine trees?"

"Yeah. The sap makes the greenery stay alive a lot longer than say a maple or oak that turns brown long before a pine does. I can't even imagine."

The thought sent a shiver up my spine. "I was just reading up on that yesterday actually. I'd never really known much about the process."

"Where you heading now?"

"Back to the library. I'm trying to track down if there were any early accounts of tree people from Heartwood Hollow's earliest years."

"You know that's how the town got its name, right?"

"It started out as Dunmore Falls, but how did its name change?"

"It's because of the dryads. Heartwood is another name for the sacred wood of the trees we merge with. But it's veiled enough for humans to not pick up on it. Pretty sure you'll read the name change has something to do with wood and lumber being the heart of our community, and since we ended up settling in the hollow of a vast forest, it only made sense to change the name as families settled in the town away from the falls, thus changing the dynamic and character of the once-logging settlement."

I laughed. "You memorize that from somewhere?"

"It was drilled into my head." She paused. "Oh, that's a terrible pun. Anyway, the festival used to include a lot more about the town's history. Now it's all about the fun and food. When I was still in school, it used to have a more reverential side to it. There had been a long poem to go with it and those reenactments things too."

"A pageant?"

"Yeah, those. Although having been in them, I'm not sad those disappeared while I was away at college."

I stepped inside the library entrance but didn't go farther into the lobby. "Okay, I'm going to have to let you go."

"Call me when you're done in there. I have an idea, but I want to run it by Alex first to see what he thinks."

That piqued my curiosity. Consulting her twin meant serious business. "Will do."

"Talk to you later."

She hung up, so I clicked my phone off and dropped it

into my purse before pushing through the final set of entry doors.

Emily greeted me with a smile. "Back to what you were doing yesterday?"

"Yep. At least for a little while."

"You know where to go. Just leave whatever books on the cart when you're done."

I hiked my bag back up onto my shoulder and headed for the local history room.

There I scanned the shelves, looking for a few more books, then settled into the same chair as before and flipped open the first book. I found nothing pertaining to dryads in the first book but did find more pictures of the earlier days of the tree festival. They used to include tree plantings and everything. It was a good idea. Why had they stopped? Recently our town improvement efforts had focused more on cleaning up the park and picking up trash along the river. Couldn't they do both?

The next book I grabbed was *Haunted Heartwood Hollow*. Maybe I'd find what I needed in there. After all, some stories were based in fact. The creepy stories of the north woods had led to me finding out about the dryads. I flipped to the table of contents. A few stories stuck out at me. "The Tree Monster of Dunmore Falls" was one of them. I turned to the first page and scanned the tale. The story recounted how in the early days of the logging industry here in town, the entire production line had to get shut down twice due to damaged equipment. The second time almost shuttered the business, but an unexpected blizzard kept the men from leaving. When they were next able to venture to the lumber site, the largest gnarly oak on the site had toppled over. In the bark, they swore they saw a face. The men believed this tree monster had deliberately tried to sabotage the lumber company and, with it gone, they were safe to try again.

They didn't experience another problem with the equipment, and the following spring, the men called for their wives and children to come to the new settlement.

If this story were rooted in truth—I chuckled at my pun—then it would seem dryads had been here even longer than anyone in the village knew. So when did they begin to settle within the town's boundaries and live as villagers? Did they avoid working in the lumber mill so waited until other industries had blossomed? Or were they like Lily, who embraced working with wood so long as it wasn't sacred?

Two other two stories involved wolves and river people. Maybe Libby's grandparents were on to something in the stories they'd told her as a child.

I closed the book, noticing the author's name. Olivia Barker. Wasn't Libby short for Olivia? How weird would it be if the author of the book was Libby's grandmother? Perhaps her grandparents had been telling ghost stories to their grandchildren to see how they'd be received before writing them in the book.

I glanced at the time. It was getting late, and I wanted to give Saffy her dinner at a reasonable time. Plus, I still had to call Steph back and find out what her idea was.

Someday, I'd have to come back to read more of *Haunted Heartwood Hollow*, but for now, I closed the book and picked up my things. Setting the books I'd removed onto the cart as I walked by, I left the local history room and headed back down the hall toward the lobby.

Emily came around the corner from the reference section, pushing another cart. "Find everything you needed?"

"I think so, thanks. And if nothing else, I learned a few things."

"Wonderful! Time is never wasted as long as you're learning."

"It was good to see you again. Say hi to Ashley for me."

"I will. Have a good one, Joanie."

"You too." I exited the library with a wave, then fished out my phone.

Steph picked up at the second ring. "You home yet?"

"Be there soon."

"Okay. Well, feed Saffy, grab a snack, and be ready to go in a half hour."

"Where are we going?"

"If I tell you, I'm afraid you'll chicken out."

"I see ghosts, remember?" I whispered into the phone so no one could hear me from inside their houses. With the nice weather we'd been having since the humidity broke, everyone had their windows open. "There's little that can scare me."

"Nope, not gonna tell you. Let me have my fun. You'll see when we get there."

"All right. See you in thirty." I clicked the phone off and picked up my pace. If I was going to have a snack, I needed to hurry.

CHAPTER 27

S affy jumped down from the couch as soon as she saw me turn down the walkway to the house. I was home earlier tonight than last, but it was still late for her.

"I know, I know," I called out to her as I put down my bag and changed into slippers. "Again."

She was staring at her empty bowl when I entered the kitchen.

I grabbed her bag of food from the cupboard and poured some out for her. "Here you go. No more waiting."

She made a short chirping noise and leaned into her bowl. The noises continued, making me laugh. She didn't let my chuckle at her expense bother her, though. Had she even heard me over her own chewing?

I turned the burner beneath the tea kettle on, then opened my fridge to see what I had. A quick sandwich with some grapes would do.

Saffy protested as she heard me pop open the can of tuna. That was one sound she never missed.

"Not until you're done. I'll give you some then."

The promise seemed to satisfy her as she bent back down

to her food. By the time I'd finished loading the tuna onto my whole grain bread, she was up on her hind legs pawing at me.

"What did you do, inhale it all? My goodness."

She spun in a circle before returning to her bowl and then tapped it three times with her paw.

I squirted a bit of mayo onto the top slice of bread, then used it to cover the tuna side of the sandwich. Then I dug in for the taste test. The first bite taken at the counter was always the best bite of a meal. I never could wait to sit down before taking one.

Behind me, Saffy's bowl rattled.

"Okay, okay," I said, turning to find her hitting the side of her bowl harder and harder. "Patience, will you?"

I set my sandwich down on the plate and grabbed the can with the remaining plain tuna in it. Saffy wrinkled her nose as I approached, feigning annoyance with me. But as the fishy smell reached her, her nostrils flared and her ability to give me attitude was overpowered by her desire for the tuna.

I'd barely gotten the tuna with the extra juice I'd strained from my portion into her dish before her head was as deep into her bowl as it could go. A drop from the edge of the can fell to her ear, causing it to twitch. The smell was going to drive her crazy since she wouldn't be able to get to it properly. I'd have to wipe it for her, but not when she was in a feeding frenzy. Catnip and tuna always made her wild.

I rinsed out the can—didn't need her to crawl into the recycling bin to get anything that might have been left behind —tossed it in the bin, then grabbed a few grapes out of the fridge as I put away the mayo. Snack complete, I took my plate into the living room to add distance between myself and Saffy, who I hoped would forget I had a whole sandwich to beg for as she licked her bowl clean.

My eating in peace only lasted about five minutes before

she joined me on the couch, cementing herself to my side and tapping at my hand every time I brought my sandwich to my mouth.

"Not happening, Saf." I popped a grape into my mouth. "Can't have one of these either. They're no good for you."

It didn't stop her from trying, getting so far as to come between me and my sandwich by sitting on my lap and half blocking the path to my mouth.

"It's not going to work. Steph and Alex will be here any minute."

She glared at me. Message received. She hopped up behind me on the back of the couch. Then two front paws found their way to my shoulder as she leaned down, hoping to snag a bite that way.

Half amused and half annoyed, I laughed and dug a small piece from the center of my last bite of sandwich. "Okay, you win."

She greedily gobbled the tiny morsel and lay down in her spot.

I had just enough time to pop the last few grapes in my mouth and rinse my plate in the sink before the doorbell rang. Saffy took off running.

"Come on in."

"Ready to go?" Steph asked as she pulled the door closed behind her. "Alex is in the car."

"Just got to get my shoes on."

"Sneakers. You're going to need them."

"Okay . . ." I preferred sneakers, but being told I had to wear them only intensified my curiosity. "Will you tell me where we're going now?"

"Nope," she said with a wry smile. "Let's go." I followed her out the door and we climbed into Alex's SUV. He put it into gear, and we were off.

CHAPTER 28

e drove to the west side of town then hooked north, following the river. It wasn't until we passed the old lumber mill that had been turned into a museum, mostly visited by the elementary school kids and summer tourists, that I realized where we were going.

"Are you two sure you want to go up there?"

"Yeah, it's fine. You aren't afraid of the stories, are you?" Steph teased.

"No, not at all. I just wasn't sure if it was something you were comfortable with given what happened."

"Well, in ordinary circumstances, we wouldn't. What happened up there was awful, and it's someplace that is better left alone. But if we want to solve this problem of yours, we need to go to the source. Remember how I talked about how long things can retain their living energy?"

"Yeah . . ."

"Well, it's not unheard of for chairs made out of sacred wood to shift or for walls and floors to creak when there be no real reason for them to. But add in a ghost too? Who knows how far a possessed sacred wood knife could travel. Maybe all the way back to whence it came."

"Did you really just use the word *whence*?" Alex asked, lightening the mood.

She lifted a finger to her mouth. "Shh . . ."

I wasn't sure if that was in response to her brother's statement or because of where we were going.

We turned off the paved road onto a dirt trail that was a little wider than the SUV. I tried to imagine teams of donkeys pulling carts of logs down the road in the town's early days, those pieces that weren't floated down the river to the mill. It couldn't have been an easy task.

About a mile up the road, Alex came to an abrupt stop.

"Are we here?" I asked, unable to see clearly from the back seat.

Steph hopped out of the car. "Almost, but this is as far as the SUV can go. There's a tree down across the road."

I opened the car door and slid down from the seat, landing on soft earth padded with millions of pine needles all around. Who knew how long it had built up over the years.

Alex stepped over the log, easily clearing the trunk. Steph placed her hand on one of the branches still sticking up in the air. It had been down for a while. Its needles were browning.

"Just a tree," Steph said, confirming it hadn't been sacred wood and no dryads had been harmed when it fell. Then she lifted her leg up and over with no trouble.

The tree seemed to get larger as I approached, and when I tried to climb over, my foot hooked one of the branches, sending me toppling over the side. Thank goodness for Alex, who caught me before I could hit the ground.

"It's easier if you go over the lower part where there aren't any branches to trip on."

"Is that what happened? I felt like it grabbed me."

"It didn't grab you," Steph said. "You're just a klutz."

I wiped pine needles off my pants. "There's a reason why I don't do this whole outdoors thing very often, you know."

"You're outside a lot," Alex pointed out as he stopped to retie his shoe. "You're always on your bike or walking around town."

"*Town* being the key word. Me and nature? Not so much."

"You just need to embrace it the same way you're starting to embrace your witchy self. Maybe it will be kinder to you if you do," Steph said.

"I'm not a nature witch." If there was such a thing. "If anything, I'm a kitchen witch. Even Gram says so."

"Everything's connected," Alex said, straightening. "You rely on nature for many of your ingredients. And all of your tea that you drink too. Where do you think that comes from?"

"You have a point. Okay, I will work on embracing all of this." I twirled in a circle, my arms out wide.

"Plus, you never know when you might offend a tree," Steph added. She began walking down the trail.

"I'm still trying to wrap my head around this whole trees-can-be-people thing. I had no idea there were other paranormal beings in Heartwood Hollow besides the ghosts."

"Well, there's you," Steph said.

"Yeah, but I just started to accept that fact too. So are there other paranormals in the village? Lily mentioned something about other witches."

"You never know, but I've never seen any. Then again, we don't go broadcasting out being dryads, so why would anyone else admit what they are? I only told you because I've known you for years and you've been struggling with your own identity. Maybe if you realized you weren't alone, that it wasn't just you and Lily, you'd be more open to, well, everything."

"I'm surprised the three of you aren't more open about it. Everyone who knows about me has seemed so easily accepting of it. Are there more of you?"

"Yes, but that's not something I'm going to reveal about others. If Alex wasn't my twin, I wouldn't have outed him. But—"

"I trust you, so it's no big deal." Alex grabbed a branch from the middle of the path.

"Do you think other people would care if they knew?"

"Well, some might find it an unfair advantage. Like with me and football." He carried the branch to the side of the trail and set it down. "I have better grounding because of it," he said when he met back up with us.

"And everyone judges that which is different," Steph added.

I nodded, everything on my mind keeping me from saying more. After a few minutes, I asked, "How much longer?"

"We're almost there. Another football field or so away." Leave it to Alex to measure distance with a sports thing I really didn't understand.

The air seemed to grow heavier the farther we walked, not quite oppressive, but something. Maybe somber. It was as if the place itself held the memory of what had happened to the six dryads and who knew how many others throughout the forest surrounding Heartwood Hollow since its founding.

Looking toward the sky, I studied how the tree limbs wove around one another and together as they reached toward the sun. It was almost dizzying.

I hadn't noticed that Alex and Steph had stopped walking, and I crashed into Alex's hard back. He didn't budge. Guess he wasn't kidding about being more grounded than others were. I could see his point about it being an advantage in football. Is that why he had returned here instead of going professional?

"What's going on? We haven't walked that far, have we?" I peeked around Alex in between him and Steph.

My mouth dropped open.

Five feet in front of us, the entire forest was gone.

CHAPTER 29

Steph gasped at the sight. The land had been stripped. Nothing remained but a few felled trees, broken branches and trunks, and sawn stumps. Fifteen feet beyond that, there were only stumps as if the trees had been hauled away somewhere. Several saplings stood a few feet high, one or two slightly higher, but it was nothing like I imagined it had once been.

I stepped out from behind my friends and took a few steps forward before Steph reached for me and grabbed my arm. I turned back to look at her and saw tears falling down her cheeks.

Alex's eyes welled with unshed tears. This was the first time I'd ever seen him get emotional. He wrapped an arm behind his sister and pulled her to his side.

"What's going on?"

"This shouldn't be like this. There should be trees here. This is wrong."

"You didn't know it was like this?"

They shook their heads simultaneously. "The last time any of us—and I don't mean me and Alex, I mean dryads in general—were here, this had only started to be forested. Those six who died... They were the last of it. All the others uprooted, and that's when we started merging with multiple trees to prevent us from dying if our tree was cut down when we weren't there." Steph wiped her eyes with the heel of her palm. "The rumors of the area being cursed caused the workers to be too scared. The logging stopped. Add in all the mishaps and they couldn't come back from that. The Singers were forced to close the mill. There's no way they could have done this. There was no one to do the work."

"Let's go back," I suggested. "We're not going to find anything here. I'm so sorry I asked for your help. If I had known—"

"We didn't know either. It's been years since anyone has been up here," Steph replied.

"Who owns this land? Does it still belong to John's family?"

Alex scoffed. "No one should own this land. Not after what happened and definitely not now." He balled his hand into a fist, and it hardened as it transformed into wood.

"Hang on." Steph pulled out from under her brother's arm. She stepped past me, dropping my hand in the process, and walked toward one of the closer stumps. "It's not recent," she said, squatting, her hand pressed to the flat surface of the cut.

I didn't know if that made it better or worse.

She stood and strode past Alex and me. "Coming?"

I took Alex's rough hand, breaking him from his trance on the barren land. "Come on. We'll sort this out. I promise." As we walked, his hand returned to normal, smoothing out and becoming flesh once more.

We trudged quietly through the forest path, all reflecting on what we had just seen. I hoped none of the wood had been sacred. They'd said they left the area after the six disappearances, but would any of them have come back now and again? I couldn't imagine what it was like for Steph and Alex to see the woods like that. Must have been like returning home after a disaster to nothing but smoking ruins or flattened posts and beams. Nothing salvageable.

But in the back of my head, I realized not all hope was lost. I had a plan but not a lot of time to make it work.

We made it back to the fallen tree. It looked far less ominous from this side. Had it purposefully fallen, trying to prevent anyone from seeing what had happened, a guard to this fallen stand of trees?

I crawled into the car and buckled up as Alex threw the car in reverse. We stayed silent all the way to my house. I almost didn't say anything as I stepped out of the SUV, but I had to acknowledge what had happened.

"I promise you," I said, leaning through the window after closing the door, "I'll get to the bottom of this. I'll talk to John to find out what he knows and call you tomorrow."

Steph nodded from the passenger seat.

"Night, Joannie," Alex said.

"Night." I stepped backward onto the sidewalk and watched as they drove away. John couldn't have been responsible for what I'd seen, but would he know anything about it?

CHAPTER 30

The next morning, Lily breezed into the kitchen, clearly unaware of what Steph and Alex had seen in the north woods. I wasn't sure if they would spread the word or keep it to themselves. If no one ever went up there, as they had said, then no one else would find out. In a way, they were acting like the fallen tree, protecting everyone from what had happened up there however long ago.

"Date go well?" Gina asked after Lily started humming as she rolled out pastry dough.

"It was magical. So much of the wood could be reused, and when I suggested that we use some scraps to make pens, he loved the idea. Said it would be a great way to promote his business." She turned to me. "And he loved the cupcakes. I had one, but I made him take the rest home."

"Wonderful! Hey, any chance we'll see him in the shop today?"

"I'm not sure. He has to work today. He's got some order for a place in Astoria."

"Could you call him and ask him to come by if he has the

time?" I smiled, hoping to diffuse any worry I could create by my request. "I have something to ask him."

"Yeah, sure. I can probably get him to bring me lunch or something or pick me up when I'm done here."

"Perfect. I'd really appreciate it." I jumped onto my station, mixing icing for the cupcakes, and then pastry cream, followed by making a big batch of cookie dough. My focus was everywhere. I couldn't concentrate on any one thing, feeling like I needed my hands in everything today. Some days were like that, always when I was working through an issue. It was a habit noticed over the years, but I wasn't sure if anyone else had picked up on it.

As I worked, I wondered about something Steph, Alex, and I had talked about during our walk in the woods. Were there other paranormal creatures in Heartwood Hollow? Could the stories I'd seen in the book actually be true? Werewolves? Mermaids? What else? And how would I ever find out? It wasn't like I could ask everyone without them thinking I was crazy, or at least those who were humans anyway. Was there some way I could get them to tell me without me having to ask?

"Muffins are boxed and ready, Joanie," Bryan said, pulling me from my thoughts.

I wiped my hands on my apron. "Fabulous." By the time I'd washed my hands, Bryan and Sam had already loaded my bike trailer.

"Thanks, see you in a bit." I climbed onto my bike and made my way out of the parking lot, hoping for a speedy trip.

Everyone was getting ready for the festival tomorrow and prepping for another busy day filled with tourists. Donna had remained true to her word, barely saying more than hello to me before writing down the flavors I'd brought for the day then shooing me back out the door. All told, the entire trip had taken maybe twenty minutes, a record for morning deliveries.

I continued jumping between tasks, helping wherever I was needed, still consumed with thoughts about paranormal beings and what I would say to John. He hadn't done this. Dale maybe. Or perhaps someone else in his family? It wasn't an easy topic to broach, for sure, and I didn't want to sound accusatory.

I rolled out the cookie dough I'd been working on, my mind going back to the dryads and other possible paranormals in town. How could I get them to trust me? How would they know they could come talk to me or that I was even looking for them? I couldn't put up a sign like I had when I was looking for information on Kate. Steph and Alex had told me the dryads weren't likely to tell someone what they were out of fear of judgment or worse.

I understood that. It wasn't like I felt comfortable running around town letting anyone and everyone I saw know that I saw ghosts and might be a witch. It didn't work that way. But was there a secret code, some phrase I could say that the average person wouldn't pick up on but supernatural beings would understand right away and know I was their friend? And would it need to be different for each potential type of paranormal out there? If anything, I figured the dryads would be easiest. That would come from word of mouth if I could get Lily, Holly, Steph, and Alex to tell the others. But what about the river people Olivia Barker had written about in her book? Or the wolves? And were they werewolves, or were they shifters who could transform at will? And what about creatures like fairies or gnomes or trolls? Did any of those call Heartwood Hollow home too?

"Joanie, everything is ready to go," Gina said quietly, tapping me on my shoulder.

I jumped. "Sorry. Didn't realize how in my head I'd gotten."

"Everything okay?"

"Yep." I gave her a big smile. "Just running through an immense to-do list. I forget how big this event is each year, and I want to get it just right."

She returned my smile with one of her own. "You'll do fine." She grabbed one box from the counter, and I took the other one.

"You've got the smaller box in one of these, right?"

"It's in the one you're holding."

"Fabulous. See you all soon. Try those scones when they come out."

Bryan held the door open as Gina and I walked down to the parking lot and loaded my bike trailer. "You sure everything's good?" she asked.

"Yeah . . . yes. It will all be okay. Just have a few things on my mind."

"All right. Safe riding."

She turned to head back into the kitchen as I pushed off on my bike, waving to Kimmy and a few of her yoga students through a window as I pedaled by. Were any of them paranormal?

I parked my bike close bear the kitchen and then, boxes in hand, pushed the door open to find Billy waiting for me. "Morning, Billy."

"Hullo, Joanie. How are you?"

"Good. You?"

He gave me a typical Billy response. "Can't complain."

I placed my boxes on the counter near the awaiting tea trays.

"Heard you were talking about the forest the other day."

"I was. Libby was a great help."

"She'll talk your ear off about anything." Of this I had no doubt. He smiled. "Thank you for the pineapple treat."

"Did you like it?"

"Might be my favorite thing you've ever made."

"Aw, good. I'm glad to hear it. I brought another one just for you."

His eyes lit up the way an excited child's would when they were presented with the toy they'd been wanting for far too long in child time. It wasn't a common sight on Billy's face. He was quiet, usually more stoic. He and Libby made a great pair. A man of few words and a woman who wouldn't stop talking. Then again, maybe Billy never got a word in with Libby around. He didn't seem to mind, though.

"Where's Libby? I have a feeling she doesn't want you around these based on your reaction to them."

He grinned wickedly. It seemed like he had a more child-like side than I'd known.

At that moment, the door from the main part of the inn swung open, and Libby strode through. "You're early!" She glared in amusement at Billy and flailed her arms. "Shoo! Away from the pastry. You'll be able to have them if there are any left after tea."

I grabbed a smaller box from one of the bigger ones and handed it to him before he could leave. "For you."

"Thank you," he said, dodging Libby's playful attempt to bat him away from the table and out of the kitchen.

Once he'd scooted out the door, Libby said, "That man, I swear. You've created a monster."

"I take it he liked the pineapple?"

She belted out a laugh. "He would have licked the trays if I'd have let him. You're going to have to keep these on the menu all summer. He might riot if you don't."

"He doesn't seem the rioting type."

"Oh, he likes his food. Believe me." She opened the other box and started arranging cookies on the middle tier of her tray. "And keep making him one extra too. Put it on our bill, of course. It will be well worth it if it can keep him from eating the rest before they make it out to our guests."

"I can do that. Hey, I have a random question for you."

She quirked an eyebrow at me but said nothing.

"Are you, by chance, related to an Olivia Barker?"

"She's my grandmother."

"I was at the library last night doing a bit of research. I came across a copy of ghost stories and folktales of Heartwood Hollow. It had a lot of the stories you'd mentioned being told by your grandparents. Thought I'd ask since you have the same first name."

"I was named after her. Better her than the other one. I'd never live down Bertha as a first name. It's been ages since I last read that book. I should reread it sometime. Maybe this winter. No time during tourist season." She smiled softly. "Grandma Libby wrote that book with my grandfather. I miss them. And I love their stories."

If she believed they were stories, who was I to tell her otherwise? I nodded. "It was a lot of fun to read what I could. I'm going to have to check some of the other tales out when I have the time."

"Yes, time, which you don't have a lot of today. Lord knows I've been running around all day catering to guests, but it's been great seeing all the returning visitors and having their families come to see them. Today will be the best turnout we've had from the villagers for tea in some time."

The Love a Tree Day Festival had always been one of Heartwood Hollow's most popular events. Until now, I'd always thought it was because it was the first one of the spring. Now knowing about the dryads and how they'd scattered after what happened in the north woods, I wondered if this was more of the reunion for them. It made it all the sadder knowing what we'd discovered up there.

"How's your prep going?" Libby asked.

"Today it's okay. Most of the decorations are done. We'll make do with the rest. There will be a lot more tomorrow with all the actual baking. That and transporting my cart to the festival." Although Bryan had declared it to be still plenty sturdy when he checked it out, I still worried about it going over the last bit of dirt path on the way to the festival clearing. Maybe I'd have John and Lily make me a new one once all was said and done.

"Don't let me keep you."

"You're not keeping me."

She raised an eyebrow at me but once again said nothing. We continued to work, chitchatting about nothing in particular, and once I'd placed the last scone, crowning the top tier, she shooed me out the door much in the fashion that she'd chased Billy out of the kitchen. "See you tomorrow," she called from behind me as the door closed.

I walked back into the bakery's kitchen and saw the progress my team had made. Everyone was cleaning up except for Bryan, who was putting his last tray of cookies into the oven.

"Great job, everyone. Go on home. Tomorrow is an early day. A long day. Get some rest. Coffee is on me in the morning."

The three bakers cheered. Sam, who had left for school a few hours ago would be pleasantly surprised in the morning. Bryan and Gina finished what they were doing and left. Lily called John, then joined me out in the shop. So we could talk in private, I sent Sarah to get her lunch.

Sarah ducked into the back before returning a moment later *sans* apron and with her purse. "See you in thirty!" She headed out the door in the direction of the coffee shop.

I didn't know where John's workshop was, but he arrived within ten minutes. The last two heralded his arrival as the ever-present tingling I experienced when matches were together stirred in my belly from just their mutual anticipation of seeing one another.

"Hey, Joanie," he said, making a beeline for Lily as soon as he stepped into the shop. She met him in the middle, and he kissed her forehead.

"Hi, John. Thanks for coming. Good to see you."

"Lily said you wanted to talk to me?"

"I do. I have something to ask you that may not be the most comfortable thing to talk about."

"Is it about my knife? Were you not able to find it?"

"I haven't been able to locate it yet, but I haven't given up. This isn't about that, though, and I'm sorry to say this affects you too, Lily."

John squeezed her hand, and she returned the gesture.

"Two of my friends revealed to me that they are dryads, and on a hunch, they took me up to the north woods."

Lily gasped.

Based on Steph and Alex's report saying that no one had been up there since the six had been killed, I understood her surprise. "I don't know how to come out and say this, but there was nothing there. The land had been stripped. Nothing but trunks, a few trees left fallen over, and a handful of saplings that are several years old. I'm not sure how many."

Lily teared up. "That's not how it was."

"No, it wasn't," John agreed. "I—I had no idea it was like

that up there. The area had only started being logged when my grandfather called off the harvesting. It should have been nearly all forest."

"Does your family still own the land?" I asked.

"They do, well, I do. It's all mine now, not that I'll ever cut anything down from it, especially now knowing what I do about the dryads. There was supposed to have been a development going through there some time ago, but that fell through and never happened. None of the trees would have been cut down for it. Nothing had been signed. It was shortly before the company closed and my dad passed. I'll have to go back into the records to see if I can find anything about the trees being cut."

"Would you let me know what you find?"

"I'll devote the afternoon to it. But first"—he let go of Lily's hand and wrapped his arm around her shoulders—"I promised my girl some lunch." He looked down at her face, her eyes still full of unshed tears. "Are you okay to grab food still?"

"I can eat." She gave him a reassuring smile.

"All right, you two, enjoy your meal. I'll see you tomorrow, Lily. Will you be coming to the festival, John?"

He shrugged. "Not so sure I'm wanted at a festival that celebrates the thing my family made a living at chopping down then nearly ruined other lives over."

"Well, I'll talk to you soon either way."

"Have a good afternoon. Good luck at the festival tomorrow." He and Lily walked out of the bakery, passing Sarah on her way back in.

"All right, your turn," she said as she crossed the shop and ducked into the kitchen. She came back with her apron, tying it on. "They really do make a cute couple, but you and your witchy ways knew that all along, didn't you?"

"Yes," I answered, not elaborating more. I wasn't ready to have that discussion with her right now. There was too much to do still.

"You're not fighting me on that. You're usually a lot more defensive when I bring it up." She cocked her head to the side and squinted at me, studying my face.

"Guess I've gotten used to it. The rumors don't hurt the bakery at all." I cracked a smile. "They help if anything."

"I like it—this new attitude of yours."

"Thank you?"

"It's a good thing. Now go have your lunch." She waved me away.

I'd only packed grapes this morning, so I snatched a scone from the back as I went to hang up my apron. Hurrying back into the bakery and across the room, I said, "I'll be in the park if you need me."

CHAPTER 31

I sat on my favorite bench, waving to Arthur and Bardi sitting on theirs. "Thank you for your help the other day. I don't think I'd be this far along without you."

He tilted his hat forward in acknowledgment but said nothing.

Popping a grape into my mouth, I looked at the sky. It was a beautiful late Spring day. Tomorrow was supposed to be as nice if not nicer. Good. Festivals were better for all when the weather was decent. One year, we'd had to postpone for snow, and it was wicked muddy from the melt the next week, but such was life in New England. It had been fun, but the dryads who were coming back to visit deserved a good day. We all did.

I sighed deeply, trying to clear my head from all the thoughts running through it, then bit into the scone. Oh my goodness! It was delightful. Thank goodness my team had convinced me to add bacon to the pineapple scone. The salty smoke of the bacon was a great accompaniment to the sweetness of the pineapple. Since I couldn't sell it in the shop due to my agreement with the town council, we'd only made a small batch to make sure it would work out. Hopefully Zeke wouldn't care about my using bacon in the festival's special baked treat. If he did, there wasn't much he could do. This was the one place he wasn't competing with me, and technically I wasn't violating any agreement because I'd only said I'd not sell savory goods in my shop.

As I sat munching the scone, Sierra from the clothing boutique across the street approached me.

"Afternoon, Joanie," she said as she sat down on the bench next to me.

I chewed my bite as fast as I could, holding up one finger. Why did it always take so long when someone was expecting a reply? Finally I swallowed. "Lovely day, isn't it?"

"It is. I saw you on the bench and thought I'd come join you in the sun. Got a minute?"

"Sure thing. What's up?"

"I had one of your lovely pastries today. I've been thinking about it all day. Delicious."

"I'm glad to hear it."

"And I don't know . . ." She grew quiet and folded her hands in her lap. "Can you keep a secret?"

"I'd like to think so."

"I'm a mermaid."

"You are?" My gaze darted to her legs.

"Well, I have legs for when I come out on land, of course. I'm not stuck waiting for an evil sea witch to trick me into having them." She laughed. "I don't know why I just told you that."

"I appreciate your trust in me. Thank you." What else could I say to that? That I'd had suspicions her kind existed?

We sat in silence a few minutes, then Sierra stood. "Well, that's all I had to say. Have a good afternoon."

"Enjoy the rest of your day."

Without a glance backward, she retreated across the street and entered her shop. I shook my head. Strange. It was as if it were any other day and she hadn't just revealed her biggest secret to me. We were friendly, always saying hello at chamber of commerce events or passing one another in town, but we weren't close. So why me?

Arthur and Bardi headed out of the park. He tipped his hat at me again as he passed. Their departure allowed Kimmy from the yoga studio to sit on the bench they'd vacated.

"Hello, Joanie," she called.

I waved. "Hey, how are you?"

"Well, I cheated today. I had one of your cookies. Don't tell any of my clients. I usually don't even let them see me eat your goodies on cheat day. With as many classes as I run, there would be way too many cookies consumed."

I made a zipping my lips motion. "I won't tell a soul."

"Good. So you won't tell them I'm a faerie either?"

I tried to keep my cool, but my eyes widened slightly. What was going on? First Sierra and now Kimmy? "Nope, I won't tell anyone about that either."

"Thanks, Joanie." She stretched all the way over, touching her toes then flattening her hands against the ground.

"Can I ask you something?"

"Sure," she said, sitting back up and bending as far as she could over the back of the bench arms stretched over her head.

"Why tell me?" Kimmy and I knew each other better than Sierra and I did, but still.

"The rumors."

I pointed to myself. "About me?"

"Yeah, that you're a witch. I figured there has to be some truth to them, especially with the way people talk about your Monday muffins and how you cured Rachael's morning sickness with scones. Plus, there's your whole matchmaking thing. That's not normal." She sat straight and looked me right in the eye. "If anyone understands how it is to be different, you do."

Kimmy stood, then placed one foot up on the bench and leaned forward onto her leg on the ground, the one on the bench straight out behind her. "You seem safe," she continued.

And she didn't even know about the ghosts. That would only prove her point even more. "Safe?"

"Yeah. Someone who isn't going to use it against me."

"Is that what you're all afraid of? That someone is going to use this information against you?"

"Well, look what happened to the dryads. They got chopped down and driven from their homes."

"You know about the dryads?"

She nodded, then turned so she could switch her position from one leg to the other. "Of course I do. I'm a woodland faerie. We kind of go hand in hand."

"Huh. I didn't know."

"I wouldn't expect you to. Like I said, we don't go around telling just anyone."

"Well, thank you for telling me. Do you know of anything else in the village?

"There were men who could turn into wolves when I was a child. Not sure if they are still around or how many of them there may be. I don't go around looking. They're a bit rough around the edges if you ask me."

"Wolves, got it."

"That's all I know." She looked up at the sun. "Okay. Time for me to head back for another class. See you tomorrow. I'm looking forward to whatever treat you have special for the festival."

"See you tomorrow."

She walked away as quietly as she'd come.

I had to go too. Lunch was over. As I headed back to the bakery, I looked down at the last bit of scone in my hand, then popped it into my mouth, thoughts still running through my mind.

First dryads. Now mermaids, faeries, and confirmation of wolves. What next? And why were they all telling me now?

CHAPTER 32

Every time Sarah walked into the kitchen, it seemed as if someone new was walking into the shop to confess what they were.

One thing became evident to me with the revelation of every individual who came in with a supernatural secret. They'd all been in earlier this morning or had eaten one of today's baked goods that someone had given them. Had my thoughts about wanting to know about other paranormals transferred to the treats as I made them? Was everyone unknowingly right about the good luck cookies and Monday muffins? Was the whole kitchen witch thing true? I'd always thought it was something Gram had called me because she liked my food, but perhaps there had been more to it all along. I'd have ask Gram when I talked to her later. We were planning to talk tonight since tomorrow's festivities would keep me out during our usual time to chat.

At the end of the day, Sarah and I made fast work of cleaning the shop. Both of us wanted to get out of there and get some rest for tomorrow. She was meeting us right after the first round of baking to help load the car to take it to the clearing and would run the first shift at the festival while I returned to finish baking with the team. Then we'd switch out, and she'd enjoy the festival for a bit while I ran the table with one of the bakers. In the afternoon, we'd swap places twice more. It was a system the team had developed over the last few years, and it allowed us all ample breaks to partake in the festivities.

Saffy met me at the arm of the couch when I arrived home. Since I was on time today, she allowed me to scratch behind her ears before she hopped down and headed toward the kitchen. She waited patiently as I got her food ready and ate it without a fuss as I made a sandwich for myself. It was quick and easy and something that required no thought to make. My brain was too full of confessions from the townspeople, of their fears for why they'd not told anyone before, and their reasons for telling me. I doubted I could stuff another thought in my head right now. All I knew was, two things were clear. Heartwood Hollow's paranormal beings were afraid of retaliation and judgment from the human townspeople, and they needed a safe place to go. With how many had come into my shop, I wondered how many regular humans the town had.

Dinner done for the both of us, Saffy and I collapsed onto the couch. She lay behind my head on the back of the couch and was asleep within moments. In slight envy of my cat, I held the house phone in hand, ready to call my grandmother. It rang. The number didn't bring up a caller name, and it wasn't one I recognized.

"Hello?"

"Joanie? It's John Singer. I hope it's okay that I called you at home. Lily gave me your number."

"It's absolutely fine, John. What's up? What did you find?"

"Remember how I told you about that development? Well,

nothing was ever signed, like I thought, but it seems that my dad believed that if the forest was cut, the development would go through. One less obstacle in its path. It was right around the time my mom left, and I thought he was going to the bar at night after work. I was a young teenager. I didn't know better. Didn't realize there was something more going on. He was taking down the trees. By himself. All of them. It's no surprise he died shortly after this happened. It took everything out of him."

My heart ached at how sad this story was for everyone involved. "Oh, John. I'm so sorry."

"What was he thinking?" Now he was getting angry. "Never mind the fact you don't start projects without signed contracts in place, but why do this all alone? And why do it after my grandfather forbade this grove from being cut down?"

"People do strange things when they are grieving. Your mom may not have died, but the relationship ended. That can be enough to cause the same emotions."

"I feel terrible about the whole thing. I had no idea this was going on."

"Like you said, you were young. What would you have done?"

"I don't know. But something."

"You can do something now, though."

"Do you have any ideas? I'd love to make this better. My family is responsible for causing more heartbreak for Lily, for your friends, for all dryads who find out about this. How do we fix it?"

I explained to him my plan that I'd been thinking about during the day when I wasn't having people come by to tell me their secrets. His agreeing sounded more and more excited the further I went on to tell him how he could be involved.

"So you'll come to the festival tomorrow?" I asked. "It's going to be the best place to announce our plan and set it into motion."

"I'll come by in the afternoon. Might take me that long to work up the nerve."

"Once people hear what we have in store, I think you won't need to worry about how they view you around town anymore. This is a good thing."

"Thanks, Joanie. I'll talk to you tomorrow."

As soon as we hung up, I called Steph.

"Hey, Joanie. What did you find out?"

I told her all about the failed development, then how John's dad had taken it upon himself to clear the forest in a fit of grief and desperation.

"I remember hearing about that development. The dryads were up in arms that the forest would be destroyed. But things settled back down once the deal fell through. The forest was safe." She scoffed. "Or so we thought. But we never actually went back to check. The deal was over. It was never talked about again. The development went up near Astoria instead. Especially once the lumber company shuttered, why wouldn't we have thought the forest was safe?"

"I don't know, Steph. But we're going to fix things. John and I have a plan, but we need your help."

"Anything."

"I need a press release written and ready to go for tomorrow afternoon. You'll be there covering the festival, yeah?"

"Yep. It's one of my favorites to cover, especially now that there are no pageants for me to get involved with."

"Fabulous." I told her what we intended to announce at the festival.

"Joanie, that's wicked amazing," she said, sniffling at the end.

"Are you crying? You're crying, aren't you."

"What? No. Allergies."

"What part of nature are dryads allergic to? It doesn't make much sense to have a tree sneezing."

She laughed, giving me the reaction I'd hoped for. I knew they were happy tears, but I didn't want her to shed any more over this. "Fine, you got me. But it does happen sometimes. Not the allergies, but the sneezing. Humans just assume that a squirrel jumped through the leaves or a bird crash-landed into the branches."

"Really?" Several times when sitting in the park I'd heard and seen exactly what she'd described. Had it really been a sneezing dryad?

"Yep."

"Huh. You learn something new every day." That was an understatement today. "All right, well, I gotta let you go. I need to get to bed early tonight to make sure we're ready for everything tomorrow."

"Sleep well. Oh, hey, can I tell Alex? It's really been getting to him."

"Absolutely. I'll see you tomorrow."

This time when I hung up the phone, it rang in my hand for a second time. "Hi, Gram."

"Joanie, there you are. I've been trying to call you, and it's just been a busy signal. Over and over again. I thought that sassy cat of yours might have knocked it off the hook or something."

"Nope, just talking to a few people to get things lined up

for tomorrow." I filled her in on learning about dryads and what had happened in the woods.

"Your town always has given off a vibe that there's something more going on in it. What, with all the ghosts and then that hairbrush a few weeks ago?"

"I haven't even told you about the knife."

"What knife?" Alarm rang clear in her voice. "You're not in any danger, are you?"

"No, not at all. The knife is how I first learned of the dryads. It was made of sacred wood."

"Oh, that's what you were asking me about last week."

Guess she had heard me after all. I shouldn't have doubted her. She was taking on her friend's murder investigation, after all. Nodding, not that she could see me, I said, "Yeah. Sacred wood is wood that was either home to or was a dryad."

"So that knife is possessed by a dryad?"

"Or the ghost of its owner. I've seen both of them around. But now the knife's gone missing, and I don't know how to summon a ghost without an object."

"You could try something else that belonged to them."

I sat up straighter, jostling the cushion and startling Saffy awake. She jumped down next to me and, after spinning in a circle three times, lay back down. "That's a good idea. If I end up needing to, I will. I'm hoping that things will right themselves soon. My couple is happy, so maybe it's already all over."

We chatted for a little while longer. She filled me in on Miss Susan's memorial service and her sending off from the witches. It sounded like it had been a beautiful sight. Then she told me what she'd been doing to help find Miss Susan's killer. She had a lead, and I hoped it would pay off.

"So she was a green witch?" I asked, stroking Saffy's soft fur.

"She was."

"And that's because she was good with plants and herbs and such?"

"And her overall good communion with nature."

"So I'm a kitchen witch because I'm good at cooking and baking?"

"Are you finally ready to admit it?" She sounded excited.

"I think so. Gram, today was so weird." I told her all about how I'd made my baked goods hoping to find a way that others would be able to trust me with the truth about who they were and then how everyone came in to tell me their secrets.

"That, my dear, was a spell."

"But I didn't know I was doing it. How does it work?"

"Exactly how it did today," she said matter-of-factly.

"So the good luck from my cookies I played off as them believing in the placebo effect? The Monday muffins that give everyone a pep in their step to help them get back into the workweek?"

"Both spells. Maybe a little bit of this placebo effect because it's been going on for so long now and everyone buys into it, but you can put what you want into your baked goods to do just about anything for their benefit. Nothing negative, though. That always comes back to bite you."

"Understood." I had no intention of ever harming anyone with my treats. Not only was that not like me but it would be bad for business. "Hey, what's on your schedule coming up?"

"Well, I've been a bit busy lately. Miss Susan's death really took a lot out of the community. What do you need? I'll help anyhow I can."

"I was wondering if you could come by sometime and

help me put the wards back on the house. Maybe Mom too? Sage everything and give it a good cleanse like you did when I moved in. Since what happened a few weeks ago with the hairbrush, I've now had several ghostly visitors inside. Miss Susan was a surprise, and I'm glad she did come visit, but overall, I'd really like for this to be my safe space, you know? Nothing in that isn't invited."

"You're okay now, right? Nothing bad?"

"I'm fine. If you don't have time for a little while, I'll manage. You're still dealing with Miss Susan's passing, and I have the Love a Tree Day Festival tomorrow and hopefully something next weekend related to this case, but maybe the next? Or the one after?"

"Oh yes, everything should be all right here by then. We'll make a day of it and go to that yummy cider mill we went to that last time I was over. Their samples are delicious and their food is even better."

"I would love that. It's been too long, Gram."

"You prepare that sassy cat of yours for my visit. Tell her Gram's bringing her some special catnip."

I threw my head back in laughter, waking Saffy up once more. This time she glared at me before grumbling and putting her head back down.

"I'm going to hold on to that bit of information or else she's going to think anyone coming to the door could be you. It would drive her crazy. If she could talk, she'd demand your presence right now if she knew."

"Surprised she hasn't yet."

"Come again?"

"Oh, nothing. She is an expressive one, isn't she?"

"Sure is. Sometimes I swear she's looking right at me ready to say something, and then she changes her mind and goes back to her business."

"That's a cat for you."

"All right, Gram. I'm going to let you go. You call me if you need any help with anything, okay?"

"Miss Susan hasn't come to you again, has she?" Her voice sounded tentative this time.

"Nope, nothing since last Saturday."

She sighed. "Oh well. All right, dear. I'll talk to you soon. Love you."

"Love you too."

The phone disconnected, and I clicked it off, flopping back onto the couch. I glanced at the clock by the kitchen door. Only seven thirty. Bedtime. I knew better than to push it with such a busy day ahead ahead of me.

As I lay down, Saffy already joining me even though it was early for her, too, I hoped everything would go smoothly tomorrow. Lily and John's match—and possibly the whole town—depended on it.

CHAPTER 33

I arrived on the festival grounds with a second load of tree and dryad themed cupcakes, pineapple bacon scones, and palmiers. A line had formed in front of the cart, Sarah and Lauren working tirelessly to fulfill orders. The festival grounds were hopping for the late morning hour, the beautiful weather helping everyone to get out earlier to enjoy as much of the day as possible. Every table had at least a small line, but nothing compared to ours.

I held my arms out as Sam loaded me up with some boxes, then he picked up a stack of three to carry. We carefully carved our way around the outskirts of the festival to our cart, placing the boxes on the table we'd been using for storage behind the cart.

"Oh, thank goodness you're here," Sarah exclaimed, throwing her arms up into the air. "It's been like this since we opened. Your scones are a hit. How many more do you have?"

"Half of the boxes are just scones."

"Might want to call and have them start on another batch. That's not going to last us through dinner."

I'd overbought the supplies just in case, but hadn't

expected to need to use them, especially not so early. Usually, I had an impeccable ability to calculate exactly what the bakery needed for the day, plus a few extras for the day-old shelf. It had to be a kitchen witch thing. Outdoor events always threw me off slightly but not like this. Was pineapple bacon that popular of a flavor or was something else going on?

As Sam refilled the cart, I shot a quick text to Gina, Lily, and Bryan back at the bakery to make another round of scones.

"Done. What's next?" I slid the phone back into my pocket.

"Okay, this is going to sound really weird, but just as popular as our scones have been, so have you. Some of these people in line have just been waiting for you."

"Me?"

"Yeah. What did you do?"

"I have no idea," I told her, having every idea but not wanting to tell her.

"Some have even left you cards. There's a small pile in the cash box." She eyed me skeptically. "Did you do something special to the baked goods you haven't told me about? High school finals are coming. Adding some extra good luck maybe?"

Lauren piped up at this. "Oh, think I could snag one for my brother? He's nervous about them."

"I hear it works better if eaten the morning of the test," I replied, embracing the rumors that increasingly looked to be true. "But you're welcome to grab one come test day for him."

Lauren beamed and returned to helping the next customer in line.

Sarah smiled proudly. "I don't know what you did, but I

like that you aren't getting defensive about it. This is progress."

I laughed, shaking my head. Sarah had been on my case about the possibility I was a witch for some time. She'd thought so even before my baked goods started having an effect on people. She didn't know the half of it.

I dug my keys out of my apron pocket. "All right, can you go drive my car around to the lot? They let me get as close as I possibly could to make this delivery, but I'm sure it'll be in the way if I leave it there. After that, bring me back the keys and you'll be free for the next couple hours."

"Fabulous. I could so use a coffee." She peeked her head past the cart toward Leafs and Grounds' pop-up tent a few stations over. At that moment, Gary looked up and smiled.

I waved at him, and he did the same, a big smile on his face. "I'm sure Gary will be happy to see you."

Sarah blushed. She wasn't ready to admit it, but I think he was growing on her. I didn't get my matchmaker vibe with the two of them, but this was the first time in ages we'd all been in the same general area for it to happen. Nothing yet, although plenty of couples didn't need my push to be perfectly happy together.

"I'm coming too," Lauren said, snapping off the gloves she'd been wearing to handle the treats and pulling me from my thoughts.

She and Sarah strode off in the direction of the station wagon, leaving Sam and me to help the awaiting customers.

"One scone please," Greta from the historical society said.

I smiled at her as I handed it to her in a paper bag. She passed me the money, and a small slip of paper poked out from the folded five-dollar bill. I opened the cashbox to make change and read the note in the process.

I'm a troll.

That was a new one.

I quickly folded it back up and then slipped into my pocket. She gave me a small smile as I handed the change back to her, and she nodded, dropping a dollar in the tip jar. She walked off, scone in hand, disappearing into the crowd.

"Delilah wanted me to give this to you," Sam said a few minutes later as he reached back for two lavender-lime cookies, handing me a small pink envelope.

I mouthed "thank you" to the anxious-looking Delilah.

"I had one of those cookies yesterday, and they were divine," she said, likely confirming my suspicions about what was inside the envelope. "I'm so glad you had some today too." Was she still being affected by yesterday's treats? Just how powerful was the spell I'd unknowingly put into them?

"I'm happy to hear you liked them. And thank you for your note. I'll read it when it's less busy."

"It's silly, really, but I felt like I should tell you. Have a good day."

"What was that about?" Sam reached to grab a palmier.

"I think I made truth cookies yesterday," I said quietly, ducking under the cart to reach for a pineapple bacon scone, allowing us to be on the same level and away from other's ears. "Or truth scones. Truth muffins?"

"Or maybe truth everything. You did do a bit of it all yesterday. Today too."

Sam and I both stood. Then he handed the pastry to Pete, and I gave the scone to Duke from Leafs and Grounds.

"You don't seem fazed by my admission," I said as I waited for Jill to step forward and place her order.

"Told you before I don't believe rumors." He shrugged. "But I'll believe you when you tell me." We both ducked down to retrieve baked goods for our customers. "If you made truth muffins, you made truth muffins."

"Thanks, Sam."

He straightened. "Nothing to thank me for. You're still Joanie. That hasn't changed at all."

Jill passed me a five. "It's special," she told me.

I looked down to see the words *I'm a faerie* written in purple pen along the bottom of the bill. I nodded. "Very special. Thank you." I reached into the cash box to get her change.

"Have a good one," she said as she took the two dollars from me but dropped the coins in the tip jar.

The next two hours zoomed by in much the same fashion. By the time Sarah returned and Lily, Gina, and Bryan had driven up with the last of the baked goods, I'd gotten dozens of confessions. I hadn't read them all. The ones that were sealed I'd wait to read until I was alone. But several had been passed to me written in folded pieces of paper like Greta's had been or written on money like Jill's. Holly stopped by, simply saying, "You already know about me, but I'm confirming it face to face." We both laughed at that. One of the high school freshmen had even come out to Sam, saying he was the first person outside of his family that he'd told he was gay. He'd picked Sam because he figured he'd understand. Sam had felt honored and gave him a hug. I wasn't sure if my baked goods had anything to do with that. Most likely, Sam's recent coming out had been the key factor in the freshman's revelation.

"All right, I'm going to walk around for a bit, but call me if it gets crazy. I'm thinking with lunch time approaching, we might have a small lull as people go for the sandwiches and hot foods being offered elsewhere." Sam and I swapped places behind the cart with Sarah and Lily.

"Lily, call me if John shows up, please. He and I are working on something."

"Sure thing," she said with a knowing smile. I wondered how much he had told her. They'd gone on yet another date last night.

I'd been up since three this morning with only a small breakfast and my usual tea. Gary gave me a coffee when I got here. I hadn't wanted to touch any of the baked goods. If what rumors said were true, and if Gram was right, I didn't want to accidentally admit my secrets to anyone. It hadn't happened yesterday after my scone, but there was no need to press my luck. Now my stomach growled, but I could hold off a little longer before finding food. Instead I took off toward a quiet end of the clearing and found a sunbaked boulder that had been recently vacated by a few kids and their parents. I sat on the boulder with a stack of sealed envelopes in my lap, but I couldn't bring myself to open them just yet. Instead, I closed my eyes and let the sun warm me, renewing my energy. Was this what Alex and Steph had meant about me embracing nature? This I could do.

The air stirred slightly, and I knew I was no longer alone. I waited in silence to see if whoever it was would tell me they were there before opening my eyes to see who it was.

I didn't know the voice once it finally spoke.

"What are you hoping to achieve with all of this?" the female voice asked. It sounded genuinely curious. Not hostile or angry, but not necessarily pleased either.

I opened my eyes. Sitting next to me was Juniper, Lily's grandmother.

"I want to heal some of the hurt that's been happening here beneath the surface for many. But knowing is only half the battle. The other is doing. John has that ability. And why not, given how involved his family was in the hurt toward you and the rest of the dryads?"

She smiled. "I'd like that. I'm Juniper, but you already know that."

"I do. I'm sorry for what happened to you."

"What's done is done. Any luck getting the knife back?"

"So you're not anchored to it?"

"It may have once been a part of me, but no," she said, shaking her head. "I'm not anchored to it, as you say. It was my body at the time of my death, but my spirit escaped. I've been wandering around in the background for years keeping an eye on things."

"Perhaps Dale's attached to it, then."

Her smile turned sad. "Perhaps." She stared out across the festival, and I turned my head to see what she was looking at. The crowd parted, and there was a clear view of Lily behind the cart. I took her *keeping an eye* answer to mean she was always watchful of her family, maybe Lily in particular, guiding her how she could after her parents left town, leaving her to live with her aunt, uncle, and cousin.

"Did you know him? Dale?" I believed I already knew the answer.

There wasn't a response.

I glanced to my side. She was gone, her energy fading in the air around me.

I sat on the stone for a while longer, reading confessions and thinking about Heartwood Hollow and its residents. So many were afraid to say what they were, but others were so readily accepting whenever I broached the subject of the paranormal with them. Ashley. Sarah. Sam. Rich. Occasionally Ken. I pushed the thought of him away. He wasn't a bad guy. He was still coming to terms with everything. Someday he would. He'd seen it with his own eyes. There had to be others who would be just as accepting if not more.

Everyone needed to come together, and I hoped what John and I had in store would allow them to do just that.

My stomach growled once more, so I crawled off the giant rock and went in search of food. If this was my opportunity to eat, I had to take it.

I was finishing the last of my chicken curry fries from one of the food trucks when Lily called.

"John's here"

"Great, be there in a few."

Cutting across the field, I called Steph after Lily hung up. "Hey, ready to get the scoop on some breaking news?"

"Absolutely. Where do you want me?"

"By the stage please. We'll be there soon."

CHAPTER 34

"Can I have everyone's attention, please?" I said into the microphone as I stood on the small center stage. Slowly conversation died down and hundreds of pairs of eyes all focused on me.

"Hi, everyone. For those of you visiting our lovely town, I'm Joanie Sunevall, the sweet treats baker. You may have visited me at my cart over there." I pointed to Bryan and Gina, who were now staffing the station. "Heartwood Hollow is a special place. I'm sure many of you are aware of that. I think we can also all agree that it has a unique history that unfortunately has some darker moments."

Several in the crowd grumbled in agreement.

"One of these moments is the disappearances that happened in the north woods. Believe what you will about the place, but it was an unfortunate event no matter what happened. And now the north woods have taken on an air of mystery, of creepiness, and to some of you, evil. But that was never the intent of the place. It was once a sacred locale, and to some, it still is." To make sure I wouldn't call anyone out, I avoided eye contact with those I knew to be a dryad. "I recently found myself in those woods."

The audience gasped. It didn't surprise me that more than the dryads had avoided going to this spot given the tall tales I'd heard about it when I first sought information on it.

"I can assure you there are no monsters or bad guys or what have you up there. However, there are also no trees."

"What do you mean?" someone called from the crowd. "It's a forest."

"Several years ago, some of you may remember it, a development was going to be built in that area."

Many nodded.

"Obviously it never happened. For what reason, I'm not here to speculate. Unfortunately, however, in preparation for this development, the forest was clear cut, leaving nothing but stumps behind."

Several gasped again, and shouts of anger came from others.

"Why?"

"The deal was never final!"

"I bet you Joe Singer had something to do with it. Shuts the business and clears the forest to try and make a profit without us."

"Yes," I confirmed, "it was Joe Singer who chopped the north woods down." As the noise level rose, I raised my hands and lowered them, hoping the volume would do the same. The crowd quieted down, and I continued. "Since he's not here to speak for or defend himself, I do not want to go into the *hows* and *whys*. What's done is done. The forest is barren. It is unfortunate, but it is not irreversible. We have a plan."

Holding my arm out to the side, I continued, "I'd like to call John Singer to the stage as he lays out his plan to set things right."

John stepped up the few stairs to the stage

I handed him the mic as he took a deep breath, steeling himself to face the villagers who hadn't all been kind in the past. No one spoke, no one moved. They just stood watching him, waiting to hear what he had to say.

"Hello, everyone. Thank you, Joanie, for being the spark for this project. When I heard what had happened in the north woods, I was dumbfounded. A young teen at the time, I had no idea my father was clear-cutting the forest. Some of you may remember my grandfather Dale. He was a good man, although he might not have had the best business sense. One thing he told me before his death was to not cut down the north forest. This was back when he thought I'd be in the lumber business, following in the family's footsteps. He'd felt strongly about it, and I'm sure he'd requested it of my father too. Why my father chose otherwise, especially after that deal had fallen through, I'm not sure. But I am prepared to take steps to remedy the black mark that has been following my family for too long, made only deeper by the recent revelations of my father's actions."

He stood a bit straighter, perhaps gaining confidence as all kept their silent attention on him. "Many of you may remember how, as part of the tree festival, we used to go into areas of the forest and replant sections that had been harvested. Some time ago, this effort became the river cleanup, and it became its own day in the spring. That is not going away, but we are bringing back the tree planting. Next weekend, I have a shipment coming in of one thousand native trees, purchased by my furniture company, and I hope that we as a town can replant them together up in the north woods. I'll do it myself if I have to, to make up for what has transpired, but please . . . join me. Let's make a day of it. More if we have to. Let's bring the north woods back to the thriving forest it once was.

He let his plea hang in the air. When no one spoke up, he concluded, "Thank you all for listening."

John waved awkwardly, then took a step back, handing the microphone over to me.

"Thank you, John. There you have it, folks. Let's extend the spirit of the Love a Tree Day Festival to next week. Come to the north woods, some of you again, many of you for the first time. Let's put our community spirit together and restore this wonderful space. I'll bring the scones."

Steph reached up and handed me a clipboard with sheets of paper on it.

"There are volunteer sign-up forms here and over at my cart. Let's get these sheets filled up with names."

I followed John off the stage to an eager crowd. For what I wasn't sure. People in the crowd quickly stripped the clipboard of all its forms, and momentarily my heart sank as I thought they were going to be ripped up.

"Does someone have another pen?"

"Give me one of those forms."

"I have a pen."

"Me too!"

The clipboard wasn't a fast-enough method. Villagers passed papers back and forth. Some used the backs of whoever was around to sign the forms on. Others struggled with whatever they had in their hands to do the same. By the time I'd cleared the stage and come around the front to talk to Steph, I couldn't see any of the papers.

"I hope you made enough copies of those," Steph said. "You might get halfway through the festival before running out of room on them."

"There are more over by my cart." I gazed across the field,

watching as the occasional sheet of paper popped into the air in the hand of a villager calling out, "Next!" or, "Who wants it?" only for it to be snatched down by a waiting hand.

I smiled at John. "You've done a good thing."

"Thanks to you." He rubbed the back of his neck. "I wouldn't have thought of it on my own. I'm only happy to help."

"You would have gotten there on your own eventually. I only helped move things along."

"I'm going to go see Lily now if that's all right."

"Go on, go enjoy the festival." I shooed him away. "We'll talk soon."

He waved over his shoulder as he disappeared into the crowd.

"Got everything you need for the release?" I asked Steph.

"I think so. You've already given me the date and time, and we know the meet-up point. Do we have other donors?"

"Can you make a request for them in the release? Perhaps we can get someone to donate water or yard waste bags. There's going to be a lot to pick up in order to clear the area for planting. Maybe see who might have chainsaws to help with the fallen trees that are toward the perimeter."

"All right. That I can do."

"And I'd like to talk to you about the supernatural population in town. It might be bigger than we first imagined. More than just dryads. But they're scared, like you said the other day. They're worried what the full human population might do if they revealed themselves."

Quirking an eyebrow, she asked, "What are your thoughts?"

"I'd like to create some sort of an outreach or support group. Everyone should be allowed to be who they are without fear. Out in the open if that's what they want."

"I'm sure I can think of something to write. Expect it to run next to this release. Maybe the dryads can lead the way. This project of yours it going to be wicked good for us. It's amazing what you're doing for all of us. To see the north woods as a thriving forest again? Wow. Never thought I'd see the day. The last time that place held happy memories, I was a little girl."

"I hope you have many more there someday soon."

She grabbed me, pulling me into a hug. "Thank you."

I wrapped my arms around her, putting my response into the hug. A *you're welcome* didn't feel strong enough for what she was thanking me for.

I wove back through the festival grounds, making my way to the cart. It took ages. People kept stopping me to thank me for what I was doing. To say how great this undertaking was and that they were looking forward to next week. To tell me how amazing my festival specials were. To confess if they were a paranormal being. When I'd finally reached the cart, Lily bolted toward me and wrapped me up in a fierce hug.

"Thank you, thank you, thank you. That is so amazing." She bounced on her heels as she spoke.

"You didn't know?"

She stepped back and reached for John's hand and looked up at him in a way that made the matchmaking tingle surge through my system. "He didn't tell me all of it. Just that he had something important to do with you. I never would have imagined."

"Well, I'm glad you liked the surprise."

By now, everyone on the team had gathered around me, and I clapped my hands. "Okay, let's get back to work."

CHAPTER 35

C ome Sunday morning, I had a strong desire to stay in bed when my alarm clock sounded. I even clicked the snooze button, something I never did. My bed was that inviting, and my body that tired.

Saffy, however, had no plans of sleeping in, not even for an extra few minutes. My movement to turn off my alarm had been her cue. If I was awake enough to press a button, then I was awake enough to feed her. She crossed my body, her little feet stepping on every pressure point. There was no chance of sleeping now.

As if to ensure that fact, Saffy lay down on my chest and batted my nose until I opened my eyes.

"Okay, okay," I groaned. "I'm getting up. But you have to get off me first."

She used my chest like a springboard and jumped to the floor with a loud thud. Then she turned back to look at me, checking to see if I was doing what I promised.

With my sassy calico giving me no other choice, I sat up and swung my legs over the edge of the bed. A few minutes later, I was dressed and in the kitchen, giving Saffy her breakfast and waiting for the water to boil so I could make tea and hopefully wake up a bit more. If I felt like this, I could only imagine how my baking team felt. Coffees would be on me again today. I wondered if Gary would already have some marshmallow rice treats ready at this hour. He'd started his summer hours this weekend to cater to the tourists and any morning runners taking advantage of the earlier daylight.

I headed outside once my tea was in my travel mug. The only way I'd fully wake up was with a good walk to stretch out the muscles that had gotten in some overtime yesterday. The festival had been a great success. All my volunteer slips had at least some names on them, and some went onto the back.

Knowing I would run a few minutes late, I texted Lily to give her a heads-up and promised I'd make it worth it. She responded immediately with a smiley face followed by a coffee cup emoji and a question mark. They all knew my pattern by now. My being late meant I was getting them all something too.

I walked into Leafs and Grounds, hoping the smell of the coffee beans would wake me up even more through some sort of olfactory osmosis.

"Joanie! Good to see you," Gary called chipperly. How much coffee had he had this morning? He seemed to have no effects from yesterday's festivities. "Hey, I want to donate the coffee for your tree planting."

"Aw, thank you. I hope you know I wasn't coming in to hit you up for donations at this hour."

Gary laughed. "No, I figured not, but I'm happy to do it. Anything to help out this community."

He took my order, and we chatted as he filled the five drinks. "You gonna be able to get all of this across the street?"

"I'll manage as long as you can get the door for me."

"Can do." He bounded around the counter and rushed to

the front door. "I'll see you again soon. Say hi to Sarah for me when she comes in."

"Sure thing," I said, momentarily jealous of the fact she was still sleeping at this hour.

Everyone was waiting for me as I came around the building, and they cheered when they saw the coffee even though all of them already had their own travel mugs full of it. Nothing beat Gary's coffee. Maybe he was a coffee witch. Or would he be a wizard? I wasn't sure of the term, though I chuckled at myself for the thought.

The morning started off a bit slow, but we picked up the pace as the caffeine set in. And despite being late a few minutes, we had everything ready on time for my diner deliveries.

We'd made a bit more than we usually would for a Sunday, but there were still plenty of festival goers in town, and after the announcement of the north woods replanting, I expected today to be busier than usual. Many came in asking if I had the festival special, and although they were disappointed I didn't, they didn't leave empty handed. Most promised they'd help at the planting if it meant another pineapple bacon scone. No one confessed to being paranormal. Whether that was due to Sarah's presence or that the spell from Friday had worn off, I wasn't sure.

John stopped in during a small lull before the after-church crowd arrived to say he'd seen the press release. He thanked me again for saying his company was at the forefront of the project.

"You are donating all the trees, after all," I told him. "Of course I'm going to give you the credit."

"You're too nice to me." He leaned toward a case and pointing to a cinnamon twist. "Especially given how this all started."

Sarah handed him the twist as I rang him out. "Aw, all of that's long forgotten. I'm glad you and Lily were able to come together after the misunderstanding." If they could do it, maybe there was hope for Ken and me after all. It bummed me out that he was the one person I didn't see at the festival. Ivy had at least waved when she spotted me, but she was playing with the other children, getting ready for a sack race.

"Any luck finding the knife?"

I shook my head. "I'm sure it will turn up, but with yesterday—"

He held his hand up. "Say no more. You've been wicked busy."

"I haven't given up the search." Knowing Juniper wasn't attached to it led me to believe Dale had taken it somewhere. But where?

"Thanks. All right. I have to get back to work on that Astoria order, but we'll talk soon. Have a good day." He waved and nodded to both Sarah and me as he stepped out of the shop.

"I was wrong about him," Sarah admitted. "I thought he was weird and reclusive, especially after he quit football in high school. Never really gave it much thought that it was because of how the villagers viewed his family due to what happened. He's a nice guy."

"People can be a lot more than what they first seem when you meet them."

"Like you being a witch?"

"Yes, like me being a witch." Still not ready for that conversation with her, I chuckled in a way I hoped would make her question my response, as if I was just playing along.

Someday I'd truly confirm to Sarah what I was. In my own time. But this overall issue went beyond Sarah and me. It went into all of Heartwood Hollow and all the villagers who people believed were human but were actually dryads, mermaids, faeries, and trolls. What we were doing with the north woods for the dryads was just the beginning, and I hoped the second notice that Steph had put in the paper would have as big of an effect for every paranormal being in town. Only time would tell.

CHAPTER 36

Sometime after lunch, the door swung open, and my heart jumped into my throat as the air shifted.

Ken.

I looked up and saw two people, one big and one small, both with their faces obscured by flowers.

"What is all this?" I asked, a smile growing across my face. As I glanced at Sarah next to me behind the counter, she waggled her eyebrows at me.

"Hi, Joanie!" Ivy chirped from behind her bouquet. "We've brought you flowers because Daddy said he messed up." She lifted her bouquet, vase and all, onto the counter.

"Oh my goodness. This is beautiful. Did you pick it out?" I leaned forward and made a show of sniffing the bright Gerber daisies and carnations.

"Yep!" She bounced on her toes. "I helped Daddy pick out his too."

"You did a great job."

She beamed.

"I'm going to go get started on cleanup and prep for tomorrow," Sarah announced with more flair than the statement would typically require, sneaking behind me and heading into the kitchen. Her face was fully of giddy delight, and I pictured her bouncing in the back much like Ivy was. Tomorrow everyone would know that Ken had brought me flowers.

"Hi, Joanie," Ken said, lowering the flowers to reveal a sheepish smile.

"Those really are beautiful, Ken. Thank you. How are you? I didn't see you at the festival yesterday."

"Got roped into working most of yesterday. I snuck out for a little bit to try to make some connections, but you looked busy, so I didn't want to bother you. Your line was huge."

"Oh, you'd never bother me. But you're right. It was a busy day." I smiled warmly. "But a good day too."

"I saw the press release this morning in the paper. This is a result of what you've been doing with John and Lily, isn't it?"

I couldn't get a read on his voice as to what he thought. His tone was even, his face a mask of calm and still partially obscured by the flowers.

"It is. They're in a really good spot right now, but I think they're only one aspect of this . . . issue." I wanted to call it a curse, but I wasn't going to with Ivy standing right there. She was young and impressionable, and she'd seen plenty of animated movies with cursed princesses to know what one was. I didn't want to scare her, especially when it involved where she lived. Somewhere she'd only moved to recently. And I didn't want her to think anything differently of me either.

"I know you're not a big fan of what I do—"

"Joanie." Ken handed his flowers to Ivy, allowing me to meet his gaze. "I think it's amazing. This whole replanting the forest. You've gotten the entire community together on this issue. This is a good thing. I get it now."

"You do?"

He stepped closer to the counter and leaned forward, extending his hand to take mine. "I do. I'm sorry I didn't before." He chuckled. "And I have to admit, I'm a little jealous."

"You are?" What in the world would he have to be jealous of?

"Yeah, look how quickly you rallied the entire town around a single cause. If you weren't so good at what you do, the hospital would be knocking on your door to give you my job. Think you can take up a cause at the hospital next to scrounge up some new volunteers for me?"

Ah, that made a lot more sense. He wasn't jealous of my ghost-seeing or my matchmaking. "One case at a time," I answered with a smirk. "But you never know when and where a match might strike next."

"I really am sorry. Can we try this again?"

"Daddy? I'm hungry," Ivy said, her voice muffled by the flowers in front of her mouth.

Ken looked down at his daughter. "What do you say we go grab an early dinner at Dawg Pound after this?"

"Yes please!" No amount of flowers could muffle her excitement. It was her favorite place to go in town.

In the kitchen, a chair scraped against the floor, and the door between the kitchen and the shop swung open. "Hope you don't mind a third. Joanie's going to go with you."

Ken didn't miss a beat. "Of course. We'd love to have you come, Joanie."

"Oh goodie!" Ivy cheered.

"What? But we're still open—"

Sarah put her hands on her hips. "And I've got it handled.

I'm perfectly capable of cleaning the shop and closing up for the evening. You go. Have fun." She tilted her head at me and dropped her chin toward her chest, daring me to say no.

Throwing my hands up in surrender, I glanced at Sarah before turning to Ken and Ivy. "Okay, you don't need to tell me twice. Give me a minute to get washed up and I'll be ready to go."

Sarah followed me as I darted into the kitchen. "Are you sure you're good?" I asked.

"You need this. He's a good guy, and it's clear you're both still into each other. You deserve to be happy. I've hated seeing you mope in the quiet moments. Go for it and have fun."

I removed my apron. "Thanks. I'll owe you."

She waved me off. "Eh, you'll get one of my Wednesdays. It's all good. Now go, will you?"

After washing my hands and making sure I didn't have flour smeared anywhere, I scooted back into the bakery and ducked under the counter to grab my purse. "Ready to go?"

"Um . . ." Ken's eyes darted to Ivy.

Laughter bubbled out of me as I realized she was still holding Ken's larger bouquet. I took the vase from her, then grabbed hold of the one she'd originally given me before moving both to the now empty day-old shelf. I'd have to come back for them. As much as I liked fresh flowers, there wasn't a suitable space in the bakery for them. Saffy was going to be so excited when I got home. She loved flowers. Not that I was going to give them to her.

Returning to Ken and Ivy, I asked, "Shall we go?"

"Lead the way." Ken swept his arm out in front of him.

Ivy took that as her cue to run out of the bakery and to the corner of Founder's Park, directly across the street from Dawg Pound.

Laughing over her show of enthusiasm, Ken and I stepped out of the shop. When we were both on the sidewalk, Ken stuck his elbow out, and I looped my arm through his.

I didn't get the tingling feeling or the swarming butterflies I always got when two people who were destined to be together were near each other, but I felt calmer than I had in days. More centered. Maybe I was meant to be with someone after all.

CHAPTER 37

After a lovely unexpected date afternoon with Ken and Ivy that turned into a date night with popcorn and a movie, the rest of the week flew by. I still hadn't found the knife, and neither Dale nor Juniper had reappeared. With so much to get ready for the tree planting, however, none of that had been at the forefront of my thoughts.

The morning of the tree planting, we all showed up early to the bakery. Unlike with the tree festival, the bakery would remain open during the event, so we needed to stock the bakery and make enough scones to feed the volunteers. Lauren, who had worked in the bakery before transitioning to the shop, arrived as backup to help with the extra load. Now that she was done with her finals, she was more than happy to get back to work.

By eight am, I was up in the north woods with the first load of scones. The event wouldn't kick off until ten, but there was plenty to do in the meantime.

John met me at the entrance to the forest, stepping out of his pickup truck. "Morning, Joanie."

"Morning. How are things?"

He smiled. "You know? It's going well. I'm excited about today." He waved me over and started walking to the truck bed. "Come, let me show you what I have."

I followed him to the back and saw hundreds of foot-tall saplings. "Are these all pines?" I really had to start learning my tree species.

"Yes. I have a guy coming closer to ten with a few other varieties and some larger saplings that will hopefully encourage these to do their thing."

"That's wonderful. Thank you again for donating all these trees."

"It's the least I could do. After all that happened with my family, I made a point to never take another living tree down to do what I do. And I haven't. Using reclaimed wood has been great, but I always felt like it might not be enough. So I donated money to various forestry charities."

He shrugged. "Still, I have been wanting to do more, and until you made me aware of the situation here, I didn't know what that more would be. This is it, so thank you."

"I think this is going to go a long way to fixing the town's opinion of you and your family. It was never fair to you because you weren't a part of it, but unfortunately, that's the way it is sometimes. I get it."

"So what do you need help with?"

"I have a table and several boxes of scones in the back that I have to set up, but that's nothing major. Have you ever done a replanting before? How are they done? I've never been to one."

He laughed. "I'll help you move your table if you'd like, then leave you to the baked goods, but don't worry, I've got the replanting logistics covered."

"Sounds good."

As I set up my table near the start of the clearing, John

dragged several more tables out from his cab and set them up in various sections of the tree-cleared area. Then he began unloading the trees, bringing them in a wheelbarrow to each of the tables.

"Huh," I found myself saying out loud at John's setup.

"He's a good one. Handsome too. Looks a lot like his grandfather did when he was younger."

"Sh . . . ugar!" I jumped at the voice, then turned to find Juniper standing behind me.

Amusement twinkled in her eyes. "I have to admit, I do enjoy doing that. Makes me wish more people could see me. I'd do it to everyone."

"I'm glad I can be of service."

"Oh, pish. You're doing a lot more than that. Look at how much you've accomplished. And Lily is so happy."

"They're really good for one another."

She nodded. "I don't have much time, but I wanted to wish you well with this today and to thank you. My kind has avoided this forest for far too long. We used to love it so. I hope we can again."

She poofed from sight before I could respond. I hoped that if she had made an appearance, Dale would as well. Once the woods started to heal, I believed whatever was keeping them on this side of existence would be resolved. Both had been harmed through Dale's and then his son's actions. Juniper had ultimately paid with her life, but Dale had never been the same, likely feeling guilty for what had occurred up in the north woods.

I finished setting up the table and then checked my phone. There was no signal all the way out here, but it could still tell the time. Gary would be here at any moment with the coffee and another batch of scones.

I was walking back toward my car when his Jeep turned

onto the path. He parked behind my station wagon, and I was unsurprised to see Lily in the passenger seat. There was no way she was going to miss this, but after a minute, neither she nor Gary had moved. As I approached the Jeep, Gary finally got out.

"She needs another minute," he called, then opened the fifth door at the back of his Jeep, disappearing behind it for a moment. He reappeared holding three large carafes of coffee, the kind you'd see at conferences or in hotel lobbies. "Got a place for these? I've got creamer, cups, and sugar still to grab."

I pointed to my long table. "There's a good start, but we can probably distribute them among the tables John's got set up so no one has to walk too far for a refill."

He dropped off the carafes and turned to go back to his Jeep.

I took a step to follow him.

"Nah, I got this. Don't worry about it."

"I have to get my scones."

"Lily can get them when she's ready. She needs a few more minutes. She, uh, really cares about nature, and this is hard for her to see."

"Gary, I know about Lily."

He stopped in his tracks. "What do you mean?"

How could I word this in case he actually didn't know what she was? "I know why seeing all of these trees cut down like this bothers her. That her grandmother was one of the six who were . . . who were reported to have gone missing. And I know there was more to it than that."

His shoulders relaxed. "You can come out and say it, Joanie. I know all about it."

I hoped he was right as I said, "I know she's a dryad."

"How'd you figure that one out?"

"It wasn't easy, but I got her to tell me."

He glanced back at the car, eyes widening. "Why didn't she tell me you knew?"

I raised an eyebrow. "Why would she tell you?"

"I'm her uncle."

My mouth dropped. "You do not look old enough to be her uncle. The one she lived with?"

"Ha, no. I'm only four years older than her. There were just a lot of us. I'm the youngest of the lot. Juniper was my mom."

"So you're . . ."

"Yep, a rare male dryad." I wondered how rare if I knew two of them. "Come on, you had to have realized the logo of the coffee shop was a dryad."

I shook my head. "Guess I need to take a closer look at my cup next time."

"Well, come on, then. Maybe you can talk Lily out of the Jeep."

I walked up to Lily's side of the Jeep and knocked on the door before opening it. "You okay?"

She nodded, although tears streamed her face.

"You ready to get out?"

She shook her head.

I patted her knee. "This must be hard for you, but when you're ready, John and I could use the help."

"John's here?" She shifted so her legs were hanging out of the Jeep.

"Yeah. He's walking around setting up tree planting stations."

She slid off the seat, jumping to the ground. She threw her arms around me. "Thank you," she whispered.

I hugged her back. "You're very welcome."

She pulled away and wiped her eyes with the heels of her palms. Then she took a deep breath. "Okay."

Lily opened the back passenger door, giving me access to three boxes of scones. I waited off to the side as Lily grabbed the remaining two boxes from behind the driver's seat. We said little on the short walk back to the table I had set up. Lily still seemed a bit overwhelmed by everything around her, but as she paused momentarily to take in John working with the trees, his back to her, the intensity of my matchmaking tingle increased.

We put our boxes down, and Lily immediately opened one. She pulled out two scones. "I'm going to go see if John needs anything."

"All right." It was good to see her smile back. She took off across the clearing, her yellow-pink ponytail swaying this way and that. He turned, and even from a distance, his grin was visible. Lily raised her arms up, and he spread his out low. She jumped into his awaiting embrace, completely unfazed by his dirt-covered hands. He lifted her up, and they spun in a circle before he set her back down. After he wiped his hands off on his pants, Lily gave him a scone as they walked back to his truck.

Gary cleared his throat, making me jump. That was twice I'd been startled here despite the quiet. Not even birds were chirping. I would have thought I'd hear anything that came near me.

He grabbed a cup from the stack and poured coffee into it, then handed it to me before pouring a second cup for himself.

"Enjoy it while you can," he said, a small smile on his face. "It's going to get busy soon."

CHAPTER 38

G ary wasn't kidding. At quarter to ten, the villagers arrived en masse, led by Steph and Alex, Rich and Ashley, and Ken and Ivy. My heart swelled.

And then I was quickly overwhelmed. I had expected a large turnout, but I hadn't expected them to all show up at once.

"Alex and Rich pulled some strings," Steph told me. "Two school buses are parked as far as they could go. We walked the rest of the way."

"Buses? Up here?" I couldn't picture it with all the dirt roads. My station wagon's ability to make it had worried me enough, nevermind buses.

"You'd be surprised where they can get to."

"But where will they turn around?"

Steph laughed. "If we hadn't stopped to come up this trail the other day, you would have seen it all loops back around. There will be no stuck buses today, I promise. This is the only newsmaker around. Ready for that interview?"

"Let's do it." We moved to a quiet section of the woods off

to the side and talked for the next fifteen minutes so she could get enough for tomorrow's paper.

After the interview, I returned to the table to finish my coffee and make sure there were still enough scones. The food offerings had multiplied while I was gone. Boxes of bananas and apples sat next to the table along with three cases of bottled water, all courtesy of the local grocery store.

I looked out across the open expanse, now full of people working together to restore what had once been here. To my right, Alex led several members of the football team in clearing some trees that had been cut down and left here years ago. He was using a chainsaw to cut them up, and the boys were hauling the sections away. Bryan had come up to the woods too, and was leading a second team of boys. Wrestlers, I was told. To my left, members of the village gardening club stood around a sapling in a hole, getting a lesson in how to prep the soil for its planting. Straight ahead, villagers from all walks of life dug holes, carried saplings, and patted the earth back into place. Earlier today, the stillness of the woods had caused me to jump at every small noise. Now the lack of noise had been replaced by happy chitchat, the occasional burst of laughter, shovels slicing into the dirt, saws cutting wood, and the occasional drilling noise. I didn't know what John was doing with the drill, but I trusted him.

After refilling my coffee, I set off in search of Ken and Ivy. I found them at the far side of the woods with several adults and children.

Ivy ran toward me as I drew nearer. "Come see what we're doing." She grabbed my free hand and hurried me along.

Ken smiled when he looked up and our gazes met. He'd been kneeling on the ground, packing the earth around one of the larger saplings John's friend had brought. He stood, wiping the dirt from his hands onto his knees.

"You came," I said, my voice barely above a whisper, betraying how touched I felt by his show of support.

"Of course I did. After having to miss most of the tree fest last week, no way was I going to miss out on this when it's this important to you." He kissed me on the forehead, then gestured toward the others he was near. "These are some of the people I work with and their families."

I recognized many of their faces and some of their names, figuring that anyone I didn't know wasn't from town. The hospital employed people from all over the region.

"I may have pulled some strings and pointed out how community volunteerism goes both ways. We can't expect people to come help us if we don't go out to help the community when we're able."

Ivy tugged on my shirt. "Joanie, I planted this tree." She pointed to a sapling, and I did a double take. It was sticking out of a stump.

"I thought the same thing when we were told to do a few like that, but John said that by digging down into the center of the heartwood and adding the dirt, the sapling could use the older tree as nourishment to grow."

"So in a way, they weren't cut down in vain," I said quietly, my heart melting at the thought John had put into this.

"Isn't it cool?" Ivy said.

"Very cool. It's great to see you two here. I'm going to go check on the others, but have fun, make sure you're getting enough to drink, and take a break if you need to."

"Dinner after?" Ken looked hopeful.

"I'm going to have to stay after a bit to help clean up, but if you don't mind waiting . . ."

"I don't mind."

"Great. I'm looking forward to it."

He reached for my hand and pulled me toward him so he could kiss my cheek. "Me too."

I walked away feeling a light stirring in my stomach. It wasn't butterflies, but it was something.

Lily was with John when I found her. They had planted dozens of trees between the two of them along with Gary, Holly, Steph, and three others from town. They were with two others I didn't recognize, but there was something familiar about them.

Lily rushed up to me. "Joanie, come meet my parents."

"Your parents?"

"Uh-huh," she said excitedly. "They came just for this." She turned and hurried back to them.

As I closed the gap between us, the smile on my face widened. The matchmaking tingle I got was stronger than I'd ever felt it. No doubt Lily's parents had been destined to be together too.

"Mom, Dad, this is my boss, Joanie. She's the one who arranged all this."

Her dad took my hand in his and shook it heartily, and as he stepped back, her mom threw her arms around me. "Thank you so much for what you've done. My mother would have loved this."

"It's my pleasure. When I found out, I had to do something. I hope anyone in my position would have done the same."

"No. You're a special one," her mom said. "We live a few hours away now, but if you ever need anything, don't hesitate to ask."

"I do have one question."

"Name it."

I looked at Lily's dad. "Are you one of those rare male dryads too?"

The family laughed. "No, not me. I'm as human as you are, although maybe more than you if my wife is correct."

"And you know I am," his wife replied, batting her eyelashes at him.

"These dryad women have a way about them. Good luck to you," her dad said to John.

"I'm learning that." John chuckled. "But I think we'll do just fine." He wrapped an arm behind Lily and pulled her close.

"Three generations of dryads and lumbermen, what are the odds?" Lily's mom commented.

I turned to Lily's dad. "You work in the industry?"

"Did. I drove a truck for the Singers. Obviously I left after what happened in the north woods."

"So your mom was the first?" I asked Lily's mom. "Your dad was a lumberman?"

"Oh no," she explained. "She loved one, but they never ended up together. My father was a teacher."

"Huh, she never told me that," I mumbled. Pieces of the mystery clicked in my head. I needed to get Dale and Juniper together in the same spot. If I could get them talking...

"I'm sorry, what?" Lily's mom studied me curiously.

I shook my head. "Sorry, I was talking to myself. I do that sometimes."

At that moment, Gary, Holly, and the three townspeople approached us after drifting away to plant other trees while we talked. "Joanie, this is Hawthorne, Rowan, and Cindy. They're also dryads."

"It's so good to meet you all. I recognize all your faces from over the years, but it's nice to put a name to them. Thank you for trusting me with your secret."

Rowan stepped forward. "We'd like to volunteer to take care of this fledgling grove to ensure that it thrives. We never want to see something like this happen anywhere near here again."

"That would be wonderful! Thank you."

"No, thank you, Joanie. Never did we imagine we'd be back in the north woods. Now I look forward to the time when I can come and exist here in my natural state."

I nodded. Together we worked for a little while, but I still had other people to see. "Thank you all for coming. I should go check in with some of the other volunteers." I repeated my reminder for them to get plenty of fluids, food, and rest if they needed it.

For the rest of the event, I bounced from group to group, planting saplings with everyone I could. By two, one of the buses took those who needed to leave back to the village, but many stayed. By four, we were done. All the trees were in the ground.

We'd started something here today, but I wasn't done yet.

CHAPTER 39

As Lily, John, Ken, and Ivy loaded up my station wagon and John's truck, I asked if they could come over to my house on Tuesday. It was too much of a coincidence that Juniper had been in love with a lumberman. It had to be Dale. If I could get the two of them together in the same room, then I had a feeling all of this would be settled. The forest, the knife, Dale and Juniper's being stuck here, John and Lily's relationship. Everyone agreed, including Ken. He'd been present for the last group summoning and had seen it work. His belief I could do it again meant more than I could say.

Sunday and Monday came and went. The last of the tree festival tourists left before the weekend ended. Lily's parents stopped in to get some treats to go. They also wanted to see where their daughter worked since this was the first time they'd been here since I'd opened. They thanked me again for my part in healing the north woods and left after promising they'd be back.

Tuesday came, and I awoke with nervous excitement in my gut. I preferred the butterflies. The feeling made me antsy, no matter what tea I had, and reading more of my book became a wasted effort. Every page or so, I'd lose my place and have to find it again. So I turned to cleaning to keep me occupied. Saffy took an immediate interest in the feather duster.

"People are coming over." She probably figured that from my tidying up. "I need you on your best behavior. There will be some catnip in it for you."

She didn't even beg for her extra meal at lunchtime. That was how badly she wanted her mouse again.

At two, the "people" came bearing pizza. It helped to have everyone comfortable, happy, and fed. Neither John nor Lily had been here before. Ken obviously had. Unsurprisingly, Saffy turned her back on him the moment he walked through the door, although she looked over her shoulder to make sure Ivy wasn't following. He was the reason I hadn't told her who was coming. I hadn't wanted the silent judgment I would have gotten until everyone arrived.

"Here, kitty kitty," Lily called, distracting Saffy from Ken. Saffy walked over to my baker and reached her head out to sniff Lily's offered hand before rubbing up against her leg. In jean shorts, Lily smiled and transformed her leg into wood. "What do you think of that?"

Saffy repeatedly ran her cheeks across the rough surface before reaching up to Lily's knee. She picked at her leg like she would a scratching post.

"Saffy, stop that," I scolded.

"Oh, she's all right," Lily assured me.

"Doesn't that hurt? Her claws are no joke." I was lucky to get one or two trimmed at a time.

"Not at all. It's a bit of exfoliation for me if anything." She laughed. "Benefits of a wooden leg."

"Okay, as long as you say so." Hopefully Saffy wouldn't get any ideas about doing this to other guests I had in the future.

Lily turned to John, putting a hand on his leg. "You know what we should make with some of the smaller pieces of the salvaged trees?"

"What?"

She pointed down to Saffy. "Cat trees and scratching posts. I think we have a good product tester right here." She leaned down to pet Saffy's head.

"You're using the wood from the north woods?" I asked, surprise evident in my voice.

"Anything the dryads deemed to not be sacred, I got their blessing to turn into something," John explained. "What was usable anyway. It has been sitting out in the elements for years. You may have noticed several trees that we left fallen where they lay. Those were sacred."

"We will have a ceremony for them when it's time," Lily added.

I nodded my approval.

"What's going on today, Joanie? Why did you want us to come?" John asked through a bite of pizza.

"As you all know, I see ghosts. I've seen both of your grandparents in the last couple of weeks. As much as we have begun to heal the forest, this won't be over until Juniper and Dale are happy. Something she said, and something your mom said, has stuck with me. Juniper said John was handsome like his grandfather when I saw her at the tree festival. And then your mom talked about your grandmother being in love with a lumberjack. I'm certain your grandmother's lumberjack love was Dale. And what if Dale's grief wasn't over what happened to the north woods in its entirety but what happened to Juniper? With your help, I'm hoping we can get the two together to talk and settle this once and for all."

"Is that why you had me bring something that belonged to her?" Lily asked.

I nodded.

"What both of you brought today still holds the energies of your deceased grandparents. It should be enough to call upon them."

John swallowed another bite of food. "So what, you have a Ouija board?"

"Oh goodness, no. I'd never bring one of those in here. That would invite way too many bad spirits to join us. No, we're doing it with candles, sage, and silver."

John nodded slowly, likely skeptical of the whole thing. I couldn't blame him. Until I had been forced to try it due to a lack of options when I was trying to help Kate, I would have doubted the validity of any sort of séance or summoning.

"Oh, I'm so excited." Lily clutched her hands together against her chest. "It would be so nice to see my grandmother again. Even if only for a little while."

Once we'd eaten our fill of pizza, we filed into the kitchen —Saffy included. I'd already prepped the table for what we were about to do.

"If you both could place your objects next to each other's at the center of the table, then we can get seated and begin."

Lily reached behind her neck, unclasping the locket she'd been wearing. She placed it gently on the table.

John dug a small leather-bound book from his back pocket. "It was my grandfather's account book." He set it down next to the locket.

"All right," I said, pulling out a chair. "Please, sit."

Ken took the chair next to me. John slid out the chair on

the other side of me and motioned with his head for Lily to sit.

"Such a gentleman," she teased. John sat in the last open chair. Saffy sat next to Lily, either still mad at me for not telling her Ken would be here or hoping Lily would turn her leg into a living scratching post again.

I lit the candles, first the black and then the white. Before dousing the match, I lit my sage stick. A plume of smoke rose from the bundle. As I blew the smoke toward the four corners of the room, "to cleanse the space" as Gram would say, I marveled at how much more efficient this was than using crushed sage spice like I had done the last two times. Then I set the sage stick off to the side of the table on a little dish, tapping out most of the smoldering leaves. The rest would die out on their own as the energy level rose within the circle, drawing strength from the remaining embers.

"Now hands together," I instructed. "Do not break your hold on one another for any reason until I say so. Understood?"

They all nodded, Lily adding in a *yes* for good measure.

"Okay. Close your eyes. I'll tell you when to open them once I feel the energy shift."

I actually didn't know if this step helped or not, but I felt it blocked out any potential visual distractions that could occur outside the circle. Or in the circle, for that matter. My first group attempt at calling Kate forth had resulted in her seeming staticky. Fortunately, neither Ashley nor Rich had seen her that time. I didn't want to risk that happening again and someone seeing this time. It wouldn't do any good for Lily and John to see their relatives like that. I wanted everything to go right for them. *All* of them.

I called the two spirits forth using the words Gram had taught me, first Juniper and then Dale.

Within moments, the energy shifted, and I opened my eyes to see the locket chain lift into the air and the account book open, the pages within flipping back and forth. So far so good.

A minute passed, then another, then finally the forms of the two ghosts appeared. Both looked around at their surroundings before their gazes stopped on their respective relatives.

"Well, hello there," I said, drawing their attention to me. They both looked good. Whole. "Okay, you can open your eyes," I told the others.

John's mouth dropped open as Lily blinked rapidly as if to clear her vision. Ken's eyes held a mix of wonder and amusement. He'd been in their position not too long ago.

"Is this really happening?" John asked.

"She doesn't even look dead," Lily said. Juniper spun on her heels to face her granddaughter. "Grandma June." As Juniper smiled, Lily's grip went slack on my hand.

I tightened mine. "Stay holding on."

"Right, sorry."

Juniper reached out and stroked her granddaughter's cheek. "Oh, Lily. It is so good to see you again."

Lily leaned into her grandmother's hand. "She feels so real."

"I am real. You have grown up to be such a beautiful young woman. And so talented." She glanced at John. "And he's not so bad himself."

Lily blushed. "Grandma . . ."

"John, how are you doing?" I asked. He hadn't stopped staring at his grandfather, the two of them locked in some sort of unspoken exchange.

"I'm good. I'm good."

"Dale?"

He turned toward me.

"Can you speak?"

He shook his head, looking a bit defeated. Why? What was preventing him now? Kate had a hard time speaking until she had the energy from the circle, but what was Dale's issue? I didn't understand it. There should have been plenty of energy to draw on from within the circle.

"Can you see that you're not alone?"

Dale quickly looked to his left and right. Then he shrugged as if he was used to the disappointment.

I cleared my throat. "Juniper, do you see who else you're with?" Dale perked up at the name.

"I don't see anyone but the four of you at the table."

I dropped my head back and looked up. What was preventing them from being able to see one another?

"I was hoping you'd be able to see that you and Dale are together."

"Dale's here?" Her excited tone was one I knew well. She sounded just like Lily.

"You loved him, didn't you?"

"Still do. Oh, how I longed to be close to him. He'd sit in the woods for hours as a boy, even into adulthood, and I always turned into a tree near him so I could be close and give him as much shade as he wanted. He had this one spot he loved to go to, which is where I regularly took root. Of course, I should have just stayed there. Following him got me killed. Not that he realized until it was too late, poor man."

"Wait, I thought the dryads only had the ability to merge into one tree, that the skill to have multiple trees was learned only as a result of what happened."

"Oh, I came from a line of elder dryads. I could do a lot more than the others could." She lifted her hands, palms up. "See how far that got me?"

"But then why did you die? I thought if you had multiple trees, you'd be fine if something happened to one of them."

"Only if you're not in the tree when that something happens. Just my luck, huh?

One thing had been weighing on me since hearing how the dryads had died in the north woods. "So why not unmerge with the tree before you could be cut down? Surely that would have stopped whoever it was from continuing."

"We could have, but it wasn't that simple. We had families to think of. Revealing our secret would have put all of them at risk."

I understood now. "So you sacrificed yourselves to keep others safe. That's why it didn't stop after the first one. The loggers never realized what they'd done."

"No. And I only revealed myself because of who chopped me down. He had the power to stop what was happening. And he did."

Dale waved to catch my attention, then made the motion of checking his watch before pointing to the sage. The smoke had stopped, and the circle's energy was waning.

"One last question, Dale. Did you take the knife somewhere?"

He shook his head. So if neither of them had taken it, where had it gone? We needed to find out.

"Thank you for coming," I told Dale. "I hope to see you again."

He nodded once more before turning to John again. He saluted and blinked out of sight, leaving Juniper alone in the circle.

"Oh, that was a rush," she said. "He left, didn't he? I felt a small surge of energy."

"He did."

"That poor man. Don't think he ever forgave himself for

what happened. He needs to, though. It's strangling him. I forgave him long ago. He didn't know." She sighed. "All right, Lily. I'm going to go now too, but we'll see each other again before this is all over."

She sat on the table and then held her hand out toward her granddaughter. Lily looked at me, hopeful.

"Go ahead."

Lily dropped John's hands and mine, then clasped her grandmother's tightly. Juniper placed her other hand on top of Lily's. She gently patted it as she slowly faded from view. The energy stilled around us. She was gone.

But not for good.

This wasn't over.

We needed to find that knife.

CHAPTER 40

A storm rolled in later that evening, charging the air. It rained throughout the night with occasional thunderstorms. Poor Saffy moved to her secondary spot, surrounding my head with hers smooshed down into the bend of my neck. She hated the booming thunder and flashes of lightning.

I hoped Dale was still around and able to soak it in. We needed him to have enough energy in case we needed to call on him again.

The next morning was still rainy. It had been a while since we'd had a soaker like this. Good for the new trees but not for my deliveries.

I parked my car in the lot behind the bakery and jogged to the back door, unlocking it and quickly stepping inside the kitchen. Only one person I knew liked the rain this much, and she would be arriving soon enough.

Only she didn't seem happy about the weather when she stomped in drenched head to toe.

"Lily, what's wrong?"

"Nothing. Give me a minute." She pointed to a backpack covered with plastic before trudging off into the bathroom.

She emerged a few minutes later, dryer, but her mood no better.

I called her into the shop as Gina and Sam showed up.

"Lily"—I placed my hands on her shoulders—"what happened?"

She sighed deeply. "John and I had a fight. It might be over."

"A fight?" My heart sunk. "What happened?"

"He called me stupid for going outside in the storm."

"That can't be all that happened . . ."

"Fine. He said it was a bad idea for me to be out in the storm. I told him I love storms. That they refresh me. I've been doing this all my life. Then he asked if I realized things like trees get struck by lightning all the time, saying that's why you don't seek cover under one during a storm."

She crossed her arms, and I pictured her doing the same during their argument. "I told him it wouldn't happen. That plenty of other things sought out the rain and were fine. Do you know what he said?"

I shook my head.

"Worms did that. Worms! Then he told me to not be stupid and asked why I couldn't just turn into a bush instead because they're shorter."

I needed her to finish her rant, but internally I sighed in relief. This could be fixed.

"Doesn't he get that he mocked me for who I am? I can't help it if being out in storms makes me feel alive. The whole earth buzzes with energy. It's amazing."

"I'll take your word for it. I'm more of a read a book inside while listening to the rain on the roof type of person."

"He doesn't understand me. If he did, he'd never have said those things." She tugged at her wet ponytail. "And a bush. Really?"

"So what did you do?"

"I went outside and found a nice tree. It was way too amazing of a storm to pass up. And all that rain! I got to drive my roots down deep and soak it all up."

Her talking about the rain seemed to restore her mood. It was now close to what I had been expecting it to be this morning. The rain always made her happy. I had to tap on that.

"There. Drink in that feeling you're in right now as you listen to me and consider what I'm about to say. Do you think he could have been afraid for you? You've been doing this your whole life. He's been doing it for what, not even three weeks? There are going to be bumps in the road with any relationship, but I've seen you two together. You complement each other perfectly. It's almost poetic. A furniture maker and the son of a lumberjack falls in love with a woman who can turn into a tree."

She smiled, but it was short lived. "But he called me—"

"I know. But think about it. He was worried that if you were the tallest thing around that the lightning would be attracted to you. And would you survive a lightning strike?"

She shook her head. "I doubt it. I don't know that any of us have been hit by lightning to say, but I've seen plenty of trees burning from the inside over the years. They weren't dryads, though."

"He may not have said the right things in the right way, but I think it was coming from the right place. I mean, if you weren't a dryad, do you really think you would have been going outside in last night's storm? The lightning was intense at times. My cat was freaked out, and I barely got any sleep. As kids, we're all told to come inside when there's lightning, not to run outside and enjoy it. I can only imagine how a storm like that might affect someone who grew up his whole life paying attention to the storms because his family was surrounded by trees that could cause a lot of damage to nearby people if they were struck.

She sighed. "I hadn't thought about it like that... Oh, I don't know, Joanie. I don't want him thinking that he can control my life if we're together."

"He let you go outside, didn't he?"

"I didn't really give him a choice, but yes."

A thought occurred to me then. "Does he know you're okay?"

"No." I gave her a look, and she held her arms out in front of her. "I was mad. No way was I calling him to tell him I made it home safe. I stayed out all night. Grabbing the bag of dry clothes was the only time I've stepped foot in my house since the thing we all did yesterday."

"Okay, well text him at least. I doubt he's slept. Or if he has, it was because he passed out exhausted. I'm not saying to forgive him but try to cut him a little slack. He's learning how to navigate all of this."

"So are you"—she crossed her arms—"but you're not calling me stupid for being outside. Even before you knew, you never said anything about my coming in soaked."

"Yeah, but I'm not normal either. I've been dealing with the whole seeing ghosts thing since I was a kid. It's a bit easier for me to accept all of this."

With a sigh, Lily let her arms fall to her sides. "I guess you're right. He was already overwhelmed after seeing his grandpa yesterday. And I was too about seeing Grandma June. I'll text him."

"Good. So are you all right now? I don't have to worry about you biting Bryan's head off for a comment about your hair being wet?"

She smiled. "I'm good. Despite this, the storm did me a world of good."

I stepped back into the kitchen, Lily close on my heels.

Everyone had gotten started without us, and it made my heart happy to see them so self-sufficient. "You all are going to make me feel like taking a vacation with how well you do without me."

"When was the last time you had a vacation?" Sam asked as he rolled out a ball of cookie dough.

"Well, we had to close the bakery for a few days during the blizzard two years ago when the garage door broke and they couldn't get the plows out."

Gina plopped her scone dough onto a tray. "That's *not* a vacation."

"Well, that's what I got. I read five or six books and stayed in bed until seven. It counted for me."

Gina looked at Sam, both shaking their heads in disappointment.

"You and Ken should get away and go somewhere."

The idea had appeal, though I didn't know what sort of time he got off at his job, and he had Ivy to consider.

"Maybe someday."

They didn't say anything but continued shaking their heads until work consumed them once more.

Wednesdays were always slow. The rain was only going to make it slower. By the time I got back from my delivery to Double Aitch and the Olde Templeton Diner, it was still raining, and I knew we were close to done with the baking.

"All right, everyone. Head home when you're finished working on the batch you have going. Sam, I can jump on your station if you want to give yourself an extra few minutes to get to school on account of the weather."

"You sure?" he asked.

"Yeah, nothing I can't handle."

"Thanks, Joanie. I appreciate it." He stepped back from his cookies, wiping his hands on his apron.

Gina cut her scones into shape. "All I have left to do is pop these in the oven and wait for them to come out."

Bryan pulled a tray of muffins from the oven, then placed it on the cooling rack. "This is it for me, then clean up."

"I can stay if you want me too," Lily offered. "Sarah's not even in yet."

I raised my eyebrow at her. "Have you done what I asked?"

"If I do it now, can I stay?"

"Yes."

She whipped out her cell phone and at least appeared to shoot a text to John.

"Thank you," I said when she slipped it back into her pocket.

She smiled, glancing at me but overall avoiding my gaze.

Within the next half hour, the kitchen cleared out, leaving Lily and me alone.

"Has he texted you back?"

"It's been vibrating nonstop since I sent it."

"You gonna call him back?"

She smirked. "When I head home. Let him sit on things a little longer."

I shook my head but didn't argue.

Together we loaded up the cases, finishing as Sarah walked in the door, a bright yellow umbrella protecting her from the rain.

She closed the umbrella, shaking it outside before pulling her arms in and letting the door close. "Am I late?"

"Nope." I stood from behind the case. "Didn't need as much today. You know how Wednesdays are."

"I'm going to take off, Joanie," Lily said, standing after she'd filled her case. "I'll see you tomorrow."

"All right. And take care of that, will you?"

She gave me a half smile. "I will. Maybe a few more minutes, though. Don't want to get my phone wet."

Thank goodness she only lived around the corner.

CHAPTER 41

The day had been even slower than I'd expected. Although it was her week to close, I let Sarah go early to make up for her covering for me when I went to Dawg Pound with Ken and Ivy. I even contemplated closing early, but I'd always said I wouldn't do that just in case there was someone counting on me to be there in those last five minutes of the day.

Ken and Ivy shuffled in six minutes before closing.

"Hello, you two. Come in for a cookie or maybe a muffin? They're great warmed up in this weather."

Ivy wrinkled her nose at the muffin idea. "Can I have a cookie?"

"If it's all right with your dad."

She looked straight up at Ken. "Can I?"

"Sure thing. Go pick one out." As she approached the case, he lifted his fist up, sticking his pinky in the air. He made a winding motion around his finger.

I stifled a laugh. Yes, Ivy had him wrapped around her finger. At least he admitted it.

"How are things going since yesterday?" he asked. "Any resolution?"

"No, and today it seemed to take a step backward." I told him about John and Lily's fight.

Rather than saying I told you so—something he likely would have the night he broke up with me at the restaurant had the fight happened then—he said, "John will come around. It's all still new to him. One minute you can accept it all, and then something will throw you for a loop the next."

We'd tried to be quiet for Ivy's sake, but clearly, it wasn't enough.

"Was she not wearing her raincoat and boots? Daddy won't let me go outside without them." Ivy lifted her leg to show off her pink and purple polka dot boots.

"Something like that."

"Well, that's silly of her. He just wanted her feet to stay dry. I hate wet socks."

"Same here, Ivy." I smiled warmly. "Decide what you want?"

"Uh-huh." She pointed at a lavender lime cookie.

"So is there anything you can do about it?" Ken asked as I dug the cookie out of the case.

I placed it in a bag before handing it to Ivy. I'd already swept and didn't want any more crumbs. "I told her to cut him a bit of slack and to talk to him, but I can't make her do anything she's not ready to do. She's not going to let anyone make up her mind for her or push her around."

He gave me a look. "Sounds like someone else I know."

Heat crept up my neck into my face. It didn't escape me that a lot of Lily's and John's issues this week had echoed mine and Ken's. No doubt Ken had been speaking from experience a few minutes ago. I was glad he had come around.

"So you told me about John and Lily, but what about Dale and Juniper? I get nothing's resolved yet, but anything new?"

"Nothing. I need to find that knife. It's what brought John here that day, and I think we need it to fix the rest of everything going on. The replanting was a big help, but this is that last missing piece. But how do you find something like that? It could be anywhere."

"Look back at the beginning," Ivy suggested, her mouth half-full with a bite of cookie. Fortunately, she was using her hands to catch crumbs as she spoke.

"What do you mean?" I asked.

"All the best stories do it. The thing's where no one thought to look because they'd already been there. But it was hiding in plain sight all along. You know, like how the wizard boy has to return home to get a piece of the puzzle even though he's not lived here since he was a little baby. Or how the one knight had to go back to the lake where he got the sword. Or how the prince had to go to all the houses to find the girl who fit the sneaker but turns out she was in the castle all along."

"That's a good idea, kiddo," Ken said. He turned to me. "It's better than any ideas we have right now. So if something was made of wood . . ."

She jumped up and down. "It would be back in the forest and the tree it came from!"

Ken's eyes widened as he turned his head toward me. "Are you thinking what I'm thinking?"

"That we have to go find a knife in the woods?" My look likely mirrored his own.

"Given what's happened up there, that might not be easy."

"No," I agreed, "but I'm going to call for backup."

"Well, we're coming too."

I pulled off my apron. It was two minutes after closing. "Both of you?"

He nodded.

"You don't have to do that. I know you've wanted to keep a distance with"—my gaze darted to Ivy—"things."

"It was her idea, and I dunno, I want to see her idea pay off. She should be there to see it too."

"All right. Well, I have to make a couple phone calls, but let's get to it."

I called Lily and left a voicemail to meet me up at the north woods no matter what time she got my message unless I'd already called back. Then I called John, hoping Lily would be with him. He and Lily had talked, but they hadn't fully made up, although she'd apologized for taking off and he'd apologized for what he'd said. Now he was mad that she made him worry for so long about whether she was okay. I'd never tell her, but I sided with him on that one. It was something they could work out, though. Of that I had no doubt.

"Can you meet me at the north woods?" I asked him.

"In this weather?" His tone suggested he thought I was like Lily when it came to the rain.

"Yes. I think I know where the knife is, and we have to find it. Now. The same way the weather energizes Lily, it may do the same thing to your grandfather, and we need him."

"Okay. Let me grab my boots and rain jacket and I'll head on out."

"Great. I'm going to run home, grab my supplies, and I'll see you there." I hung up the bakery phone and turned back toward Ken and Ivy. "Shall we?"

CHAPTER 42

The north woods was a giant mud puddle thanks to all the rain, and I was grateful Ken offered to drive us in his SUV. I wasn't sure if my station wagon could have handled the trip.

We pulled off the side of the pathway leading to the woods, parking behind John's truck, Gary's Jeep, and Steph's SUV.

I stepped out of the car into a heavy drizzle that could change back to a rainstorm at any moment. The trees buzzed with energy, a noise I'd never heard before. Something between a hum and a cicada song.

As we walked toward the forest, passing the other vehicles, John got out of his truck. The others were unoccupied. "They were empty when I got here. Do you think they're out here to get energy?"

"It's possible. You can hear the noise too right?" When he nodded, I continued, "They have been coming up here regularly since the replanting to keep watch over the new trees."

Ken, Ivy, John, and I stepped foot into the newly replanted forest.

Before our eyes, Lily emerged from a tree along the perimeter.

"Oh my gosh!" Ivy cried. "I live in a fairy tale. Daddy, did you see her? She just came out of a tree! I love it here!"

I smiled. She'd taken the truth better than any of us had when we first found out.

"Joanie? John? What are you doing here?" Lily asked. "Is everything okay?"

"Did you get my voicemail?"

"No, I've been here since you let me leave this morning, soaking this all in. The others not as long, but they're here for the same reason. What's going on?"

As I explained my hypothesis, Holly, Gary, Steph, and Alex separated from their trees and approached us, wanting to know what was happening.

Ivy was beside herself with the revelation that there were more tree people. She walked around each one of them, studying them.

"I know you," she said to Gary. "You make really good hot chocolate."

"Why, thank you. So what do you think about the fairy tale you live in?"

"It's so cool!" She hopped up and down, the mud splashing out from under her.

He squatted down to get on her level. "Well, now that you know the secret, you get to become a character in the story."

"I do?" She practically vibrated with excitement.

"Uh-huh. And it's a really important character too. You get to be a guardian and help protect our secret. Do you think you can do it?"

She nodded solemnly. "I *know* I can."

"You can't tell anyone or talk about it with anyone who isn't here."

"I won't." Ivy crossed her heart and took a step back to be at Ken's side once more. Then she tugged on his jacket.

"What's up, kiddo?"

"Daddy, I'm a guardian."

"That's awesome, kiddo. I think you're going to be a great guardian. You're great at keeping secrets."

"Okay, so how do we do this?" John asked. "We can't really light candles out here or keep your sage burning."

"We're just going to have to trust that the energy from the storms has been enough. With the extra bodies here, I think we can do it. That's if you're all staying, of course."

"And miss out on whatever this is?" Steph said. "No way am I leaving."

"Same," Alex agreed.

"Juniper was my grandma too," Holly added.

"And my mom." Gary smiled. "You're stuck with us."

"I'm thrilled to have you all. Okay, I'm going to need us to all stand in a circle. Join hands and don't let go for anything." I looked at Ivy. "Think you can do that?"

"Of course I can. I'm a guardian."

"That a girl." I was glad to see her taking her role so seriously because I was about to entrust her with my secret too.

We all joined hands, Ken on one side of me and John on the other. John held his hand out for Lily, and she took it, a gentle smile on her face. She mouthed the words "I'm sorry" to him. The tingle in my toes grew stronger. They'd be okay.

We all stepped backward until we were stretched out as far as possible. The only time we broke hold on one another was to encompass one of the taller saplings in the circle as we crossed its path.

"Okay, all of you, close your eyes. I'll tell you when to open them." As I spoke the now-familiar words from Gram, the air whipped around us, enough so that the leaves stirred even though they were heavy with rain. The energy shifted, and I opened my eyes. In the center of the circle stood Dale.

"It's good to see you again, Dale." When I determined he was okay, I said, "Everyone, you can open your eyes."

Dale smiled as he looked around the circle, his eyes lighting up as his gaze fell on Ivy. He waved at her, and she giggled.

"I hope you can help us."

He turned back to me and nodded.

"I think this is where your missing knife is."

He looked around.

"Somewhere around here. Not *here*, here. That's where you come in. Where was your special spot? The one you'd come to, to get away from everything during your time off?"

He took a step forward, then another and another until he reached the edge of the circle, stopping in front of Gary and Steph's joined hands.

"Joanie, we can't all walk as a circle through the woods," Steph said.

I agreed but hoped Dale was strong enough to withstand the circle being broken.

He had to be.

CHAPTER 43

This was the moment of truth.

"It's okay. Drop your hands."

I held my breath as Gary and Steph let go of each other's hands but didn't move otherwise, maintaining the circle. Dale stepped out from the inside and remained strong and visible. My breath escaped as a relieved sigh when he took another step forward.

He waved over his shoulder, beckoning us to follow.

"Well, let's do as he says."

The circle broke into pairs and triples. Steph stayed holding Alex's hand. Lily had John's. Gary had Holly's. I held onto Ken's, who kept his hold on Ivy. We led the group with John and Lily hot on our heels, but no one was far behind.

Dale led us farther north into a section of the woods that hadn't been clear cut. But the area soon thinned, highlighting a ginormous tree with branches that swooped down low. It reminded me of the tree mentioned in Libby's grandmother's book. The one that had destroyed the first logging camp in Dunmore Falls. That one had fallen, but this one was still going strong. Majestic in a way. Were all elders' trees like this?

Ivy pulled out of Ken's hold and ran toward the tree as Dale reached it. He put his hand on the trunk and patted it as if greeting an old friend. Ivy climbed on the lower branches to circle the massive trunk. Ken followed his daughter, likely making sure she didn't slip from the tree.

John and Lily searched the higher branches as did I.

"What are you looking for?" Gary asked.

"John's knife. It has a wooden handle made from your mother's heartwood."

"There's nothing here," Lily called, her hands on her hips.

"Might I point out that this tree is standing?" Gary said. "This was her main tree, but it's not where she died."

We were in the wrong place!

"Dale." He looked at me.

"How are you feeling?" I was worried that another walk through the woods would drain him of his energy before we could find the next spot. "Ready for another walk?"

He gave me a thumbs up.

"Great. I need you to take me to where you chopped the tree down that you made the knife out of."

Dale's shoulders slumped, but he nodded. He took off toward his right.

Ivy jumped from her branch and took off after him. We all did. We'd come this far, and we weren't going to lose him now.

There were no paths this time showing us where to go, but five minutes later, I knew we'd reached the spot.

Sitting cross-legged nearby was Juniper, her head down as if dozing. As we drew nearer, she lifted her head and opened her eyes.

"I see something," Ivy yelled, then took off.

"Don't touch it," I called after her.

She ran up to a spot right next to Juniper without even

glancing at her. I likely was the only one who could see her at that moment. She'd come on her own, not because we'd called her.

"It's here! It's here!" Ivy dropped to her knees and cleared away some of the wet leaves, revealing a short stump cut close to the ground's surface.

Stuck inside the center of the trunk was the knife.

We'd found it.

Juniper stood.

"How are you doing, Juniper?" I asked her. At the name, Dale perked up and looked around. Gary, Lily, and Holly did the same.

"I'm tired, but I'll be all right."

"Is there any way you can show yourself? We might need you."

"I can try." She closed her eyes and took a deep breath.

A moment later, the others gasped as she came into view.

"Mom?" Gary ran toward her, followed by Holly and Lily.

She reached out and caressed Gary's cheek before pulling him in for a hug. She extended an arm and pulled in Lily and Holly. The sight brought tears to my eyes. I let them have a moment and walked over to Dale and John.

"Dale, are you able to speak?"

He made a throat-clearing motion, then shook his head.

"How about Juniper? Can you see her?"

He peered over at the group hug and frowned. Somehow we had to get them to see each other and allow them to communicate. It had started with them. It had to end with them too.

"Oh, how I've longed to do this," Juniper cried after a minute or two. "I've missed you all so much. I've been able to check in on you, but to do this"—she squeezed them tighter

—"and actually hold you. It's more than I could have hoped for."

I patted Dale on the shoulder before approaching the still-hugging family.

"I hate to break this up, but I need to borrow Juniper and Lily." I wished I could give them all the time in the world to catch up, but I didn't know how much longer the ghosts' energies would allow them to remain.

They slowly released one another, and Gary and Holly stepped back to join Steph and Alex.

"If I could have the four of you stand over the tree stump."

"Do you know what you're doing, Joanie?" Lily asked.

"Honestly? I making this up as I go along." But it felt like the right thing to do.

"Well, I trust you," she said.

"Me too," added John.

Dale nodded.

I instructed the four of them on how to stand, two on one side and two on the other. Once they were in position, I told John to pick up the knife from the tree and hold it out for Lily to take as well. He closed the blade and set it in the palm of his hand. Then I asked both Dale and Juniper to touch the knife as well.

The moment they did, Juniper gasped. "Dale!"

"J-Juniper?"

She beamed, but tears began to run down her cheeks.

"I-I'm s-sorry for what I did to you."

"Oh, my love, I forgave you long ago. You didn't know. I just wanted to be close to you. I loved you since you were a little boy, following behind your father in the woods. You sat under my mother's shade and talked about your day. You didn't know that either, but I was nearby and heard you. It was something you did often as a child. I always enjoyed hearing about your day, but it made me shy to talk to you at school. I didn't want to say the wrong thing and have you wonder how I knew something you'd not told anyone but the trees."

"Y-you were always so kind to me even though you were quiet. I think you would have been easy to talk to."

"Eventually you did talk to me." She blushed. "You didn't stutter then."

"No. Never with the trees."

"I loved you, you know. Even after I married a wonderful man." She turned then toward her family. "I loved him too. I don't want you to think I didn't." Back to Dale, she added, "But you were always my first love."

"I-I loved you too. Both as a human and as a tree. When I saw your face appear on the trunk of this tree after cutting it down, I was devastated. That's why I made that knife. So I could always carry you with me. I didn't know your kind was real until then. I'd grown up hearing the stories, but that's what I thought they were. Stories."

"I don't blame you. How were you to have known?"

"I vowed to never touch this forest again. It destroyed me when I realized you hadn't been the only one killed up here."

As he spoke, the ghosts of five other dryads appeared. I only recognized Chrys, but I assumed the others were the fallen dryads. "We don't blame you either," Chrys said, "and neither do the others who got sick and died after their trees were cut down."

"Had you known it was possible, you wouldn't have done it," said another.

The next nodded. "Or we could have shown you what trees were safe to cut down."

"We should have been more forthcoming when it happened," the fourth one said.

"Maybe it's time more people knew we were real," Chrys said, the others nodding. She turned to me then. "Thank you for figuring it out." Then she glanced at John. "Sorry for taking your knife."

I knew I should have summoned her to ask about it. "Why not just tell me what you needed me to do that night?"

She looked at John and Lily as she answered, "Do you think they would have gone along with all of this if I had?"

I considered it a moment. "No. They would have had no reason to trust me about this then. Or work together."

Chrys smiled. "See? It all worked out. And just in time."

They five ghost dryads joined hands, then reached for Steph, Gary, Alex, and Holly, hugging them before disappearing. They wouldn't be back.

Dale sighed as if a weight had been lifted off his shoulders. "When I found out what my son had done, it crushed me. Would have killed me if I hadn't already been dead. I'd told him to leave the forest alone. I never supported that development and routinely turned them down in my later years. My son knew that. But his wife left him, and the business was failing. When you're desperate to have something go right, you'll do things you wouldn't have before."

He turned toward John. "You're such a good man, my boy. She's perfect for you. Don't let a fear of what's happened before stop you any longer," he said, referring to the Singer family's string of failed relationships either by accident or argument. Then he looked at Lily. "I wish I could have gotten to know you. I see the resemblance between you and Juniper."

Lily smiled through her tears. "Thank you. Everyone who knew her says that."

"She's a sweet girl, Dale. Feisty and sometimes a bit stubborn"—she patted Lily's cheek—"but deeply rooted in her beliefs and commitments. How about we get out of here, and I tell you all about her and you can tell me more about your grandson."

"I'd like that, but first, if I may be so bold." He took a step in her direction, and she did the same. They intertwined their fingers on one hand and leaned into one another, kissing each other for the first time. It was short and sweet. Juniper broke it off with a giggle.

The two pulled their grandchildren in for a hug.

Gary and Holly rushed over to Juniper and Lily. This time, it would be for a goodbye hug.

The energy surrounding us shifted as the two ghosts released their loved ones. John stepped over to Lily's side and grabbed her hand.

Dale and Juniper reached out for one another and then turned toward me. "Thank you for what you've done. Us, the forest, our grandkids. It's more than we could ever repay you for," Juniper said.

"I don't do this for payment," I replied. "I'm just glad you can both move on now. Together."

"Together," Dale affirmed.

Dale waved at Ivy. "Thank you for knowing where to look."

She gave a shy wave back and leaned into Ken's side. I hoped this hadn't been too much for her.

"We love you. Take care of one another," Dale said as he and Juniper looked back at their families. The four—three dryads and one human—nodded.

"Thank you," Juniper mouthed to me as they two faded from sight, still hand in hand.

We stood in silence staring at the spot where they had been.

"Are they gone?" Lily asked. "Like *gone*, gone?"

"They are," I confirmed. "It's all over now."

"Do you think they'll be okay?"

I opened my mouth to speak, but Ivy said, "Of course. They're together now. They've gotten their happily ever after." She let go of Ken and came bouncing over to me. "This is the coolest fairy tale ever! You really are a good witch!"

"I'm glad you think so. Now, remember what Gary said."

She nodded firmly twice. "I'm a guardian, and I have to protect their secret."

"Think you can protect mine too?"

"I sure can! But can I be a witch too? A guardian witch?"

"Anything is possible. It is a fairy tale, after all." And she didn't even know about the mermaids, wolves, trolls, or faeries yet. And neither did Ken. I'd tell him at some point, but it wasn't something I could discuss without knowing more about them or without having their permission.

We all came together in a large group hug before turning away from the tree stump and starting our trek out of the woods.

CHAPTER 44

I opened the town paper Tuesday morning to see a front-page headline that made me smile.

North Woods Donated to Town as First Forest Preserve

John Singer, furniture maker and heir of now-defunct Singer Lumber Company, has donated family holdings in the north woods. The donation comes after town-wide replanting efforts spearheaded by Singer and local baker Joanie Sunevall.

The rest of the article talked about the history of the lumber company, the mysterious circumstances surrounding the disappearances of the six villagers, and the recent discovery of the forest having been clear cut.

The final line concluded that the preserve would be dedicated to the six individuals who had last been seen in the north woods and a dedication ceremony would be forthcoming in the next couple of weeks.

I folded the paper back up and dialed Steph. "Congrats on the front-page news."

"Isn't it awesome? All of it, I mean. Not just the front page but the actual story. I can't wait for it to be an enjoyable spot once again for everyone."

"It's a great result, I agree. Have you been back up there since . . ." I'd meant to say since Dale and Juniper left, but let my voice trail off instead.

"Almost every day. The saplings are already growing, and the entire forest seems brighter, more vibrant. Actually all the woods around here feel like that. Nearly all the dryads have said something about it."

"That's wonderful."

"Speaking of all the dryads, are you coming tonight?"

"Wouldn't miss it." Inspired by the revelations from my baked goods and the advice of the six dryads who'd died in the woods, some had begun to be more open about what they were, not with everyone, but at least with those closest to them. In addition, tonight was the town's first paranormal support group meeting. I didn't know if the paranormals would ever be fully trusting of their human neighbors, but this was a start.

"Great. I'll see you then."

We hung up, and I stared at Saffy, who was eying me as she lay on my feet.

"Lily's coming over soon," I told her.

She jumped up onto the back of the couch, sat, and peered out the window, her head darting to the left then right as if already waiting for her to arrive.

"She's helping me with a baking project. I'm trying a new spell, or I guess it's a take on an old one that I didn't know I was doing."

Saffy looked over her shoulder at me.

"We're going to a meeting tonight, and I'm providing the snacks."

She made a huffing noise.

"I know. It's not a surprise. But this gives me an opportunity to practice my spell. I think everyone could use a boost of confidence tonight, don't you? It will be the first time many of them have told others what they are."

I picked my book back up, flipping open to where I'd left off over a week prior. These last few weeks had been so busy I'd barely gotten in any reading time, and the book was due back to the library soon. I'd already had to renew it. A rarity for me. I looked forward to things settling down again.

For now at least.

A couple hours later, Lily knocked on the door, sending Saffy into a tizzy.

"Come on in," I called, standing from my seat on the couch. I had a few more chapters to finish.

The door didn't open. I walked over to it and could not believe my eyes when I looked through the glass. "Oh my goodness!"

"Would you mind helping me get this in?" Lily asked when I opened the wood door.

"Of course." Pushing the storm door all the way open, I locked it into place so I could help Lily. She tilted the bulky object forward, allowing me to reach out and grab the top. "Wow, this is heavy."

"Real wood is like that." She chuckled. "Unless it's balsa."

I stepped backward into the house. "Saffy, look what Lily brought for you!"

Saffy had seen the whole thing through the window and had jumped to the floor. Her tail shook rapidly, and she spun in circles as we lugged the cat tree inside.

We pulled it all the way in, and then Lily shut the door behind her. "Where do you want it?"

"Somewhere in here. I don't want to have to bring it upstairs."

She laughed. "I'd definitely be calling John for that."

Really, the decision wasn't up to me. "Saffy, where do *you* want it?"

She ran around the room, sliding to a stop by the kitchen door.

"There?"

She tapped at the spot the way she did with her empty food bowl.

Lily laughed again, then bent down, wiggling her fingers. Saffy trotted over to her. "I think she's spoken."

"All right. There, it goes."

We pushed the cat tree into place, and Saffy jumped right onto a lower perch. Then she stretched up the central pole to scratch.

"I'd say she likes it. Thank you so much for this, Lily. You didn't have to."

"It's the least we could do after all you did for us. But that's not all." Lily reached into her pocket and pulled out a knife.

"Is that . . ."

She shook her head. "It's not *the* knife, but we made it to match, just not out of sacred wood. John thought you should have something to symbolize what we all went through. And you never know when you might need a knife. I have one too." She handed it to me.

I turned it over in my hand and ran my finger along the wood. "Thank you so much."

"You're welcome." She gave me a quick hug. "And thank

you. Now before I get all emotional by thinking about everything that happened again, let's get baking."

We headed into the kitchen as Saffy got comfortable on one of the cat tree's beds. It was probably the first time she didn't come running into the kitchen demanding food while I was cooking. I wouldn't be surprised if she switched her spot from the back of the couch to her new perch.

As we baked, we chatted about the new forest preserve and how in love Lily was with John. Their match was so strong my toes tingled just with her talking about him.

Then our conversation turned to tonight's paranormal support group meeting. Lily was nervous about it. Until John and me, only other dryads had known about her. I understood. After all the rumors about me since I'd moved here, I'd be confirming some of them as fact tonight.

Lily spread flour onto the counter. "So how are going to introduce yourself tonight, Joanie? A matchmaker? A psychic?"

"Nope," I answered, chopping some nuts to go into the cowboy cookies, a chocolate chip cookie with chopped pecans and shredded coconut.

"Then what?"

I took a deep breath. "I'm going to say, 'Hi my name is Joanie, and I'm a witch.'"

I smiled. It felt freeing to finally say it out loud and mean it.

Joanie must decide if she can be a baker and a witch or if it's time to hang up one of her hats in *Weddings and Witchcraft*, available now.

WHAT'S NEXT?

Wedding bells are ready to ring in Heartwood Hollow... maybe.

When a bride-to-be asks me for help with her haunted "something old," I'm is thrust into a bitter family dispute. The key to solving the decades-old mystery behind it is helping the trapped ghost. If only she could remember who killed her.

The more I dig, the more it becomes evident that not everyone is happy about the upcoming union. There are those who don't want the truth revealed, and they aren't afraid to go after my bakery to keep it hidden.

With my livelihood threatened, the couple's impending nuptials on the rocks, and a possible murderer on the loose, I must decide if I can be a baker and a witch or if it's time to hang up one of my hats.

Weddings and Witchcraft **is now available.**
Grab it today to start uncovering Heartwood Hollow's secrets.

ACKNOWLEDGMENTS

I could almost repeat the acknowledgements section from Cookies and Curses here. Thank you to my family for their continues support of this dream of mine, especially my husband, Rob. And to my daughter, Kahlan, who continued to be a great napper while I wrote this book.

Thank you to Frankie Blooding at Real Indie Author for your continued awesomeness. Thank you to Kay Springsteen, my editor, for not so much helping me dot my Is and crossing my Ts but making sure I have everything where it's supposed to go. It means so much that you like Joanie's story.

One of my biggest fears when I started this books was welter I'd be able to keep the writing momentum going. I'd written Cookies and Curses for NaNoWriMo, and that had helped tremendously. I feared that I'd peter out and have a half-finished book. It almost happened when my writing took a summer hiatus. But then I stumbled upon an amazing website. Thank you to the website 4thewords.com and the awesome writing community that I found there. It was so much fun writing this book while battling monsters and exploring a new world. I look forward to writing many more books with the motivation from that platform. It's been such a life changer.

And finally, thank you to *you* for reading this book.

About the Author

Rosie Pease is a native Rhode Islander but has lived in Vermont, New York, and Ohio. She uses the places she's traveled to as inspiration for the settings of her cozy mysteries, pulling the theater from one, the cider mill from another, the river from another to create a fictitious town that feels familiar.

She collects Funko Pops of the Harry Potter, Hunger Games, Doctor Who, DC TV, and Marvel variety, with a few others thrown in for fun. Her desk is a mess, but she can find everything on it, so it works for her as long as things aren't falling onto the keyboard as she writes.

When she's not crafting cozy mysteries, she's playing with her daughter, hanging out with her husband, or being amused by her two crazy cats.

Come find Rosie online:
Website: https://rosiepease.com
Facebook, Instagram, Twitter, and Pinterest:
@WriteRosiePease

ALSO BY ROSIE PEASE

The Matchmaking Baker

Coffee and Calicos

Sweets and Santa

Mixing Up Magic

Cookies and Curses

Scones and Spells

Weddings and Witchcraft

Potluck and Powers

Purrfect Travel Companion

Catastrophe on the Road

Catastrophe in the Kitchen